ANOTHER DAY IN
NeverLand

ANOTHER DAY IN
Neverland

ANTHONY AMADEO

Another Day in NeverLand

Copyright © 2019 by Anthony Amadeo. All rights reserved.

No part of this publication may be reproduced, stored in a retrieval system or transmitted in any way by any means, electronic, mechanical, photocopy, recording or otherwise without the prior permission of the author except as provided by USA copyright law.

This novel is a work of fiction. Names, descriptions, entities, and incidents included in the story are products of the author's imagination. Any resemblance to actual persons, events, and entities is entirely coincidental.

The opinions expressed by the author are not necessarily those of URLink Print and Media.

1603 Capitol Ave., Suite 310 Cheyenne, Wyoming USA 82001
1-888-980-6523 | admin@urlinkpublishing.com

URLink Print and Media is committed to excellence in the publishing industry.

Book design copyright © 2019 by URLink Print and Media. All rights reserved.

Published in the United States of America

ISBN 978-1-64367-855-9 (Paperback)
ISBN 978-1-64367-854-2 (Digital)

13.09.19

To my mom and dad, you're in my thoughts every day. Pluto who crossed over the rainbow bridge to be with his big brother Amadeus.

To my loving wife Helene for all her support, friendship and love, always and forever.

"I believe in everything until it's disproved. So, I believe in fairies, the myths, dragons. It all exists, even if it's in your mind. Who's to say that dreams aren't as real as the here and now?"

John Lennon

CONTENTS

Chapter 1: "Danny's Mission" 9
Chapter 2: "One Summer Night" 13
Chapter 3: "Till We Meet Again" 19
Chapter 4: "Crossroads" 23
Chapter 5: Danny, "Good times" 26
Chapter 6: Jimmy "Fortunate one?" 32
Chapter 7: Jimmy "This is not the real world anymore" 38
Chapter 8: Danny, "Waiting for a Girl like you" 44
Chapter 9: Jimmy "Where have all the soldier's gone" 52
Chapter 10: Jimmy "Chain of Fools" 56
Chapter 11: Danny "Always and Forever" 60
Chapter 12: Jimmy "Welcome to the Jungle" 67
Chapter 13: Jimmy "Sweet Soul" 73
Chapter 14: Jimmy "Night Fever" 77
Chapter 15: "Last Hoorah" 80
Chapter 16: Danny and Jimmy "Reunited" 83
Chapter 17: "Science Fiction" 92
Chapter 18: "Memories" 96
Chapter 19: "Just a Dream?" 102
Chapter 20: "Nightmares" 105

Chapter 21: "Another Life" 113
Chapter 22: "Suspicion" 121
Chapter 23: Danny "Alternate Universe" 124
Chapter 24: "Two Different Worlds" 137
Chapter 25: "Evil" 144
Chapter 26: "Not so friendly" 152
Chapter 27: "Believe" 157
Chapter 28: "Pure Evil" 162
Chapter 29: "Do the right thing" 166
Chapter 30: "Psycho" 174
Chapter 31: "Brother Aiden" 177
Chapter 32: "Cabin in the woods" 190
Chapter 33: "Destiny" 197
Chapter 34: "Careful What You Wish For" 199
Chapter 35: "Déjà vu with a twist" 204
Chapter 36: "Miracle?" 207

Acknowledgements..211

CHAPTER 1

"DANNY'S MISSION"

It's hard to believe that I'm sitting here waiting to board a flight to the UK. Not only am I going to England, but instead I should be with my real wife, Maria, on a vacation. I am traveling with an eighty- five-year-old priest who I just met two days ago. Believe me, this makes no sense. All I can think about is why am I doing this? My life is good as I dreamed it would be. I had a great wife, two beautiful kids, my business was doing well enough and I'm flying to England in the middle of the night with a stranger. I should be just putting down my book, shutting the light, kissing my wife and falling asleep in my soft safe bed. I should blame my mom, God rest her soul, for preaching to me over and over again "Do the right thing." Well, not just my mom because my dad said the same thing "Danny, just do the right thing and you will be happy." Well my dad is with my mom in heaven, I hope. If they were here, I wonder what they would say if I told them what I'm about to do. It's just another day in never land since this craziness started.

Well, if I was going to change my mind, this would be the time to do it. They just announced our boarding and I knew this was it. I nudged Father Thomas, who was in a peaceful nap and said, "We are boarding Father, wake up." He looked at me and smiled, "Good, I think I will have a nice nap on the plane." We picked up our carry on and made our way on to the plane. We walked towards the back of the plane and sat two across with Father Thomas by the window. I like to stretch my legs so the isle works for me. As the plane was moving onto the runway, I knew this was it and there was no turning back now. I'm not a great flyer so this was not what I really would prefer to be doing right now.

Father Thomas was already asleep as I dug my nails into the arm rests as we started to surge forward. In a few minutes, we were airborne. Once we were at cruising speed and the unfasten seat belt sign came on, I was able to exhale a bit and was beginning to settle down. I needed to go over the plans again so I tapped Father Thomas and then nudged him a few times before he finally opened his eyes. "Father, I'm sorry to bother you, but I need to talk." "Yes, Daniel what is on your mind" My Mom was the only one to call me Daniel but this is what Father Thomas calls me. "Look Father I want to be honest; I'm scared."

"About what Daniel" "Everything that I'm going to have to do, the more I think about it, the crazier it sounds. We are going to meet a monk who was kind of kicked out of the church. He is in a Monastery that no one knows exists. This is a monk you never met and he is going to give me the way to go back and fix this whole mess. I mean I could just go to the police and tell them what I know and let them do what they do." "Daniel, yes, you could, and if it's what you want to do, I will understand and accept your decision. Justice would be served but there are the five women and other innocent people who died and that would never change." "I know Father, but this whole thing is just bizarre, it can't be done. I really think it is impossible." "But Daniel you already have done it." "Yeah, I know, well, I think I know, but I don't know how, this whole thing is crazy. If someone came to me with this story I would laugh in their face and think they went off the deep end. Why do you believe me Father?" "I believed you from the first time you told me when you sat in my confessional. I believed you then and I believe you now. I know this is hard to believe, but I have seen a lot in my lifetime. I know when someone is lying or hallucinating or just telling the truth. In your case, I knew you were truthful. This is not the first time that I have heard of a messenger calling on a person. In this case, a dark messenger, and yes, it is the first time I have heard the story of events like this. But I have had many dealings with dark messengers and the good messengers interfering with events and interactions with humans. Yes, I have seen many things, and heard many stories and I am not alone. I also believe in alternate reality.

The Monk we are going to see is one who deals with these occurrences before. His methods have pushed the boundaries and he did lose his standing with the church. As a matter of fact, his case went right to the Vatican and I have been told that the Pope himself made the final decision. The Monastery, which he is part of, works outside of the church and is not recognized by the Vatican; it is in fact a separate entity. Originally Brother Aiden was part of the Monastery called North Umbria during its "golden age." It was the most important center of religious learning and arts in the British Isles. The Monk we will be visiting is also known now as Aidan he took the name in honor of the founder, Saint Aidan." I looked at Father Thomas a little confused, saying, "How long has this Brother Aidan been at this Monastery?" Father Thomas smiled and shrugged his shoulders saying, "I have no idea and there is no record of his birth or any details on his life or his age." "What actually does this Monastery do and believe in?" Father Thomas put his hand to his weathered face and stroked his thin gray hair and said, "This is kind of a gray area, they are very secretive. They allow no visitors except on an individual dispensation from their governing body, which no one knows anything about. From what I've learned over the years, they believe, practice, and study a combination of "Divine utterances." To make this as easy as possible, Brother Aiden believes and practices methods of inviting messengers or angels, who at times, act in helping change and alter events. The Bible and associated texts have been widely received as divinely oracular by various religious sects where verses can be interpreted as supporting desired ideas of "God", reincarnation, spirit communing, extraterrestrials and the afterlife. To answer your question in the simplest of terms, Aidan and the Monastery he resides in, study and practice this combination of beliefs." Wow! Listening to Father Thomas made my head spin. All of this is way out of my league. This whole situation has made me feel powerless about what has happened and what is going to happen. I am heading to some remote Monastery on the northern tip of England just below the Scottish border.

Father Thomas will lead me to this Monastery to meet a rogue Monk who practices some kind of channeling or whatever he does. He will hook me up with some kind of good messenger or angel-like being and I was able to go backwards through a portal and fix the mistake I made twenty years ago for the third time. Okay, I know I don't do drugs. I don't drink, except for a beer and a scotch once in a while, so can you believe what I am saying? But the reality is there are five women dead, other innocent people murdered and I know, if it wasn't for me, they should all still be alive. Listen, I never killed or even hurt someone in my life, but I am responsible and I know down deep, I have to do the right thing and try to fix what I have done. I still can't believe it, but it all started twenty years ago and, as I close my eyes I can relive the whole dam thing. I have a life I want to get back to. I have been living a nightmare and this is my only chance to make it all right. Danny sat back, and closed his eyes.

CHAPTER 2

"ONE SUMMER NIGHT"

The year is 1967, and it's a summer night in July on Long Island, NY. My friends and I decided to try something a little different that night. So, Stevie Bracken, Jimmy Cetano, Ray Freed, Sal Ritello and I went to a new club in Lido Beach. I was driving as usual, because I didn't trust any of them to get behind the wheel even back then. My name is Danny Amendola. We were all around the same age, all within a year. I had just turned twenty and I liked the idea I was the youngest. I was three weeks younger than Jimmy but still I was the youngest. We all grew up together, known each other since we started in Grammar School together. We lived all around each other the furthest away was Sal and he lived two blocks away in the same development. This was the craziest thing that our town, it was predominantly Jewish but the only one of us that was Jewish was Ray. The rest were all Italian Americans and we're very proud of it. Stevie's mom was Italian his dad was Irish. Ray the only Jewish one loved to eat with any of us Sundays because all our families made lots of Italian dinners and Ray loved it. We headed for the club and as usual we all were in a good mood. We loved to go out on Friday nights, loved the night life and the challenge of maybe (hopefully) picking up some nice- looking girls. The one challenge was keeping Stevie in line. When Stevie had a drink, his whole personality would change. After he had that first drink, then he had to have a few more real fast. After the buzz got to him, he would sometimes get out of control. All of us took turns watching out for Stevie but for some reason I was the one that always felt that it was up to me to take care of him. Stevie was different than the rest of us. His Father was an alcoholic and he was a real nasty drunk. There many times Stevie would call me and the other guys to come over and get him because his father was drunk and started punching everyone around him. He hit Stevie's mom, his two younger brothers. He was big, mean and violent when he was loaded.

We bailed Stevie out many times. I would get Stevie and he would come with me and stay at my house until a few days went by and his father would dry out, for a while. Although his father would hit all of them, it was Stevie, maybe because he was the oldest that he really went after the most. The last time his father went nuts, I was the only one who could get there and just as I pulled up to Stevie's house a big TV came flying through the front window. His father also loved to bust up all the furniture and throw it at Stevie. I told them to call the cops, but they would never do it. It was a really bad situation. Most of the time Stevie was normal and his family life had some weeks of calm. The bottom line was Stevie needed help and I loved the guy he was special so I always was there for him. He would be a hand full at times, but he had a great heart and would do anything for me and the rest of us. Stevie was the one kid that even when he did something wrong and got caught, he would just look at you with a scared puppy dog face and you would forget about what he did. Of course, Stevie knew it and played that card many times. My parents loved him, he was so polite and cute. The girls would always be drawn to him with a devil personality, but an angel look for him. Sometimes he just wouldn't think things through before he went and did something stupid. Like a job! He bounced from one to the other. He never had any money and when he did get some he would give it all to his Mom. That was the thing about him, he would do anything to make a buck, any way possible except holding a regular job. As soon as he got the money, he would give it away. The money meant nothing to him, but when he gave it to his mom and made her happy, he was happy. Like I said he was a handful, but he had a great heart. Every time he met a new girl, he would fall in love with her.

After the first date that's all he would talk about that this one was the most wonderful love of his life. The problem was that love affair would last about three more dates and Stevie would fall out of love just as fast. He had such a way about him that, when he ended the relationship the girl felt so bad thinking it was her fault and everyone, including myself, would console him. Stevie was a special combination of lovable, funny, conniving, gambling, walks on the edge and a guy that you wanted to choke, hug and then help him. I loved the guy like a brother, the fact he was ten months older than me meant nothing. I still looked after him like he was my kid brother. We pulled up to the parking lot and as I shut off the car and opened the door to get out, Stevie said to wait up and relax before we went in. He pulled out a brown bag from under the seat and opened a bottle of the cheapest Vodka money could buy. Stevie took a big slug and passed the bottle around. I was last and I took a small amount and swallowed, it tasted more like lighter fluid than vodka. They kept on passing the bottle around, but on my turn, I faked it, no way was I drinking that crap. After a little while we all got buzzed except me, I faked that too. We made our way out of the car and were pretty content on laughing and screwing around then going into the club. We all had a lot of the same physical appearance, Jimmy, Ray, Stevie and myself were all around six feet tall around the same weight hundred and seventy to eighty-five pounds. We all had nice hair. Ray and Stevie had dark hair, Jimmy and I had lighter hair. Sal was the only one who was short and stocky maybe even a little too heavy. We always did everything together since we were kids. None of us had steady girlfriends just dated and went out to clubs almost every Friday and Saturday nights together. We all loved to dance, party, and laugh and try to get some phone numbers and maybe a make out session, if we got lucky. We weren't very complicated or overly sophisticated guys. This was just another Friday night, just like any other Friday night out with the guys.

After about an hour of hanging out in the parking lot, we decided it was time to make our grand entrance into the club. We managed to kill most of the shitty vodka; with Stevie doing most of the heavy damage. We all tried to look as cool as possible as we walked into the club. Our entrance into the club was a big deal, this would be the first time all the good-looking girls would see us and hopefully like what they see. Well, that was our thought process back then. Look cool and hope for the best. As we entered the club it was a typical dark, smoky, noisy scene. It was a rush to be young having my buddies all around me and the excitement of maybe meeting that one special beautiful girl who would take one look at me and fall in love right then. As much as I liked hanging out with the guys, my real desire was to find the perfect girl. The rest was all bullshit. I knew it, but I would never tell my friends what was on my mind, that would not be cool. We made our way to the bar and I ordered my usual Dewar's and water. We made our way across the room to be near the lady's room, which was Ray's idea. Ray said it's the best spot because all the girls would come this way one time at least as the night went on. To be honest, he was right. We hung out there and drank, smoked our Marlboros looked cool and tried our luck with the girls as they passed by to the ladies' room.

 Later that night Jimmy had hooked up with a cute blond and Stevie was dancing up a storm with a very attractive brown-haired girl in a very short dress. Ray, Sal and I were not as lucky, but we were still having a great time. As the night flew by we were making plans to meet at mid-morning and were going to Jones beach to spend our Saturday. Where else would you go on a Saturday in the summer on Long Island? It was getting late and the place had really thinned out. There were about three or four couples on the dance floor. It was getting to that time when we would hit the closest diner, stuff our face with some hamburgers and head home.

 I was happy that Stevie was so into the girl, he was no problem at all. It was nice to have a night out with no problems, all is good. Jimmy came over to us, his girl left with her friends, but he scored her number and he was happy. Now we were waiting for Stevie. He was slow dancing to what was the last song of the night. We decided as soon as it was over we would grab him and hit the road. As the music stopped Stevie walked over to us, arm and arm with his new love. Her name was Jennifer she was pretty and very friendly. I pulled Stevie over and told him to get her number because we were ready to go. He was cool and knew it was time. He took Jennifer by the hand to a corner they spoke a while and he was writing down her number, a score for Stevie. Just as he was writing down her number two guys came from what was I guess was the back door. One of them pulled Jennifer by the arm and away from Stevie. I knew right away this was not good. I knew Stevie was into her big time and he would not let this go. I told Jimmy to get the car and get ready to pick us up so we get the hell out of here real fast. Jimmy grabbed Sal and they went to get the car. I was watching Stevie waiting for him to do something stupid, but he didn't move. He just watched as Jennifer and this guy were in a heavy conversation. I told Ray to come with me and we would get Stevie out of here. Ray and I went over to Stevie and I told him to be cool and let's get out now. Stevie smiled and said he was good he just wanted to wait just to make sure Jennifer was okay with this guy. Stevie seemed calm, so I started to relax a bit and said I would wait with him. Ray went to the door to see if they were ready with the car. Jennifer waved at Stevie and mouthed to call her. Stevie smiled, nodded his head. We both turned and started for the door, thank God, no problem. I guess my instincts were wrong.

I thought this was going to get ugly, but just another Friday night out with the guys. As we walked away and were a few feet from the door this jerk yells out, "You better get the out of here, you asshole." Stevie stops short he starts to walk towards this guy. I see where this is going so I get in front of Stevie and tell him, "No, don't be stupid, just forget it and let's go." Stevie stops, looks me in the eye, smiles with that angelic look on his face and says, "You're right let's go home." I take a deep breath and move away from Stevie towards the door. The rest happened so fast it was surreal. Stevie instead of following turns back at the guy and goes right at him. I was way too slow to react. I believed Stevie was coming with me and in a second, he goes the other way. I turn to try to go after him, but he was already on the guy's face. Stevie punches him in the stomach and they both fall to the floor, and a second later, as I tried to get to them, I hear "Pop, pop, pop" The guy gets up and runs out the door. Jennifer screams and I see blood pouring from Stevie's chest. It all happened in seconds, I fell to my knees, grabbed Stevie and screamed to call an ambulance. I cradled Stevie in my arms pleading with him to hold on. About fifteen minutes later the ambulance showed up, but it was too late; Stevie bled out and died in my arms. He had no chance three bullets tore him apart. It was not just another summer Friday night on Long Island.

CHAPTER 3

"TILL WE MEET AGAIN"

We all had to spend hours with the cops detailing the events that went down. Jennifer was there and her account was right in line with mine and the rest of the guys. There were other witnesses, mostly the waitresses and bartenders. There was no question what happened, but the law is slow and detailed. After hours at the station they finally let us go. No way could we have gone home so we went to the nearest diner. Jennifer came with us and we sat around in a daze. Jennifer knew Stevie for just a few hours, but she really was upset. We questioned her about the jerk that shot Stevie but she did not want to talk about him. She did say that she had dated him a few times, but realized he had a bad attitude. She said he was a wannabe wise guy and did some work for the local mob guys. After she broke it off, every time she ran into him, he would be a pest asking why she won't go out with him. A few times he got a little too pushy and she threatened to go to the cops. He would back off saying it was her loss. At the club when he came in and saw her with Stevie he was pissed. He was telling her that he wanted to try to prove to her that he liked her and to dump Stevie and go with him. She said he seemed to be high and even threatened he would hurt Stevie if she went with him. That's when she got scared of Stevie and mouthed to Stevie she was okay. She wanted Stevie just to get out before the jerk would do something stupid. As she spoke, tears were rolling down her face and she started saying it was her fault that Stevie got killed. We took turns telling her that was crazy, she was not responsible for what that piece of shit did.

Sal and Jimmy said we should take care of this guy for Stevie. Of course, we were no wise guys or were we any tough guys so this was just some emotion mixed with some macho thing for Jennifer's sake. I jumped in and said we all want to see this guy get what he deserves, but all we can do is testify and let the courts punish him. Hopefully they get him put away for the rest of his short life. After talking almost all night we drove Jennifer home. She lived on our way home so it was no problem. We dropped her off and she hugged each one of us and whispered in our ears how truly sorry she was. She ran up to her house in tears. All this time I was like some type of a movie or something because this whole night seemed unreal. It really did not register that Stevie was really dead. We drove home in silence; we had nothing left to say. A few days later we all attended the wake for Stevie. The whole neighborhood showed up. Stevie's mom was a mess and his two brothers did their best to console her. Stevie's asshole father was bombed and staggered his way around the funeral parlor before he passed out. One of Stevie's uncles took him home. The general words that were said were pretty much the same. One by one, all his aunts and his mom's friends said he was so young and way too soon to die. He was a beautiful boy and he was now in a better place. We all took turns crying up at the casket kneeling over Stevie. I was numb and had trouble getting any words out. I had a sickening feeling that it was my fault. I was the one who always watched over him and I should have known better. I should have grabbed him and dragged him out of there and he would still be alive. I just kept on going over the sequence over and over in my head. I should have, I could have saved him. Dam it was my fault, if I only could go back and do it all over he would be alive.

The next day we all were there for the funeral it was a rainy-day fitting for the way we all felt. Jennifer showed up with her mom and once again told us how sorry she was that this happened. Even at a funeral and the saddest of time I could not help to notice how good Jennifer looked. She had real thick black hair, tanned skin and looked unbelievable in a simple black dress, not as short as the one she wore at the club. I couldn't help thinking that Stevie was watching from somewhere thinking the same thing. As much as I loved Stevie I knew down deep that if I was the one killed and Stevie was here he would-be all-over Jennifer. I know he would be sad, but Stevie was Stevie. After the final prayer that Stevie walked through the valley of death and fear no evil, I watched Stevie's dad. He was sober and he was even in tears as he said his final goodbye at the grave. Stevie's mom held his hand and fell to her knees crying over the grave. I couldn't fight off the tears and cried like a baby, so did the rest of the guys, it was brutal. As we were all leaving the cemetery Jennifer told us she was notified that she would be called soon to testify at the hearing for Carlo. That was the dip shit's name that killed Stevie. I knew we would be there too. At the local Italian restaurant Jimmy, Sal, Ray and I sat together watching all the mourners stuff their face on penne, chicken francese and some kind of fish special for lunch. It's kind of weird that a few minutes ago these same people were crying and as sad as can be but now they are eating, talking politics and even laughing. I'm not judging them, it's just strange how these funerals go. Not just for Stevie but just about everyone I had been to. When I was a kid they were much more dramatic, at least one of my aunts would throw themselves on the casket or into the grave. The others would be passing out after a screaming contest on who could mourn the loudest. My dad used to tell me that they would pass out the smelling salts like they pass out mints today.

  He also said they collected cash instead of flowers and the closer the relative the more cash they would give. At the luncheon, winded down Sal gave a little speech to the rest of us that we are like brothers and we had to stick together no matter what. That he loved Stevie and all of us. We all took turns hugging each other and knew Sal was right. I felt a deep hole inside knowing that it was just the four of us and Stevie is gone. Sal once more suggested that if this prick didn't get the life we had to take justice into our own hands take him out. We all looked at Sal and he knew he was full of crap. We said we know what you mean and smiled. Sal was just talk. Like I said, we were no wise guys, we were just hurting and grieving the only way we knew. We took Stevie's two brothers aside and told them that if they ever needed us to just call any time day or night, we would be there for them. Robby just turned fourteen and Billy was eleven. We all walked out together and we weren't sure what we would do next. What should we do Friday and Saturday now that Stevie is gone? We had no idea so we just left off we would talk and see what happens.

CHAPTER 4

"CROSSROADS"

Carlo, Stevie's killer layered up with a top- notch asshole and gets five years for manslaughter, up for parole in eighteen months. What a joke! Like I said before, we were just ordinary guys. We loved Stevie but we all knew there was nothing we could do about this piece of garbage. We had no choice but forget about him and move on with our lives. That is exactly what we did. We started just hanging out at the local diner on the weekends and just shooting the bull. We went to a few bars, but we just couldn't get back into the club scene anymore. Since Stevie has gone, it just wasn't the same. We were all hurting, but we tried to be as cool as possible. A few months after Stevie died the shit hit the fan. I get this shitty letter with the words "Greetings" on the top. I knew right away what it was. I was being drafted in the stupid Army. We all knew it could be coming but you don't really believe it until it hits you in the face. We were hearing all the stories about Viet Nam and you couldn't help but see it on the news. We loved our country, but Viet Nam? What the hell is that all about? We never heard of the Dinky little country in middle of some jungle that means nothing to any of us. Me and the guys sat around just looking at the stupid letter and none of us could figure out what to do. Ray says, "This sucks, we all should go to Canada. "Yeah, that's a great idea. I could see me telling my Mom and Dad, I'm off to Canada to evade the Army. I'd rather go to the jungle than face them. I appreciate what you mean Ray, but you know none of us can go that route. Jimmy says "I am not waiting for the letter.

I am going down to Hempstead Turnpike and enlisting. If you go, I'm going. If I don't enlist I'm getting drafted anyway, so what's the difference." Ray and Sal joined in saying that we will all go together and kick some Viet Nam asses. Great talk while we are all sitting around Ray's house. But a few days later they really did it. Jimmy was accepted right away and the Army was happy to have him. Ray and Sal had some medical and psychological problems and were classified 4F. These were some crazy times. Another friend of ours Benny gets classified 3 something. I can't remember exactly what it was but it meant he wouldn't be drafted. We all laughed and told him how lucky he was. Benny said maybe he should call and make sure it was Okay. We told him no way just leave it alone, it was their mistake, not your problem. The same day Benny calls anyway. They thank him for calling and three days later he gets the wonderful letter, Greetings Benny come and join the party. We are all on the express train to some shit hole called Viet Nam. A week later I'm on a broken-down bus headed to Whitehall St for the Army physical. The guys on the bus were going pretty nuts. Everyone was laughing and making fun of the whole thing. I think that was the way we all were dealing with nerves because nobody wanted to think this was for real, just another school like the trip. Next thing I know we are all walking up this old ugly building. Now I'm thinking, I really don't want to do this. As I'm walking around in my shorts and tee shirt having all these guys in white coats looking in every opening in my body I'm really getting scared. I don't want any part of this. Now I'm sitting on a chair with some Army guy showing me all these different colors. I remember reading somewhere that if your color blind, they don't take you. Bingo, this is my way out. He shows me red I say orange. He shows me blue I say green. He shows me yellow I say red. Next, he yells, "Next, you're done" I say, "Did I fail?" He just smiles. There is no way out of this. I'm going to die in Viet shit Nam.

Now here comes the twist to this whole thing. A week later I find out I am doing basic training in Fort Dix New Jersey. Jimmy is sent south for training. I don't realize it at the time, but what that meant was that Jimmy was on the fast track to Viet Nam. My dear and loving Mom spoke with her brother, my Uncle Joe. Uncle Joe was a small- time politician, but was the president of the Republican Party in Queens. He had some good buddies and I don't how but they pulled some strings and I get a cushy assignment in Fort Hamilton in Brooklyn. I mean this was unbelievable. I was an hour drive to my Mom and Dad's house. At the time, I knew nothing about this and didn't find out how this happened until years later. It wasn't fare to Jimmy and I felt sick about that. But I have to admit I was happy I was not going anywhere but Brooklyn. My time in the Army was anything but dangerous. I was assigned to a data processing unit. My job was to run old Kimball readers, processing cards to be transferred onto tape and into computers. Not so dangerous and not so exciting, but nice and safe.

CHAPTER 5

DANNY, "GOOD TIMES"

The hardest decision I had was to choose one of the two girls I was dating. Before it blew up in my face and lose both. Ronnie was dark skin with dark hair and a thin but very great body. Sandy was younger, dirty blond and a great body. I would spend every Friday after my day at the grind in a local motel with Ronnie. She would bring some homemade pizza; cookies and I would pick up a cheap bottle of wine. We made great love and watched TV and ate all night long. Saturday was Sandy, same routine different motel. She wouldn't bring the food but the sex was crazy. My Sargent was a women hound and was always trying to put the make on both of them. They would blow him off but never said they were seeing me. We all worked in the same building so it was kind of crazy. I didn't know it at the time, but Ronnie was seeing some other guy.

Not only was she seeing him. but she told me one night while we were eating her pizza, lying naked together. She told me his name was Dave and he was stationed at the same base. Well, I was surprised she was dating someone else and to further complicate things I knew Dave. He was a good guy and I liked him a lot. We put the conversation on hold for another game of naked wrestling and after finishing on the floor we both crawled back into bed. She then springs the news that this good guy Dave asked her to marry him. Now this was getting awkward. She wanted my opinion on what she should do. She also wanted to know where I stood as far as her relationship with me. I told her I was nowhere ready to settle down. I liked her very much, but I was not looking to marry anyone in the near or distant future. She was a great girl but I knew she wasn't the one. I gave her my advice and told her she should marry Dave if she loved him. She said she wasn't sure about love, but she did like the idea of getting married. The more I thought of it the more I wanted out of this situation. In the weeks to come, I kind of made excuses why I couldn't see her on Fridays. Now to confuse things even more I was seeing Dave as part of my job and I felt pretty bad about the situation. Dave starts telling me he is seeing Ronnie and what I thought of her? "Great Girl" That was my answer every time. I kind of dropped out of the picture with Ronnie but a few weeks later she told me she wanted to meet me she had to talk. I didn't want to get involved, but she said please, she had something to tell me and it was important. Now I was a little nervous and needed to find out what was up.

Friday night comes and she picks me up outside the building. It's a pretty wet night out, but she says we are going to the park. She pulls into a secluded spot off the belt parkway and shuts the car off. I ask what's up, is everything all right? I'm starting to think that maybe she is pregnant but I knew we were smart about that. She then says that Dave asked her once again to marry her and she needed to hear it from me that it was okay. As I take a deep breath and look out the side window I exhale and just about to give my blessing she opens her rain coat and is naked under there. She swings her leg over me and with the hands of a magician my belt has been opened and my pants are coming down. The next thing I knew the talking stopped and I had no choice but to finish what she started. After we were done, we both got ourselves back together. She looked at me and said, "What do you think?" I was at a loss for words so I said the first thing that came into my mind and I replied, "The Flesh is weak, but it's okay." She looked at me like I lost my mind saying, "No stupid, not that, should I marry Dave?" Well not seeing any reason why I should object, I simply said, "Yes, I think you should. You will make a great wife and he will be a great husband and I will be happy to sing at your wedding or dance." She looked at me, shook her head and started the car. Back at the base or should I say the office everything was business as usual. Ronnie was busy planning the wedding. I was seeing Sandy on a regular basis just as I was with Ronnie. I became real good friends with Robbie, who also came from Brooklyn. I'm not really sure he had any connections to be placed here or he just got lucky. Robbie was the same age as me. He had black curly hair, six feet tall and an Italian American look. Sargent Tullo took a big time liking to Robbie and me. He was quite a character. I'm not sure how old he was but I would guess about forty- seven or forty- eight. He had a wife and three kids. His family lived in a house in another section of Brooklyn. Even with a family being so close this did not stop the Sargent from carrying on with any women, he could get his hands on.

He was notorious for squeezing, touching, hugging, and flirting with every female that came near him. He had this way about him, that as much as he was oversexed, he was not in any way dangerous or offensive. He was impossible to get mad at. He was always smiling and full of compliments. He would complement anybody about anything at all. If the women were very heavy, he would complement her hair or what great lips she had. He could find something nice to say in any situation. There was a female soldier Anne, who was a disaster in the way she kept her office. She was always a mess, always looked like she just rolled out of bed. She couldn't do anything right. He tried having her feeling, but she couldn't alphabetize. He had her answering, phones but she never took a message right. He just couldn't find anything she could do but he kept on trying. The one thing she had going for her she was blond and had very large breasts. Well, for Sargent Tullo that was a good reason to keep her around. He had no problem complimenting her on her beauty or her hair or just about any other part of her. The one thing he could never compliment her on was her work. One day we are having a meeting and she was in charge of setting up the room and all the necessary reports, papers, files, coffee, donuts to make a meeting work. She messed everything up, the files were wrong, the reports wrong, the coffee was disgusting, and the donuts were like bricks. We all looked at Sargent Tullo like you have to be kidding with this one. Even he looked almost annoyed with her. But as she came next to him and bent over to pour him a glass of water, he glanced at her breasts, sniffed her hair as he picked up the glass and took a big swallow and then said, "This is the best glass of water I ever have tasted, great job!" That really said it all. Sargent Tullo was true to himself and was not going to change. We learned later that the Sargent was a little more than friendly with Anne the big chested blond.

We kind of thought something was up with them, but knowing the way he was, it was hard to tell for sure. After our duties were done and with any free time we had, it was Robbie, me and the Sargent out all the time. We were regulars at the local bars around the base. The Sargent had his own routine. Every night out he would start the night with normal conversation, but when he had his first drink it was all over. He then would start circulating trying to pick up a woman for the night. His philosophy was quite simple, he always said he would start with the most attractive women in the bar and work his way down. By the end of the night, most of the time, he would end up with someone he could take to the corner motel. The weekends that we were not on duty he would spend at home. At home, he was the perfect husband and Father, of course, when he sobered up. Many times, his formula would not work and I and Robbie would drive him home. We would just about have to carry him to his front door where his wife would take him in and put him to bed. Even his wife couldn't stay mad at him. I kept in touch with Sal and Ray but didn't have much time to get out to the Island. I would speak to my Mom and Dad once a week. I even hear from Jennifer once in a while. Jimmy was doing basic in Washington and it looks like they're getting ready to ship him over to Viet Nam. We have been writing back and forth so we know what we are each up to. I can't help feeling guilty about Jimmy and what he is going through now and what was going to happen to him. I had nothing to do with what had gone down, but still felt crappy about it.

The following weeks went by pretty quick and before I know it, Ronnie's wedding was coming up on Saturday. I end up taking Sandy. Robbie is not seeing anyone so by the Sargent's request, he takes Anne. Sargent Tullo comes with his wife Bee. We all sit at the same table and things are quite pleasant. Ronnie comes over and sits on my lap. She had a few too many and was showing it. I was feeling really uneasy with the way she was acting and moving around in my lap. Sandy was shooting dagger looks and Dave came over not looking so happy either. This time Sargent Tullo bailed me out. As the band starting playing Rock Around the Clock, Sargent Tullo grabbed Ronnie and said, "Let's dance." He pulled her up on the dance floor. I took a deep breath and with a big smile I grabbed Sandy and joined in on the dance floor. Robbie did the same with Anne and we all danced our heads off. Dave cooled down and was even smiling as he joined in dancing with Bee. After all the times I pulled Sargent Tullo out of the fire this time I owed him one. I was never sure if Ronnie ever told Dave about me, but I did get the feeling she did. Ronnie was very attractive lots of fun, but was not the smartest. The night went pretty well from there for a while. As the night went on, Sargent Tullo was drinking a bit too much. As the wedding was coming to an end, so was the peace. Sargent Tullo kind of forgot that his wife Bee was still at the same wedding he was. He was slow dancing with Anne which was one of the last songs of the night. He was really out of it. As we sat in horror, his hands were grabbing Anne's butt. I mean he was right in front of the table, right in front of Bee. He started kissing Anne's neck and at the same time squeezing her butt with a grinding motion around her. It was like we were watching a standing lap dance. I kept an eye on Bee but I was frozen in body and thought. I couldn't open my mouth or do anything to stop the inevitable. In a split- second Bee sprung up screaming as she grabbed Anne's hair. Anne had beautiful blond hair in a big high hair style.

As Bee grabbed the top and went to swing her around half of the big hairdo was in Bees hand. Anne turned as she let go, with an equaling blood wrenching scream of her own and it was go time. It was quite a sight watching them in a hair pulling match in the middle of the dance floor. Everyone gathered around like it was the Friday night fights at the Garden. Nobody knew what to do as we all kind of just watched. After a few minutes, which kind of felt like a ten round bout some staff jumped in to break up the main event?

Anne was a mess; half of the front of her dress was ripped off and most of her very large right boob was hanging out. Sargent Tullo always the gentleman was the first one to her as he held her breast gently and very slowly put it back into her bra. Of course, true to form this gentlemanly act lasted too long. Bee smashed him in the head with a lovely flower vase from our table. Ann had enough and headed out the door. Bee the ever-loving wife felt bad about what she did to Sargent Tullo. She pushed everyone out of the way to be with her man. After things settled down and we propped Sargent Tullo onto the nearest chair, he smiled and said, "It's good to see my wife fight for her man. That's the way it should be. Danny, can you hand me my scotch. I think that is my drink on the table." Before I could turn to get his drink, Bee had it in her hand and gave it to him. Unbelievable, like I said before, you can't get mad at this guy. The next day I sat down and wrote Jimmy a long letter bringing him up to date. I know Jimmy would love what has been going on. I really miss the guy.

CHAPTER 6

JIMMY "FORTUNATE ONE?"

I was not as lucky as Danny. It was a bitter cold day as I got off the bus on Whitehall Street in Brooklyn. I was feeling sick. I'd rather be hanging with the guys back home, then going through this shit. I knew I had no choice but to just do whatever they say and get it over with. This was going in my life for the next couple of years. The next thing I know they put us on a train heading south. The first few days dragged on getting needles stuck with me, listening to loud barking shit heads screaming at me. The Army introduction welcomes you for a little bit, then get in your face and break you down. They did everything they could to make you feel like dirt. I started to make some friends, but I was so close to my guys back home it was not easy. I met a kid from Nassau County named Andy. He was really quiet and seemed kind of scared. He seemed to just always be right behind me wherever I would go. We started eating together and hanging out. He wasn't a cool kid, but I had the feeling he needed me to take care of him a bit. The haircuts were brutal. I mean I would spend an hour combing and fussing over my long thick hair and now it was gone. I was dam bald with a touch of fuzz. This Army shit really was not for me. The barracks was old. It was so old they had coal heat and a guy would have to stand guard all night to make sure there were no fires. I was always cold. I knew this would be ending soon and we would get assigned to where we would be going to do our real training. That day came soon enough. This Sargent comes in with this long list and starts backing out names and where they are going. I was kind of in limbo on where I wanted to go so I just waited for my name to be called. Then I hear it loud and clear James Cetano and my assignment, "Fort Lewis Washington." I turn to Andy, "Hey, not so bad, Washington, that's a five-hour drive." One of the guys behind me says, "Not DC that's the state of Washington, asshole." That's just great. I have to go across the whole country. As luck has it, Andy is going with me. Well, it's Okay he's not a bad guy just a little needy. Andy was medium height, a little over weight, light hair and had chubby cheeks.

All the way out to Washington, Andy can't stop talking. From day one he hardly spoke now he is a chatterbox. He tells me his life story. He has two older sisters; Mom, Dad and Grandmother live in a small ranch house. He doesn't have many friends and he doesn't like sports. He does like to bowl and he says he is good at it. The flight has been forever and I hear every bowling score he ever got. He also has this nervous habit of swinging his legs from side to side in and out. I'm sitting so close that every time he does it, his knees are banging into mine. After a few hours, this can drive you crazy. I tried to tell him politely as possible to shut up so I can get some sleep. I close my eyes for ten minutes and then he says are you asleep? Well not anymore because you just woke me up for the tenth time. Halfway out there I just gave up and let him talk his brains off. We land in Washington and guess what, it's raining. It always seems to be raining there. Eight weeks of basic training, then, sixteen weeks of advanced infantry training. Rumor has it they are not training us for any parades. Were all on a fast track to Viet Nam. As the days go by I start hooking up with a bunch of really good guys. Peterson from Pittsburgh, Henderson was a Mormon from Utah, Vogel a real tough guy from Philly, Maytag, we could never say his last name so someone just called him Maytag and it stuck. Moo was a big sloppy guy from a farm in Ohio. Red said he looked like a cow so he nicknamed him Moo. Red was from my area on Long Island. Gordan was a black guy from Philly. Boomer, Flipper, and the Italian guys Rega, Gulli and Sonny from Manhattan. And of course, there was Sargent Willie.

Sargent Willie could have been a perfect character in an old-world war two movie. He was a tough, hardened, older, and a big drinker. He was on the thin and small side with the typical GI buzz cut. Wrinkled face with hardened skin. Hands were like vice grips. He was all Army, but once he drank, he was all but crazy. He would rip into us and push us to the limit. But every one of us knew he had our backs. He believed in training as hard because he wanted to make sure we would be good soldiers.

Good for the Army and good for us, so we would all stay alive. One night in the middle of our training, he came back real late. He was out with one of his drinking buddies and he was wasted. On the way, back he placed a bet with his drinking buddy the Sargent of another platoon. We of course knew nothing about what was going on because we were all asleep for hours. In the middle of the night all the barracks lights are turned on. We then hear Sargent Willie screaming, "All right, you lard asses get up on your feet now! Everybody up and grab your mattresses and fall in outside." I was trying to rub my eyes and see if this was a dream but it was not. Crazy Sargent Willie ordered us all outside in the pouring rain of course to win a bet. Him and the other Sargent bet on which of their Platoons would win the mattress race around the barracks. We are outside in our shorts in the dam rain and we have to carry our mattresses over our heads and race around the barracks. We had to beat the other Platoon so Sargent Willie could win his bet. Once again this was the Army so we did what we were ordered to do. We raced around the barracks. I had to stop and help Andy up a couple of times. We stomped through the mud and beat the other Platoon by two guys. Sargent Willie was extremely happy with us all. He told us to get cleaned up and have a good night's sleep. We did go back to bed on our soaking wet mattress and were screamed at to get up an hour later, it was morning. Well, we all decided to give a little payback on Sargent Willie. We agreed with Reds idea to short sheet the Sargent's bed the next time he is out with his drinking buddy. A week later Sargent Willie was out drinking up a storm, so it was payback time. We fixed his bed sheet so it was folded in half. He came wobbling in and went right into his bed. A few minutes later we are all around him watching him trying to stretch out his legs on the bed. He could only go half way and he starts tossing, turning, kicking and cursing. After a few minutes, he realizes we are all around him laughing. He throws his whole mattress and blankets on the floor. Gets up screaming every curse word ever heard and tells to get back to bed or he will court martial every one of us. The next morning, he greeted us all with a big smile and had nothing to say. That was Sargent Willie. He was all Army, but he was one of us. He was a higher-ranking Major Sargent until, one day when he was drunk and punched an Officer. He was busted down a few stripes, but survived. Advanced Infantry training was pretty intense. I learned to fire all types of weapons from M-16s to mortars and machine guns. They trained me as a forward observer (Foxtrot Oscar.) For some unknown reason, I was good reading maps and coordinates. I had the honor to head up an advanced patrol to locate and call back positions and coordinates. My information would set coordinates for the desired mission and the type of fire on the enemy. I would call in to designate Smoke to set and spot the location. Illumination, would light up the area at night to spot the enemy. Willie Peter was white phosphorous, which when it hit the skin, it would just keep burning through. It was a brutal weapon. Heat, was for big destruction. Pretty heavy stuff for a kid from Long Island who just a few months ago was hanging out in clubs with his friends. The Army had its own way of assigning M. O. S (Military Occupation Specialist). Like Peterson, he was a tough hard nose guy that cursed and drank as much as any of us, if not more. His M. O. S. was Chaplains Assistant. As the training went on we all knew that the days in the States were growing short. The stories of Viet Nam were getting on every one's nerves. I know I had to wake up Andy many times from nightmares. He was really scared of going over. We all were but we showed it in different ways. Vogel, he just kept on telling everyone how he was going to kick some Viet Cong ass. It sounded like he was going to go GI Joe and destroy the Viet Cong by himself. Every guy had his own way of dealing with it. Some were really quiet, others talked big and others showed their fear. I guarantee one thing we all were not happy about going over there. I tried hard to make a joke out of everything and every situation. That was my way of dealing with it. Laugh, laugh and laugh some more. One day we had some big inspection with this tough ass Puerto Rican Officer named Lopez. We were lined up two lines face to face. He walked down the middle busting everyone's balls on the stupidest little thing he could find. Halfway down the line he stops and faces Boomer. Boomer was big and very strong, but he was pretty gentle. As Lopez was reaming him out, he had his back to me. I started making these stupid faces and hand gesture to Boomer. I could see I was getting to him so I did it more and more. Boomer couldn't hold it back, he went from a small smile to laughing. Lopez did not appreciate it so he told him to go into the back of the barracks and wait for him. After the inspection Lopez goes after Boomer big time. Gets in his face and curses him out. Asking if he thinks Lopez is so funny he should take a punch at him. Boomer says he would never hit an Officer. Lopez takes his hat and shirt off and tells him it's off the record, just hit him. Boomer says no. Lopez then pushes him, cursing him over and over. He slaps him in the face and says, "Come on coward, hit me, it's man against man no rank now." Boomer finally breaks and throws a punch toward Lopez's face. Lopez grabs his hand punches him in the gut and picks him up and throws him upside down onto the ground. Boomer just lies there the wind knocked out of him and could hardly catch his breath. "Not so funny now big guy is it. Just consider this combat training" Lopez puts his shirt and hat on and leaves Boomer there. Soon as he leaves we rush in and pick Boomer up and attend to him. After he starts breathing again, I apologized over and over again promising I would never make him laugh again.

As we got closer to our training coming to end you could feel the tension in the air. We knew in a few more days that we would be heading over to Viet Nam. One night this guy named Prinsky climbs up on the roof and starts howling at the moon. I didn't have much to do with him, he was very quiet and kept to himself. Everyone knew he was kind of weird and not too smart, but no one expected this. He just stood on the roof and howled like a wolf. Over and over he wouldn't stop. All the Sargent's were out there ordering him to come down, but he didn't stop howling. One, Sargent was so annoyed he wanted to shoot him. After an hour, they sent up a detail to bring him down. The next day Prinsky was gone and we never saw him again. I thought maybe he was a lot smarter than we were. He found a way out of going, but we all knew he wasn't that type of guy. He was for real. He just broke down and needed some serious help.

Later in the week the day we all feared was upon us. We were headed for Viet Nam. Seventy Five percent of the guys were sent by ship. Finally, I lucked out and was going over by military plane. I was dreading the ship because I knew I would get sea sick so the idea of flying was a lot better. The whole weapons Platoon went by air because of all the heavy weapons we carried. My buddy Andy was right next to me and all the other guys too. My happiness didn't last very long. When we landed I walked off the plane and I almost got sick right there. The smell was disgusting; my Italian nose was very sensitive to odors. The smell was overwhelming. They were burning garbage and human waste. It was hot as hell and the air was like soup. This was my welcome to Pleiku, Viet Nam.

CHAPTER 7

JIMMY "THIS IS NOT THE REAL WORLD ANYMORE"

Here I was in Pleiku, Viet Nam 4th Division, 12th Infantry, Company B, 4th Platoon. I was a Sargent E5 NCO with more responsibility than I had in my life. What did I get myself in too? Andy was always a step behind me and the guys would rib me good about it. They would break my chops about it, but they all knew Andy was helpless and he was like our mascot. The heat and smells were relentless. When the monsoons hit, the rains were, at times, unbearable the gear was so damn heavy that the backpack weighed about fifty pounds and felt double that in the rain. One day we were going from one shit hole to another. We were in a transport truck sitting on the hard- wooden benches. I had only been there about a month. As we were driving on a broken potholed dirt road, the backpack would bounce up and down. We all were miserable. As we drive by, there were village women and children all around. We knew that anyone of them could be hiding a weapon or a grenade and could come at us anytime. Bad enough, we had to worry about the NVA (North Vietnamese Army) and the Viet Cong, but anybody else could take a shot at us. We all heard the stories from the guys who were there awhile. We have also seen the death and the damage they can do. It did not take us long to understand the environment we were in. This was war and the enemy were not so easy to recognize. We had just past a bunch of Vietnamese and I was telling Red and Andy a funny story about my buddies back home. I was actually relaxing a bit as I told the story. Half way through a blast shoots us all straight up. I was propelled straight up and came down on the corner of the truck bench on my tailbone. The force of the fall and the weight of the backpack sent a shooting pain across my lower back and down my legs. We hit a mine trap. We all were stunned and swarmed off the truck ready for an attack. We waited for any sign or movement, but none came.

That was it, we hit a trap, but no attack was coming. Red, Vogel and Maytag helped take my backpack off. They could see I was in a lot of pain. From that day on my back was never the same. The medic gave me some pain pills and it was back to the war. Maybe I should have asked to go to a hospital or something to be checked out, but I couldn't leave my buddies. We were in this together and we all knew it. Crazy as it sounds, not every day was hell. I mean we all knew we were in hell but there were some days we would make the best of it. The days we got mail we would have a break from the jungle and the danger. We sat around reading about back home and the real world. I got lots of letters from the guys, especially Danny. We would share our letters so we all could escape a bit. Some guys were happy to read their letters, others were more private. Girl stuff was kind of off limits and personal. We all loved when Henderson would read his mail to us. He had a buddy back on some farm in Utah. He would read the letter out loud and we all would listen as this guy went on and on about absolutely nothing. He would write how he was sitting on his porch drinking lemonade. I mean the letters were pages about the sky the birds the cows. Henderson just kept on reading and we just kept laughing. We were constantly on the move hiking through the jungles up and down hills. We were close to the Cambodian border and headed up country towards Da Nang. At night, we would dig in and set up camp. Every night was the same. Dig in and wait. The darkness was pure black. There were never any lights anywhere. If you lit a cigarette you could see it for miles. We couldn't light up we couldn't make a sound. If you coughed it would carry forever. It was black and it was pure silence at night. We would break out the rations that were just awful. I was used to eating some great Italian food and to live on this was brutal. They were labeled from World War Two, how the hell does this stuff last that long.

As the days went on each day you survived, you thanked God. As we marched through the heat and brush every now and then there would be some sniper fire. So far there were no casualties and I prayed that we could get out of here with none. A few weeks went by and I didn't know where we were. It all looked the same. As the sun went down, we dug in for the night. Now we were really close to the heavy Viet Cong presence. You can smell them; you can have sense them watching us. At night, we set up Claymore mines about twenty yards around the perimeter of the camp. They were set to blow outward so when ignited, they would blow the shit out of the VC. The VC were getting smarter and smarter on our methods. They would watch us set up the Claymores. At night, they would crawl to them and be able to turn them around so the explosion would come back our way. To counteract, we would set a grenade under the Claymore, pull the pin and secure it. When the VC would crawl up and try to turn it around, they would pull up the Claymore the grenade would go off, "Bang!" one less shit head to worry about. This one night a guy named McCloud from Texas had set up the mine and the grenade. He was a quiet kid, real thin, blonde hair from Plano. He had a cute Texas girl he married just before he left for the Army. He showed us pictures of her and he would love to talk about how much he loved her. After one month, he gets a letter from her that she is really sorry but she can't wait for him and will be filing for a divorce. One month could you believe this shit? Well, after the letter he was destroyed. This kid was very careful in everything he did, from Basic to Advanced Training to Nam. He was by the book and told us he had to stay safe, so he could go home to his beautiful new wife. After the letter, he was volunteering for point for any advanced patrol. It was like he stopped caring about his safety. The next morning, he goes out to retrieve the mine and the grenade. I don't know what he was thinking, but he pulled up the Claymore and the grenade goes off. We went to him and there was blood and pieces everywhere.

The medics wrapped him and called in a chopper. By some miracle he lived but lost the bottom half of his body. I was sick and so were the others. Andy went to the ground for an hour and wouldn't move. He was shaking and moaning. There went my prayers for us to all survive with no casualties.

After McCloud's injuries, we all were badly shaken. Sargent Willie did everything he could to keep us together. One problem we didn't have was staying close. After what happened, we bonded closer together now we were like family. These guys were my brothers. I kept a close eye on Andy to make sure he didn't fall apart. My back was killing me and then marching through the jungles with the backpack was torture. My buddies would try to help me as much as possible. Red would take half my pack and stuff into his to lessen the weight. Sargent Willie one late afternoon gathered us around for a little briefing. It was off the record as he told us about Colonel Stevens Battalion Commander. He told us that it was Colonel Steven's second tour in Nam. His first was a disaster. He lost way too many men. The word was he pushed hard, but stayed far away from the front and they nicknamed him Chicken Shit Stevens. Now he was back with something to prove. He was a classroom trained and all Army. He was big on volunteering his men for all the dangerous missions. He was unsuccessful the first time now he wanted to make a statement. He was out to impress the brass and that meant we were in for some bad shit. Sargent Willie couldn't stand the guy, but he had to follow the orders that came down the chain. I looked at Red, "Hey is this just bad luck or are we cursed?" "I hear you Jimmy. I can't believe we get stuck under his command. We have to watch out for each other and get through this. I want to go back just as pretty as I came in." "Any damaged you take can't hurt you, if anything they might improve that ugly face of yours." Red just smiled, "I always knew you were falling in love with me. Sorry buddy, you're not my type. I like big boobs." I laughed for the first time in weeks saying, "Good to know."

The next few days went by uneventful. Days had no more meaning. Monday or Friday it didn't matter anymore. I had no idea what day it was all I knew it was the same shit. It was raining, muggy, smelly and I was sick of being there. Our Captain leads us to set up in a valley for the night. I look at the Sargent, "In the valley no high ground?" He looks at me with a small grin, "Chicken Shit made the call we follow." Andy pokes me in the back, "Jimmy, I heard what you said. We should take high ground right. Maybe you should talk to the Sargent to let us move." Red says to Andy, "That's a good idea, maybe Jimmy you should get on your radio and see if we could find a Holiday Inn for the night." "Okay cut the crap we do what the man says." So along with the rest of our Company of about two hundred men we dug in for a long night. My back is killing me as we dig the hole and set up the sandbags. The other guys see I'm in a lot of pain, but no one says anything. They all do a little extra to try to help. We set up for the night. The night is as black as you could possibly imagine. The silence is unnerving and sleeping is almost impossible. After a few hours, we start hearing these clanking sounds. Like metal smashing against a railroad track and it's coming from both sides of our position. The sounds vibrate through the night and it's making us all pretty jittery. I hear Andy whispering "What is that?" Boomer puts his hand over Andy's mouth and whispers to him, "Shut it." The sounds are continuously for about a half an hour and then they stop. Silence once again. I take a deep breath and try to relax. A few minutes go by and then we see a light in the distance. The light is moving slowly and then another light, then ten more. The numbers keep on rising twenty now thirty, forty. I start counting there has to be like a hundred moving lights or more. It must be torched or candles they were carrying. We all have weapons ready, waiting for an attack. But it didn't make any sense. The VC won't come with lights to mark their position. I was on my radio with Sargent Willie asking for orders, but all he says is just wait. The lights are making us all squirm and getting ready to fire on anything. Then I get the call, "Put those lights out, and put them out now!" He screams loud and clear. I call in the coordinates and for, "Willie Peter." Round after round we watched the flashes light up the sky. As the White phosphorus hits, the smoke fills the air. Then the screams echo through the night. The phosphorous was doing serious damage. The screams kept on filling the air as we just watched in silence. Andy says, "Are the VC or regular Army?" I shake my head saying, "I don't know" Red says, "They are more likely just village people that the VC make do their dirty work. I bet you they were just women and kids." My stomach sickens as what Red just said is probably true. Those bastards force them out to play mind games with us and they don't give a damn what happens to them. The night just gets worse as the sounds make everyone edgy. On the other side about ten yards away a green guy (a name for a new recruit) I didn't even know fell asleep. He was a fill in who just joined up with us a few days ago. After the screams had finally stopped some guys from sheer exhaustion mentally and physically fell asleep. This guy was one of them. Just as the morning light was breaking through, a couple of guys in his fox hole shake the new guy's legs to wake him up. He wakes up with his rifle in hand and fires, killing the poor guy who tried to wake him. The Captain decided not to charge him. He told Sargent Willie to keep him. He wanted him put out on any and all patrols and take point. If that poor schmuck makes it out alive, it would be a miracle. We were sent out to check on the body count, but there was not one body there. They cleared all the bodies away or buried them somewhere.

CHAPTER 8

DANNY, "WAITING FOR A GIRL LIKE YOU"

While Jimmy was off fighting Viet Cong and the horrible conditions in Viet Nam, I was still doing my thing at Ft Hamilton. After the wedding, me and Sandy kind of faded. She started seeing some old boyfriend that she never got over. I was happy for her because I knew she wasn't the one for me. Ronnie and Dave were doing great. I made it a point to stay as far away from Ronnie as possible. I kept our interactions friendly, but distant. I was still hanging out with Robbie and Sargent Tullo doing the same routine. I took Robbie with me one weekend and went home. Mom and Dad loved Robbie and they were very happy that we stayed. I introduced Robbie to Sal and Ray and they all clicked right away. We told the story about what happened to Stevie. We sat around drinking some beer and talking about Tommy. Saturday night we decided to go to a club in Oceanside. The Page Two was a cool place with a great bar a big dance floor and plenty of young girls. Ray talks to the lead singer of the band and convinces him to let Sal sing a couple of numbers. Sal was really a good singer and did some great Sinatra songs just about everywhere we ever went. He was twenty-one, but looked, dressed and acted as if he was forty. We were all into the Stones, the Beatles, Four Seasons and all the popular groups at the time. Sal was more Sinatra and Tony Bennett. He also was very sensitive to any criticisms of any kind. He did try out once for a singing part for a show. At the audition he did really well and sounded great. Just by accident, Ed Sullivan happened to be in the same theater and actually listened to some of the performers. At the end of the auditions Ray, Sal and I all went outside and who is waiting in front of the building was Ed Sullivan. Sal couldn't resist but to go over to him. He told Mr. Sullivan that he was a big fan and loved his show. They had a pleasant conversation for five minutes. Sal told Mr. Sullivan he wanted to become a professional singer. Mr. Sullivan listened to him and smiling asked Sal if he had a good day job. Sal said yes, he was a liquor salesman and was doing well. Mr. Sullivan smiled, again saying, "That's good news hold onto it because you are going to need it." He shook Sal's hand and jumped into his limo. Sal was in a daze as he watched the limo pull away. After a few minutes Sal turned to us and said, "Did you hear what Mr. Sullivan said, can you believe that. He actually gave me advise. Mr. Sullivan told me not to quit my day job. How cool is that." We all busted out laughing. He took the tough news great. That is Sal, just when you think he is going to go nuts, he laughs it off and loved it. After the band was on a break the lead singer announced that a local singer was going to sing a number for them. We all gave Sal a big applause as he stepped onto the stage. Now Sal could sing but he could also get rattled if things didn't go just right. The band started and Sal went into one of his favorites "Summer Wind" By Frank, of course. He nailed it. The crowd loved it, the band agreed and it was a beautiful thing. Then they asked him to do one more. He chose "Come Fly with me" another Frank standard. Sal was feeling it. He was moving with the beat smiling and then something went wrong. Half way through he forgot the words. He started to get nervous and messes around with the mike on the stand. The adjustable lever on the stand gets loose from him screwing with it. As he is faking the words the mike starts sliding downward. Sal keeps on singing as the mike slides lower and lower. Now you can't even hear him. The mike is just about on the floor and he is bending almost to his knees trying to sing into it. The band tried to save him by cutting the song short and ended it. The same crowd that cheered him a few minutes ago were now laughing at him. Sal does not take this well at all. He jumps off stage and we try to go over to him. He wants nothing to do with us and just pushes past us and out the door. We were having a good time, so we decided to let him go. We thought he would just cool off and come back when he is done with his feet. Robbie and Ray started to do a slow dance with two girls they had met. I started for the bar. A few minutes go by and all of a sudden, we hear this roaring sound. It sounded like a jet was coming through the front door. I looked in disbelief as I see this big ass rear end of a Chevy Impala backing through the front door. "Holy shit, its Sal." He backed the rear of the car up to the open double doors, throws it into park and starts revving the engine. That is a big engine spitting out enough fumes and smoke to wipe out the whole dam club. I grab Robbie and Ray and run to the car. We open the doors I smack Sal in the head and scream at him to get the hell out of here. Thank God he listens and throws it into drive and peels out flying down Long Beach Rd. We take turns yelling at him that he is crazy. He yells back that they made a fool out of him and that he just wanted to mess up their stupid club. He then got all emotional crying that he was sorry and he never would have hurt anyone. A few minutes later he is hysterically laughing. I ask him where are we going now and he says, "The diner, where else."

    The weekend ended and it was back to the Army. I and Robbie went back to Fort Hamilton Sunday night. A few months fly by and everything is the same. I write to Jimmy a few times a week and his letters get more and more depressing. The poor guy is going through hell. There is not a damn thing I can do about it. I speak with Ray and Sal every week. Ray is the same but Sal is seeing a girl now and seems to be getting serious. Ray says Sal is in love! Our off night this month is a Friday night and Robbie and I are alone this time. Sargent Tullo has a family party to go to and is in his good husband and father mode. We head to a Brooklyn club called the Penthouse. I gave Ray and Sal a call and they meet us there. The night is your typical bar night out with the same old talk and drinking. Of course, we keep an eye out for the nice-looking girls. That is a standard we all keep. As much as like screwing around I always know deep inside I am always looking for that special one. As crazy and a fool around a guy I might seem to be on the outside, it's just the opposite on the inside. I am really a one women guy. If only I could find the right one. The night is moving along as usual and then a group of girls catch our attention. There is six of them laughing by the bar. I look at Robbie and before you know it Robbie moves in at the bar. The rest of us keep on talking, but my eyes never leave Robbie and the girls. A few minutes go by and here comes Robbie escorting all six girls to our table. We pull another table over and some chairs as they all sit around with us. We order a round of drinks and we are all joining in on some light conversation. One of the girls, Karen has just got engaged and they are having a night out to celebrate. I'm sitting next to Ellen who is nice, brown hair and better than average looking. Next to her is a beautiful girl with thick black hair, big brown eyes. Kind of tall maybe five nine or so with a great smile and her name is Maria. Ellen keeps a steady conversation going, but I can't stop looking over at Maria. She is in conversation with her friends and I am not getting any looks from her. As the night goes on, I get the feeling Maria is out of my league. She is going to Brooklyn College. That was about all I could get out of the group conversation. I kind of give up hope on Maria because she won't even make eye contact with me. I can't get her attention, so I get the sense she is not interested in me. I do the only thing I know how to do, so I start hitting on Ellen. She seems into me enough, but I'm not really sure. As the night is coming to an end, we all get up and walk outside the club. I keep close to Ellen and decide to make a move on her. I ask if she would like for me to drive her home. She smiled nicely and says she has to go with her friends. That's it for her. No, call me or anything, just walks away. Shut down for sure. It was a fun night but I was kind of down. I really was so drawn to Maria and couldn't even get a look. I kind of settled for second choice and get shot down pretty hard. Not a good night with the ladies for me. I don't show it but I take rejection real hard. I am not Sal, so I don't do anything crazy but I do get hurt pretty bad. I guess I'm the sensitive type and getting my feelings hurt stings. As we have said good night to all the girls, I wish Karen best of luck on her engagement. Maria is standing next to her. I gave up on Maria and knew she wouldn't even notice me leaving. I turned and started to walk away. Maria calls out, "Hey, what about me. I don't get a good night?" Wow! She actually acknowledged me. I was stunned. I smiled and tried to speak but nothing came out. After an awkward minute or two I mumbled a low good night. Instead of walking away, I just stood there like a statue smiling at her. She smiled back at me and I was like mush. I said that I was sorry, but I didn't think you cared or even noticed me. She shook her head saying, "I didn't want to interfere with your obvious attempts of hitting on Ellen." I felt like I got caught cheating on a test or in trouble for doing something wrong at home. I looked into her big brown eyes and spoke so honest that I couldn't believe it was me. I put my head down and shrugged my shoulders saying, "I took one look at you and I wished that I could just spend the night with you and everyone else would just go away. I had no interest in Ellen but I didn't think you even noticed me. So, I did what I always do. Not to look like a fool. I made believe I was into her but I kept on looking at you hoping you would notice me. I know that sounds so corny but it's true." Maria looked at me saying, "That's amazing. I felt the same way about you. I liked you as soon as I met you. I did get the impression you may be one of those players that just likes to sleep around. You know the lounge type of guy. I kind of backed off. As the night went on, I really wanted to get to know you. Are you a lounge playboy type, Danny?" "Are you kidding, me, no way. No, I could care less about that stuff. My problem is that I am kind of shy, especially around someone like you. I mean your kind of a; I don't know how to say it." Maria smiled saying, "What am I some kind of snob." I was turning red and getting nervous and said, "No. That's not it. I think you are like perfect, sought of." Maria said, "You're not so bad yourself, you know." Well that was it. I was like flying as high as you can get without any alcohol or drugs. Man, that was a great feeling. "I know it's getting late, but can we walk for a while and talk?" She said, "Sure, I just have a small problem, I came with my friends. I don't have my car." I quickly replied, "I can drive you home if that's Okay?" She nodded her head up and down smiling, "Yeah, that would be great. Let me just tell Karen." Wow! This was like I was having some kind of dream or like I was in a movie. I mean she was everything I ever wanted in a girl. This was too good to be true. I drove Maria home and we talked the whole way. We could not stop talking for a second. She lived in a row house on Avenue D around Kings Highway Brooklyn. I parked across the street from her house. We talked for hours. She was the oldest of three. Her Grandparents lived upstairs. Her mom and dad were Italian- American, just like mine. She wanted to be a teacher. I told her I was stationed in Brooklyn and lived on Long Island. In a few hours I felt like I knew her my whole life. Talk about connecting, this was as connected as it gets. At the end of the night she said it was late and she should go in. It wasn't easy, but I got the courage up to lean in and softly kiss her. She returned the kiss and we stayed an extra fifteen minutes or so, just making out. Nothing more than kissing and hugging but I didn't want the night to end. Maria said goodnight and I told her I would call her. She said with a smile, "When." I said, "How about tomorrow. It's Saturday and I could see you if you like." She said, "It's a date." Not a question but a definite confirmation. I drove back to the base and had the radio blasting all the way. I forgot about my friends and just about everything else. I had only one thing on my mind and that was Maria. The next few months flew by. I was seeing Maria every chance I had. When I couldn't get off duty I would be on the phone as long as possible with her. I was in love with her from that first night. My hanging out with Robbie and Sargent Tullo was cut down a lot. We remained good friends but I was not going out at all. Those days were gone. I was a new guy. A one women guy that was all I ever wanted and now I found her, Maria.

    Sargent Tullo didn't change. He was up to his old tricks. One day our C.O. came looking for the Sargent at around nine thirty. Captain Monroe was a good friend of Sargent Tullo and they went back a long time. But he was a hot headed, power hungry and egotistical dick. He had scheduled a meeting for nine and was furious that Sargent Tullo was not yet on duty. He screamed at me to let him know the second I heard from the Sargent. I was sitting at my desk when I get a call from no other than Sargent Tullo. I picked up the phone, saying,

"Where the hell are you. You have a meeting or should I say had a meeting at nine." The Sargent in a very low voice almost whispering says, "I know. I might have screwed up. I need a favor. In my draw I have a razor and some shaving cream. Can you get it along with my tooth brush and tooth paste. Oh, also my hair brush and deodorant. Can you bring it across to me? I am in the Brookdale motel. I kind of drank a little too much and spent the night." I replied, "You got to be kidding. Don't bother answering me I know you're not. What room, I will be right there." I grab his stuff make an excuse and run over to the motel. I knock on the door and he comes to the door wrapped in a towel. He opens the door halfway. It's a real small dumpy room and I can't help but seeing a dark haired very young girl. She was lying naked on the bed with a sheet covering a small part of her. She had to be half his age or younger. Not bad looking either. The Sargent did well last night. One of his better overnight guests that's for sure. I just shook my head and handed him a bag of what he asked for saying, "What am I suppose to tell the Captain?" "Nothing." He replies, telling me he would be there in a few minutes. I can't help myself and take a nice look at the girl in bed. I turn around and have to smile you just can't get mad at this guy. Well not me anyway or just about anybody else but not the Captain. He is going to go nuts when the Sargent comes in. Sure, enough about twenty minutes later in comes the Sargent. All looking sharp, hair combed, uniform all snug and a big huge smile on his face. He says good morning to everyone as he passes down the hall. He marches into his office, like he does not have a care in the world and closes the door. He is unbelievable! A few minutes later, my phone rings and the Captain is asking if I heard from the Sargent. I tell him he is in his office and I was just going to call the Captain. He slams the phone down sending a bang through my ear. About two minutes later the Captain bulls by everyone in his way as he heads right to the Sargent's office. This lateness and missing meetings are nothing new with the Sargent. He has been doing it since I got here. Each time the Captain threatens him over and over. He gets so mad he curses and breaks everything in his path. The Sargent just smiles and apologizes. He promises it will never happen again, over and over again. It is the same way he apologizes to his wife. He promises his wife it will never happen again. With his puppy dog face and sincere apology, he gets out of it every time. The Captain charges into the Sargent office and I rush to the door. I wait just outside the door listening to what's going on. I hear the Captain speaking very loud but not really yelling. I then hear the Sargent telling him this crazy story that he had an emergency and he had to take care of it. He then said he was sorry and it won't happen again. I shook my head and thought that he has done it again. Just as I started slowly walking away from the door, I hear a loud bang. The next thing the door comes smashing down almost knocking me out. The Captain has the Sargent by the throat and both their bodies come crashing down. The Captain was cursing and choking the Sargent as they rolled around the floor. I reacted pretty quickly and grabbed the Captain by his back and tried to pull him off. It took a while, but I finally was able to get the Captain to release his choke hold on the Sargent. After a few minutes both of them brushed themselves off and adjusted their uniforms and hair. The Captain looked at me but said nothing as he walked away. The Sargent looked at me and with a big smile and said, "Did you see that, he tried to kill me. I don't know what's wrong with that man. Can you call my wife and tell her I am okay? I couldn't call her because I was on one of my special assignments." I answered, "Sargent, why can't you call her?" He smiled, saying, "I am late for a very important meeting." I took a deep breath and walked back to my office.

CHAPTER 9

JIMMY "WHERE HAVE ALL THE SOLDIER'S GONE"

More days go by and then weeks. Same routine march and dig in at night. Trying to track down and find VC was almost impossible. They fire, attack and disappear. They would run around in their black pajamas, a canteen of water, a bag of rice and a AK-47. They were small and quick.

They had all kinds of caves that they would disappear into. We had all our uniforms, gear, field packs, extra rounds of ammo and most of us were kind of big and tall. They also were smart and cunning. One day on patrol we take sniper fire but thank God no one was hit. We return fire and then chase. It was me, Andy, Maytag and Red following two VC through the dense jungle. We come upon an opening and find a tunnel hole. The opening was so small that it was hard to believe they could fit through it. Andy was way too big he had no chance. Maytag was taller than me and Red, so it was us two that went in. I squeezed through the small opening and hit the bottom. It was dark and I could hardly see. Me and Red had to crouch down so low we could hardly walk. We had our rifles and couldn't even get in any position to fire if we had too. As we are crawling and moving through Red says, "Don't move just stay down." I don't see anything but I do as he says. "What's up?" Red says, "Don't move and slowly start going back real slow. There are two viper snakes nailed above you." I froze with fear. One, I hate any kind of snakes and I know these suckers can kill you. I do exactly what Red says and in unison we both start real slow backing out. My legs were shaking, I was so scared. Slowly we back up and I keep my eye on them. The tunnel is so small I had no chance of even lifting my rifle to shoot them. We just keep moving backwards until we are away from them. We both jump up and out of the hole. I can't stop shaking and felt so rattled I just fell to my knees. Andy and Maytag together ask, "What happened?" Red tells them what was down there. "Oh, shit Maytag says in disgust." Red says to me, "Are you okay?" "Yeah just give me a minute. I tell you one thing I am not going in those shitty tunnels again. You hear me. I don't care if Colonel Chicken Shit himself ordered me too. I'd tell him to drop dead before I do it. They can court martial me, I don't care. Do you hear me?" "Okay Jimmy calm down, we hear you and we are with you. No more tunnels. If they go in there good-bye Charlie, let them go." Maytag said. Red and Andy shake their heads in agreement. That night we decided the next chance we have we will get pistols to carry with us. As my story spread every one of the guys were writing home to send them a pistol. It took a little while but the whole Company was carrying them. The Army didn't issue them so we did it ourselves. It was kind of funny after a while you could tell the difference from who came from the East or the West. The Eastern guys wore shoulder holsters and the western guys wore them cowboy style on their hips.

 I read the letters from the guys back home over and over again. Danny would tell me everything. He told me all about Maria and how much he loves her. I was happy for Danny, but I was getting more and more distant. I liked getting the letters, but I could hardly write back anymore. I couldn't put into words what was going on over here. I knew they wouldn't understand. They couldn't relate to this hell that I was in. So, there was no use in writing. They knew nothing about this shit country. They didn't know any of the guys I was with. So, what was the sense? I had nothing good to say so I decided not to say anything.

As time went on, I could feel myself changing. You get to the point you don't seem to care anymore and are ready for anything. But then shit happens and you feel the pain again. We all thought we were tough guys now. There were days, even Andy started to talk like Vogel. He said he was ready to kick Cong ass. One sticky day just about twilight we were on patrol. This kid from the Midwest named Conners was walking a few yards in front of us. He was a big kid strong and built like a linebacker. Well, he actually was a linebacker. He played for some Midwest high school and was some kind of Friday night hero. At least that's what he told us. He was proud how strong he was. He asked to carry all the extra ammo we needed. He wrapped them around his neck and shoulders. Looked like some Mexican desperado. He was also a nice kid. He would write his mom every chance he could. He told us he had to go to work to support her and his three younger sisters. He said he could have gone to a big ten college on a full ride for football. He had to say no because he had to work. He knew his mom needed him to help support them. Then he gets drafted and had to leave anyway. Instead of getting a free education and playing football, he ends up in this shit. Man, life is weird the way it dishes this crap out. As we approached the village there was no moon and it was so black we couldn't see shit. Conners was out in front, but we were in a pretty safe area according to intelligence. So, we are not too uptight and kind of relaxed. Red's telling me about some of his girl conquests and I'm listening as best I could. As Red is talking away I hear a strange sound. "What was that?" I said to Red. He says, "Maytag where did that come from?" Boomer yells out, "It came from up ahead where Conner's is." We speed up to see what was going on. I yell out "Conners what's going on?" No reply, but we hear what sounded like someone was yelling help but very faintly. We all run ahead. I hear Maytag yell, "He fell. He fell in a well" I run to the site and I see that Conners fell in a well and it was really deep. He was weighed down with all the gear and the extra ammo. Maytag yells in a panic, "We need some rope or something to throw down to him. Hurry, we need it now!" I look at Red, "What do we have?" He looks down, saying "Pants, shirts give me them." We all take our shirts and pants tie them together. Red grabs one end and tosses it down the well. I Scream, "Conners grab the line! Grab the line! Conners!" All the guys were yelling the same thing, but it was too late. He had too much weight and it took too long to get the line down to him. He was gone.

CHAPTER 10

JIMMY "CHAIN OF FOOLS"

The days and nights dragged on. We were fighting off everything from VC to NVA (North Vietnamese Army) to every type of bug, snake, and disease known to mankind. Plus, the weather was disgusting, along with the odors it was worse than I could have ever imagined. Just when you think it can't get any worse it does. We were off US 1 as we dig in for the night. Sargent Williams tells us there is a big battle going on with Company C. They are trying to hold some piece of Crap Hill. We are losing more guys trying to take or defend these hills in the middle of nowhere. It's really screwed up when you think about it. We try not to think about it. As the night goes on we hear the sounds of heavy fighting. Andy crawls up to me and whispers, "That sounds like some heavy stuff going on up there. Do you think we will have to get involved in the battle? I know I sound stupid Jimmy but I just have a hard time dealing with all this." "I know Andy, we all do. You are not alone we are all scared and sick of this shit. I know you think I am some kind of GI Joe but I'm not. I am just as worried as you and so are all the other guys. All we can do is wait it out and hope Company C kicks their ass really good and we have to go in and do a little clean up. Try to tune it out and get some sleep. We all need it." The next morning after a sleepless night we wait for our orders. Sargent Williams tells us we are moving out. We are relieving Company C. They took heavy

Another Day in Neverland

casualties but held the hill. They were just about run over but they held. Chicken Shit Stevens volunteered us to relieve them. As we are listening to the Sargent a chopper circles us and lands in a clearing just a few clicks from where we are. Red yells, "Holy shit, look who is joining us in the fight, it's our fearless leader, Stevens himself. Now I have seen everything." Colonel Stevens calls us all around and gives a rousing speech maybe he copied from Vince Lombardi's half time talk to the Green Bay Packers. "Let's go get them men we need a victory so let's win one for the old USA, go Army!" I mean not quite those words but just about. After his moving speech, our leader gets into the chopper and off he went, to some safe place to watch the show. Maytag yells out, "This is bullshit. Do you believe what just happened?" If we all weren't so scared and sick, it would have been laughable unfortunately it wasn't. Sargent Williams shakes his head and off we go up the hill. As we are going up, Company C is coming down. They were in bad shape. There were way too many casualties. There was no reason to ask because it was all over their faces that they just spent a night in hell. We all knew it so we just nodded as they passed us by. We are marching up this steep incline and my back is killing me. I'm carrying this field pack and all the ammo, its torture. It was early morning but the heat and stale air made it hard just to breathe. The signs of damage and the stench of death were all around us. We had no choice but to follow orders so up the hill we go. We finally reach the top and the Sargent tells us to take positions and wait for orders. After we are settling in and we are taking a smoke break I hear a lot of loud talk coming from the Captain. He is screaming back and forth on the radio. After it ends the orders are in, "Get the hell off the hill." The Colonel was screaming at the Captain that he misunderstood the command. The Colonel ordered air strikes on the hill at eleven hundred hours. So now we drag all our gear and equipment back down the hill. We are a few clicks away from the hill and we all sit around watching the air show and fireworks. As we watch, the Air force bomb the hell out of the hill that we were just on and secured. I looked at Maytag and Red, "Do you believe this shit?" Red says, "Oh yeah." Maytag puts his head down and just starts laughing. In a few minutes, the whole Company was laughing and smiling. Even the Captain was laughing. You can't make this shit up. No one would believe it. Now, in the burning sun, it's time to march back up the hill. Off we go dragging our asses up the hill. After the dust settles there were villager's, all women and kids around the hill looking for I'm not sure what. Maybe watches, rations, gold teeth anything that they could grab. We are warned about the women in those big hats could be hiding grenades or whatever to take us out. We watch for any kind of movement, but nothing happened.

As the day goes down the Sargent comes over to me and says, "The Colonel says the hill is secured so we are leaving. But just in case the VC or NVA decides to come back, he wants to leave a small squad of fifteen men to set an ambush." I look at Sargent Williams with utter confusion, "Fifteen men to do what? If the NVA comes back how are fifteen men going to be able to hold the hill? They will be over run." "Colonel says they can ambush the VC and stop them. If it's the NVA, you can call for heavy artillery from the Navy in the China Sea. We need a forward observer to be one of the fifteen of course." I just shake my head and look at Maytag. We both know that is one of us. We were both forward observers, so we decided to flip a coin on who stays to possibly die up here, or go down and live at least another day. Well Maytag won the flip and I get to stay. Maytag says he sorry, we hug and I watch all my buddies start down the hill. Andy was one of the last to move out and says, 'Do you want me to stay with you. I will volunteer to stay." "Andy thanks, but no. Get the hell out of here. I will join up with you and the guys in a day or so. Thanks for saying that I appreciate it." Andy smiles saying, "You're like my brother Jimmy, I can't have anything happen to you. I don't know what I would do without you." Andy it's Okay I will be fine. Now get the hell out of here Brother." After they all left it was me, Jordan, Rega, Gulli, Sonny and Red. The rest were new grunts. We spread out around the mountain but it was way too big of an area to secure. We decided to take the highest point with our backs to US 1. It was way too steep for anyone trying to come up that way. As the night rolled in we dug in and we knew we were in for a long night. The night before Company C was almost overrun by the NVA so we knew we had no chance of survival if they decided to come again. Maybe we could hold off a small amount of VC from our position. Rega looked at me saying, "Do we have any chance of calling in the heavy artillery and mortars in time to stop an NVA attack?" I just shook my head. Red said, "Yeah of course and we can call in John Wayne or the Calvary to help out while we are at it. This is bullshit, the Colonel has his head up his ass and we have to pay for it with our lives. There is no way we make it through an NVA attack. If they come we are all dead." Jordan joined in saying, "Shut it down Red, we will be fine. The NVA is long gone. They saw the firepower and they want no part of it. If the VC comes, we can handle them." Gulli adds, "Right on brother, good talk Jordan you are the man." We all smile and quiet it down. The night drags on slowly. Time just seems to stand still. I put my hands around my face and silently pray. "Lord, please gets us through the night." My mind starts to wander to my life back home. Big decisions were where we would go to on a Friday night. What diner do we hit after the club? That world is long gone. Sometimes I think it was all a dream, there is no real world anymore. This is it. I can't see myself ever getting out of this country. Red says, "Everyone stays still don't move, I hear something." We all freeze and wait. A few seconds later rapid fire fills the air. The bursts are coming from us. I call out to see what was going on. Red checks it out it was one of our guys thought he saw something move and opened fire. Thank God it wasn't VC, it was a false alarm. The night crawled by and we made it through. Morning came and we all felt a lot better as we watched the sunrise and we were all still alive. They brought in some choppers and got us out that day.

    The Army was always good with surprises as we were taken to Taipei, Taiwan for some R and R. I was reunited with the other guys and Andy greeted me with a hug that could have squeezed the last bit of breath from my lungs. But I was so happy to see him, I kissed him on the head. We were told to go to a couple of bars, one was the 63 Bar on Min Chuan Road in W. Taipei. The other was Pink Bar on Min Chuan west road Taipei. They treated us like "Number one American GI," As they would say. Plenty of cheap booze and women to cater to our needs and it was just what the doctor ordered.

CHAPTER 11

DANNY "ALWAYS AND FOREVER"

As the months went by, I was seeing Maria every free time I had. I brought her to my Parents house on weekends whenever I could. My parents took her right away. My brother Alex was also in the Army stationed in Germany. Maria became the daughter they never had really fast. They both loved her and you could tell she felt the same. I spent a lot of time at Maria's house with her Family. All I ever heard from them was when we were going to get married. They were very nice, warm, loving Italian American family. One summer night I took Maria to our favorite place. It was the same place that we went on our first date. It was an amusement park in Far Rockaway. It was different than the current parks. There was no admission, just lots of rides and games, set by the water in the Rockaways. We called it Rockaway Play land. I'm not sure if that was its official name but it was to all of us. After doing our usual rides and games we took a walk along the boardwalk. It was a beautiful summer night and the stars were as big and clear as you could ever want. We stopped by a bench facing the ocean and sat. I was so nervous my legs were shaking. I told Maria, I had something that I had to tell her. She looked upset, saying, "I knew it something bad, right? You're being shipped to Viet Nam; I have always been afraid that was going to happen." I said, "No, that's not it." She spoke before I could get another word out, "You're in trouble, you're married, tell me I can't take it." "No, nothing like that; I love you and I want you to be my wife. I want to spend the rest of my life with you." She started to cry saying, "You're asking to marry me." I held her and said, "Yes, I love you." She looked into my eyes saying, "Yes, Yes of course yes. I love you." We held each other close for a long time. Then Maria looked at me saying, "I am so happy but just one question. Is there a ring maybe down the road?" I throw my hands up and said, "Of course, I am so sorry. I was so excited I forgot the ring, my speech, everything I rehearsed over and over again all week." I reached into my pocket, took out the box and opened it. I took the ring and placed it on her finger. We both cried and laughed at the same time. She whispered, "I love it and I love you." After that night the months flew by. If anyone had it all it was me. I was happy in love and I was still safe, away from the hell in Viet Nam. I wrote to Jimmy told him all about the engagement. He wrote back that he couldn't be happier for me. His words were sincere but I could tell the pain and fear he must have been enduring. He never would write about any bad stuff just a few words about some ugly things that he was dealing with. I could tell he didn't want me or anybody to know what it was like over there. I felt mixed emotions when I wrote or even thought about Jimmy. Here I was living a dream while he is living in a nightmare. The truth was there was nothing I could do about it. Sal and Ray were happy for me. My Mom and Dad were over the top with joy. All my Mom wanted to know is when did I think I would be having her first Grandchild. I explained that I thought it would be the right thing to do was to get married first and let Maria be the one that has the baby. She laughed and said that I knew what she meant. The time went by and the next thing I know my wedding day was coming up. It was just over a year from the night we met to our wedding day. That was fine with me. I couldn't be sure of anything than my love for Maria. I knew she felt the same so there was no reason to wait. The money was going to be a problem but we would manage.

 The wedding was your typical Brooklyn wedding. Her parents picked the hall, it was Sirico's on Thirteenth Avenue. Maria's Dad knew one of the brothers that owned the catering hall so it was perfect. All my friends were there all except Jimmy, who was still serving in Viet Nam. There were around one hundred and fifty guests, so it was a decent size affair. Maria looked like a beautiful angel in her flowing white wedding dress. My brother Alex was back at home. He was done with the service and was a rookie New York City cop. I had Sal, Ray, Robbie, Sargent Tullo and my other buddy Chuck along with their dates at one table. Of course, Sargent Tullo was with his wife Bee and not his date. The night went along great. The band played and we all danced and drank. My Mom and Dad were at the table with my aunts and uncles. After a few extra highballs (Whisky and ginger ale) my Pop was feeling no pain. He tried to get my aunt Jenny to have a drink but like she always refused. My Aunt Jenny was around Fifty years old but was on the heavy side, all grey, very conservative, wore no makeup and dressed ultra-frumpy. My Dad was working her good, "Come on Jenny let me get you just one highball, its Danny's wedding." Finally, she caved in telling my Dad just a very weak one. My Dad was delighted he called me to come over with him to the bar. He asked the bartender for a ginger ale and a couple of red cherries. He squeezed the cherries into the ginger ale and added a straw that had a little whistle at the end of it. The whistle straws were a little take home for the guests. It had Maria and Danny and the wedding date written on the side of it. My Dad told me that Aunt Jenny never touched a glass of liquor in her life. The cherry juice will give the soda a different taste and she won't know the difference. I asked him why he doesn't give her the real thing. He said, "What are you crazy. She might get sick or pass out. This will make her think she can drink and be part of the fun group for a change." I agreed, "Whatever you say Pop sounds good to me." My Dad was one of those guys that when he drank, he became very happy and a little bit of a prankster. He loved to laugh and make others laugh along with him. He always reminded me a little of Lou Costello of Abbot and Costello. We brought the soda over to my Aunt and my Pop says, "Now just sip it Jenny you don't want to get drunk." She replies, "Absolutely not!" As a little while passes we were watching her as she sips the soda through the straw and likes it. I kind of smiled and nodded to my Pop. I danced with Maria a few fast numbers and went to the bar for a cold beer and walked over to my Mom and Dad's table. My Dad is laughing his head off because Aunt Jenny seems to be carrying on like she is drunk. She is laughing (which she never does} and singing aloud to the band. She looks at me saying, "Danny your Dad is very bad. He gave me two of these highballs and I think I am getting drunk." On top of that now every few minutes she keeps blowing on the whistle. Every time she does it makes everyone laughs and she loves it. I look over to my Pop and he can't stop laughing. Well, I guess that old saying mind over matter is true. Aunt Jenny believed she was drinking so she was getting drunk on soda with cherry juice. Sal sang a couple of Sinatra numbers and everyone loved it. He was on and he knew it. A minor problem was when Jimmy the owner came over to me and asked if I could speak to one of my friends to behave. I asked him who? He pointed out my buddy from high school Chuck. Jimmy said that he was eating the place cards and the flower arrangements on the table. I smiled and walked over to Chuck and asking if he would please stop eating the place and cards. Chuck smiled and said in a voice that was very slurred, "I'm so sorry was I not supposed to that? I answered it would be better to stick to the food and deserts if he didn't mind. Chuck nodded his head up and down in total agreement. After his final nod, he placed his head on the table and in seconds he was fast asleep. The band played on and we were all dancing like crazy. Sal, Ray, Robbie and Sargent Tullo were all on the dance floor together smoking cigars and throwing their hands in the air going crazy to the song "Shout." It was pretty late in the night and everyone was feeling really good. All the drinking hit them pretty hard. Even my seventy- five- year old Aunt Nancy was out on the dance floor. She was dancing with a portable oxygen tank connected to her side. Just as the band was winding down to the end of the song, down goes Aunt Nancy. Everyone stops dancing and they form a big circle around her. Someone yells out to call a doctor and an ambulance. Sal jumps down next to her to attend to her. He leans over her yelling are you alright. As he is talking, her daughter screams out, "He has a cigar in his hand, she has oxygen." Sal looks up saying, "What's wrong?" As everyone is yelling at him to get away from her, Ray yells, "What are you nuts you have a lit cigar and she has oxygen." Sal realizes what they are saying so he jumps to his feet and throws the cigar into a glass of beer at the nearest table. Aunt Nancy comes back to life and says she just passed out but is now fine. The band starts to pack up and the wedding is officially over. Everyone starts leaving and I see my Pop still at the table. Now he has a white linen table cloth draped over his head and shoulder as he says he can see the future and is now a fortune teller. There was no one left at the table but my Mom who was just smiling at me and my Dad shaking her head. "What am I going to do with him Daniel he will never change?" I smiled at her and said, "I will help Dad get into the car. Uncle Joe is driving you guys home."

As I am helping him up Maria comes over to help him on his other side. We follow Uncle Joe and my aunt Jenny out the door. My Dad keeps commenting to us to check out Aunt Jennie's legs. He says they look like tree trunk stumps. And Uncle Joe the big shot politician. I said to my Dad to keep it down or they will hear you. He just laughed. Well, that was it. Maria and I put Mom and Dad in Uncle Joe's car and off they went. All my friends kissed us goodnight. Maria's Mom and Dad, Grandparents kissed us and everyone was gone. We were the last ones out. I know that was not the usual but we had a great night and just kind of lingered in it. I didn't get much time off. I was still in the Army but we managed a few nights in Atlantic City for a honeymoon.

After my two years in the Army, I was out. We didn't wait very long and Maria gave birth to our first Daughter Lucia. Maria was a sweetheart and she agreed to name our baby after my Mom. My Mom was Lucy but in Italian it was Lucia. We liked that better and my Mom loved it. Lucia Gabby (Gabby was short for Gabriella for Maria's Mom) Ray and Sal were still around. Me and Maria ended up in a small apartment on Long Island. We agreed we wanted the suburbs to raise our kids and not Brooklyn. Maria had her teaching degree from Brooklyn College but for now she was a stay at home Mom. Sal and Ray have been always around and Maria would cook for them every other Sunday. Robbie and I stayed close and we went into business together. We started small and opened a used car lot. It was small time but we did okay. We kept in touch with Sargent Tullo who was still in the Army. Jimmy's tour was up but for some unknown reason he extended the service and went to military police. He was stationed in Saigon. I wrote to him all the time but his letters went unanswered. With him now everything was a mystery. Once again there was not much, I could do but to keep writing him and keeping him up to date with our lives. Once again, I had to say it was like I was living a dream. Lucia was a beautiful little Maria, looked just like her. We had our second Daughter, Angelina Sofia named after Maria's Grandmother. The business was doing great. We doubled the size and our sales were through the roof. I was on a super roll ever since I met Maria. Then as we all know in life nothing lasts forever. It was an ordinary Tuesday and I worked kind of late. I came home and we had dinner. I watched a little of the Yankee game. Maria had been already in bed and so were the girls. I flopped into bed and fell asleep. The stupid alarm goes off at seven just like every other day. I jumped in the shower and after a few minutes Maria comes in. She tells me my Brother is on the phone and he needs to talk to me. I know right away that it's not good. He never calls at this time in the morning. I wrap a towel around me and go to the phone. I say, "What's wrong?" "It's Dad, He had a heart attack." I start shaking, "Is he alright?" There's nothing but silence and I knew. Just like that, one phone call and I would never see my dad again. It was brutal the more it sunk in, the worse it got. I wish I could just see him to tell him how much I loved him. It was difficult but the reality was he was gone. We had the funeral back in Brooklyn where my Parents lived most of their lives. The funeral hall was on the corner of Forty First Street off of Fort Hamilton Parkway. The wake was packed for three days and nights. Everybody that knew my Dad and loved him. No one ever had a bad thing to say about him. The doctor told us he didn't suffer; it was a massive heart attack. Not much of a consolation when you lose your Father who you loved so very much. But what can you do, life goes on.

My Mom moved in with my Brother who lived in Brooklyn. He had a two- family house along with my Sister-in-Law Joan. They lived in a nice area off the belt parkway not far from where I was stationed at Fort Hamilton. It was tough on us all. At least my Dad got to see his two Granddaughter's. He was so proud of them. He bought Lucia this wind- up swing. We would strap her in it, winded it up and she would swing back and forth nice and slow. She loved it. She would go right to sleep just about every time we put her in it. My Mom was heartbroken, but at least she was taken care of had a good home with family. Just as they say life goes on. I was back to work and our life was back on track. There isn't a day that goes by where I don't think of my Dad. When it hits me, I need to go somewhere and cry it out. Maria has been always there for me and so are my daughters. As difficult as it was, I was still happy because I had them.

CHAPTER 12

JIMMY "WELCOME TO THE JUNGLE"

After the R and R, we were sent just south of Tuy Hoa, not too far north of an Air Force base in Nha Trang on the China Sea coast. It wasn't bad around there compared to what we just went through. One day the company was deployed to a hill which overlooked the river down below. Sargent Willie comes over to me with a big smile and says, "Do you see the VC in the two small shits floats in the river?" We look at the river and we see what are older village fisherman sitting two in a small pontoon boat. I turn to Sargent Willie, "No way are they VC, they're just a couple of old fishermen catching something to eat for dinner." Sargent Willie grabs my binoculars, "Bullshit they're VC. I know Gooks when I see them. Cetano turn the mortar around and blow those VC shits out of the water." I look at Red who was right beside me, "They're no VC or am I nuts?" Red says, "Hell no they're just fisherman." I say to Sargent Willie, "Come on Sarge let's get out of here no way their VC." Sargent Willie yells, "Turn it around and fire on my command." "No way, Sarge I'm not going to kill fishermen." Sargent Willie grabs the mortar and starts dialing in the coordinates himself. I look at Red and we both know he's never shot the damn thing himself. He is acting crazy and there was no way we could stop him anyway, so we let him do his thing. He starts dialing in, sets the mortar and fires. The first rounds splash down 100 yards off to the right. The fishermen start waving their shirts yelling at us. We don't understand what they are saying and we couldn't hear them anyway. It was obvious they were scared and saying no VC just fishing. Sargent Willie readjusts and fires again, this time further off to the right. He starts cursing and repeats a few more rounds. He does get a little closer as they were rowing farther away. After a few more minutes it was obvious even to Sargent Willie he isn't going to hit them so he gave up. He was pissed at us and didn't say a word to us the rest of the day.

One thing about Sargent Willie the next day it was all forgotten, like it never happened. A few days later back at base camp, Sargent Willie was at it again. He had a few afternoon belts and he grabs me. He tells me he wants to visit an old buddy at the Air Force base. I start following him to get the jeep but he says, "No, I don't want that thing I want to use that over there." I look where he is pointing and I just shake my head, "That's a tank." Sargent Willie looks at me, "Of course it's a tank. What are you, stupid?" Tanks were of not much use in the jungles and we did not see too many of them. Sargent Willie was very familiar with them because he was in a tank division in the Korean War. So, he did know how to drive them. We go over to the tank and he says to get in. We climb up onto the tank and he says, "Cetano, you drive." I answer, "What? I don't know how to drive this thing." He looks at me and smiles, "Just get down there in the driver's seat and I will guide you through the headphones it's like driving a jeep. Just start her up and listen to me. There you go, just start her up and let's get going." I think to myself this might just be the end of my Army tour. If I take out someone or some expensive piece of military property, it's a court marshal and I'm out of here. That's so bad. I have nothing to lose. I listen to Sargent Willie's directions and start it up. Next thing I know I have it moving, but I can't keep it straight. I'm all over the place. I start to straighten out a bit but I over compensate the move and now I'm headed right for the dump station. I see the racks of 55-gallon tanks of crap waiting to be burnt. Sargent Willie yells, "Cetano, What the hell are you doing, go left shithead." I try to slow down and turn left but I panic and I'm heading right at the barrels. Sargent Willie Pushes me away and turns as best he could but it was too late. We take out the rows and rows of barrels and really the shit hits the fan. The tank is covered in crap and I look at Sargent Willie and he is fuming. I don't know what to say so I say, "Sorry Sarge I screwed up. I guess we're in some deep shit now." As I said it, I couldn't help it, I just started laughing. After a minute of watching me, Sargent Willie started to laugh along with me. Needless to say, it was a shitty day and guess who was assigned to clean it up, Not Sargent Willie but me. Of course, the jokes never stopped after that. "Hey Cetano, I heard you had a shitty day." Hey Cetano, Sargent Willie says you're a shitty driver or you can't drive for shit. I was famous everyone laughed as soon as they saw me. I knew Sargent Willie was at fault. He should never have told me to drive it but I bit the bullet and said I wanted Sargent Willie to give me a lesson to drive it. I said it was a dream of mine to drive a tank and Sargent Willie just wanted to grant my wish. I went through a lot out in the field and he was rewarding me for it. What a great guy he was. Sargent Willie liked that I had his back and I knew he appreciated it.

After our stay in Tuy Hoa things were not so funny. We received new orders and we were headed to Pleiku. The helicopters took us towards Pleiku. They dropped us off and we marched through Happy Valley and headed toward the Cambodian border. We left the lowlands where there were all rice patties, farmland and jungle. Northwest was mountains and totally different. On one of our first missions in the area, we came across a large tribal village. It had these large wooden twelve to fifteen-foot-high stake fence around the village. The tips were sharp, obvious for defensive protection against intruders. It reminded me of the movie King Kong. Our interpreter told us they were Mountain Yards Natives (Degar Montagnard). Usually no one bothers with them not even the NVA or the VC. They have been there forever and they know the mountains and the jungles very well. Captain decided we would go to the front gate and try to speak with them. He felt they might have helpful information on the enemy and their location. It was known that have spoken to the US Army before. As we approached the gate a few of the natives came out. They were small, muscular, dark skinned, with bones in their ears and nose. They reminded me of the Aboriginals of Australia. Some women came out and they were bare chested with little grass like skirts. The men wore skin shorts and bare chested. The interpreter communicated for the Captain and they made a good connection. The Captain and a few officers were invited into the village. The gates were closed behind them. The rest of the Company about one hundred and sixty men were in a defense mode and waited outside. About thirty minutes went by and no sign of the officers. All of us were starting to get a little worried about what was going on in there. The general buzz was what was taking so long? Red yelled out, "Hey, they're probably boiling big pots of water and serving US Army Officer stew for dinner." Gulli added, "Yeah, they could have the Captain on a spike rotating over the open fire." We all had a good laugh. After a few more minutes went by the Captain and the Offices came out. They gained information where the VC and the NVA were located. They were wearing brass bracelets that they received in a ceremony while they shared rice wine. Most of the natives came out and we sat in circles as they offered all of us these brass bracelets and their rice wine. Unfortunately, not all of the guys participated. They did not trust them and looked at them more like they were VC. My buddies and I enjoyed them and it was a great experience. A while later we were back on the mission. Wearing our new brass bracelets.

About eight months into my tour, our Lieutenant Skippy was promoted to first Lieutenant executive officer and second in command of the company. We were happy he was promoted he was a great guy and deserved it. His replacement arrived a few days later. He was all gung ho right out of officer's candidate school in the states. He had an attitude that he was going to win the war by himself. His first course of business was to call our platoon for a full out inspection. Sargent Willie introduced him to us as Lieutenant Burley. We hadn't had an inspection since we were in the states. We all started mumbling what a bunch of bullshit this was. The Lieutenant was wearing a baseball cap with the big letter "B" on it. He was from Boston, but he explained the "B" was for Burley's rangers. Guess what? That was what we are going to be called from now on. I turned to Red and said, "Oh shit what an asshole." All the guys around started to laugh. Sargent Willie called us to attention and to get information. The Lieutenant started to tell us that we will lead the way. Night patrols, ambush missions, whatever it took, he will lead us to get the job done. These were the worst missions that he was going to volunteer us for. We were lined up in formation for the inspection and he walks down checking our gear. He comes to my buddy Gordan where he stops and looks at his rifle, "Soldier this rifle is unacceptable." He takes the rifle and sticks its muzzle down in the sand about six inches. Then barks at Jordan, "I want to see this weapon cleaned in a half hour, now pick up your weapon and get back in formation." The Lieutenant stood face to face with Gordan. Gordan was an African American, over six feet tall and built solid. He came from a tough area and did not take shit from anyone. The Lieutenant was five feet nine, black hair, good looking, in perfect top physical condition. He looked like he came out of a movie poster. As they were face to face, Gordan just stood his ground and you could see steam coming from his ears. One unwritten rule is that no one screws around or even touches another soldier's weapon. We all knew our weapons were cleaned, oiled and could pass any inspection. We had been here for long enough and knew our weapons were keeping us alive. This asshole was trying to show he was now in control and was a tough guy. Even Sargent Willie was shocked at the action taken by the Lieutenant. Gordan looked the Lieutenant in the eye, "You stuck my weapon in the sand so you fucking clean it." Gordan's eyes were glued into the Lieutenant and you could see he was about to kill him. Burley started to respond to Gordan, but Sargent Willie stepped in between them, "Lieutenant, we have to talk." Sargent Willie then ushered Lieutenant Burley into the tent. We could not hear everything that he was saying but we heard enough. He told him that that is not the way to treat soldiers like that. If he wanted to have the respect of his outfit he better change his attitude quickly or he would not survive over here. Sargent Willie's talk definitely worked because Lieutenant Burley came out of the tent, pulled the rifle out of the sand and apologized to Jordan for his actions.

After a few weeks went by' he did adjust to us, but that did not stop him from volunteering us for all the shit assignments. On one of his self-serving missions of search and destroy, backfired on him big time. What was different on this mission was we had the use for the first time of a canine unit. The unit consisted of a trained team of a German Sheppard and his Corporal handler. The duty of the Corporal and his German Sheppard were to be up front and lead the patrol. The canine was trained to sniff, hear, and see for traps, VC, and ambush. If the dog sensed any of these he stops and points to the danger, he signals to the unit to take proper action. The Corporal uses hand signals to communicate. As we moved up the mountain and through the jungle bush and elephant grass the dog got excited indicating there was something in front. The dog then started to slowly run heading towards the top of the hill. At that point Lieutenant Burley was positioned behind the dog and his handler instead of where a squad leader would normally be which was in the middle. Now our fearless leader decides to run ahead of the dog and his handler. The dog was in a controlled run gets excited and begins to chase Lieutenant Burley. He jolts ahead and the Corporal trying to keep up with them trips and falls. His rifle goes off accidentally and shoots Lieutenant Asshole in the ass. He goes down with a loud scream. We all gathered around our fallen hero setting up a perimeter of defense. Our medic checked and bandaged the wound and it was just a graze and not life threatening. He called in a chopper anyway and our leader was evacuated to the base camp at Pleiku. I'm not sorry to say that was the last time we ever saw or heard from Lieutenant Burley. We were sure that Lieutenant Burley was going to be very proud when he gets the Purple Heart medal pinned on him. Back in the states we were sure he would put quite a spin on how and where he was wounded. I'm sure it will be in a fierce battle. A few weeks later we got a replacement for Lieutenant Burley. He was a seasoned Lieutenant who immediately earned the respect of our platoon. It was after his first speech where he said it was his number one priority to get us home safe. We will do our share and only our share and we will survive. He was not here to win medals just do his job and keep us safe. He was the total opposite of Lieutenant Burley. His final words of his speech were a bronze star doesn't look good on a mohair suit. Amen.

CHAPTER 13

JIMMY "SWEET SOUL"

On our next mission, it was another rainy, hot humid day as we are marching through some heavy bush following single file over a narrow path and we come to a sudden stop. One of the guys on point must have heard or seen something and held us all up. We wait a few minutes and we start moving on again. I'm walking with Red in front of me, Maytag ahead of him and just in front of him was Moo. Behind me were Andy, Rullo, Sonny and Gordan. As we continued walking it was the same old crap, and a little chatter a lot of bitching. We all enjoyed the complaining about being there and the Army in general. We were also talking about home and what we were going to do if we have got back to the Real World. The Real world meant home and the real life not this nightmare that dragged on and on. As I'm walking I stumbled just a bit on a rock and almost go down. Andy holds me up from the back and as I turn to thank him I hear popping sounds of bullets bouncing all around us. As I am turning towards Andy, he falls into my arms. We all go down on the ground. There was return fire from all around me, but I am looking at Andy. He is motionless in my arms. "Andy are you okay? Andy, Andy!" I yell at him, but there is no response. As I was holding him there is a stream of blood running down my arms. I look at his head and I could see he was hit through the neck. I scream for a medic and help. I just stared at Andy as I cradled him in my arms. I started to cry and curse, "Look what these bastards have done. Andy, Andy no, not Andy." The medic came and they moved Andy off of me but there was no hope. Andy died instantly. I just stayed on the ground and I couldn't move. Moo comes running back a few minutes later saying they killed the two snipers that fired on us. Red, Sonny, Rullo, Gordan, Maytag, Boomer, Flipper and Rega all sat around me. They all felt the same about Andy. Rega said, "This can't be, not Andy, he didn't belong here. He shouldn't have been here. This was no place for Andy." Red looked at me, "Buddy I'm so sorry. We all knew you looked after him but there was nothing you could have done. Rega is right Andy didn't belong here. He wasn't a soldier; he was a Muppet. I don't mean that in a bad way. I learned to love the kid. The Army should have known that he didn't belong here. He was a soft, kind, loving and an annoying beautiful kid." Wise ass Red couldn't help himself as he kneeled down by me. He held me and cried just as hard as I did. Sargent Willie hugged me and said, "I'm sorry kid, we loved the guy. We will miss him, but we will never forget him. He has to be in a better place, God rest his soul."

The days passed by as we continued on. I was mostly in a trance like state. A big part of me felt like giving up. In my head, I was almost hoping for a sniper bullet to put me out of my misery. I was sick of the smell, the heat, the rain, the blood, the pain and the death that was all around us. My stomach was sick. I hurt bad inside over Andy. In nine months, he became my brother and I loved him. He was so happy anytime I would spend time with him. I can't forget his face when I came down off the mountain. The plane ride over to Nam when he never would shut up. I promised him when we got back, I was going to beat his ass in bowling. He wanted me over for all the holidays. He promised that his Grandmother would make me Italian food that I would die for. He even said that I could come live with him. But he did make me promise not to touch his sisters. Every few steps I take I look around and it tears me up that he is not behind me anymore and never will be. I was always complaining to him, if I stop short, he would end up in my ass. He just laughed and said he was sorry. Now I would rip my arm off to have behind me. It's crazy, but in the months you form a bond with your buddies that would take a lifetime to do in the real world. No one knows what it's like unless you were here. Only the few of us that have walked through this hell understands. We're not soldiers, we are just kids. We can't even buy a drink in the States. We would be still in school if we weren't here. We are here for what reason. The Politicians send us here, but for what. The VC are fighting for their country. This is their country and we are the invaders. The farmers want no part of us or any war. This hell is turning us all into mindless killing machines. We have no idea what we are doing here. All we want is to get it over with and go home. Andy's death was ripping me apart. He was a gentle soul and he should not have been forced into a war in a country that hates us. He shouldn't have been sent here. I couldn't sleep at night until I was exhausted. I kept waking up all the time because I heard Andy call out for me. I couldn't write home anymore. I started to just stash the few letters I did receive. I couldn't deal with the little everyday bullshit that was happening in the real world. More days and weeks went by. We settled in Pleiku and we knew there was something bad going on. We were surrounded by the NVA and we're constantly hit with VC. We dug in on a hill for the night. Me and Red was just talking about the usual BS as the night passed on. Red knew I couldn't sleep so he tried his best to keep me company until he couldn't take it anymore and fell asleep. The morning sun was up and we broke camp. I was having a last precious sip of my morning coffee when all hell broke out. All around us was rocket fire and mortar rounds. We had no cover so their attack was perfect. They waited until we were out in the open and packed to attack. Now we had to scramble to dig in again. This was a full attack by the NVA and the VC. The ground was shaking as the mortars and rockets hit all around us. I dug in next to Red, Gordan, Moo and Sonny. We were being hit really hard and we knew we were taking heavy casualties. After a few minutes of silence, the VC came in hard in a human wave attack. The crazy bastards came in screaming and firing their AK47's. We returned fire and were shooting anything and everything in sight.

 I thought we were going to be overrun any time now. We kept on firing away. Bullets were flying all around me and guys were screaming out in pain. The VC kept on coming. The mortars pounded them and our fire took its toll, slowing them down. Just as I thought we were holding them off, they come again. I had no choice but to bring in our fire support, so the rounds could hit closer. I called in my fire mission to our mortars to hit all around our location and perimeter. I also called back to base camp for artillery support. The tactic worked as they started to back off. One small problem, we were running very low on ammo & needed some sent ASAP. Problem was they would never send in the choppers to a hot landing zone. We got lucky because Lieutenant Skippy heard the call for help. He was in base command. Lieutenant Skippy was a small guy from upstate NY. He was short of stature, but very large where it counted. He comes in on a chopper and he and his crew start throwing down boxes of ammo. Their taking fire, but he doesn't give a dam. As we were looking up, gesturing our thanks you could read his lips saying, "It's no big thing." If there was music playing this could have been a movie. Lieutenant Skippy saved our asses by dropping all that extra ammo. We were able to hold off the NVA and the VC. We took heavy casualties. Not only from the NVA, the VC, but our own mortars did some bad damage to our own. We lost over two dozen men and many more wounded. By some miracle none of my guys were killed. Moo took a bullet in the arm and that was it. One guy I did know was Phizer he was a big kid with a high-pitched voice. He took a direct hit from a mortar round. He and two other guys were lost instantly. The next day we searched the area and found all these tunnels a few clicks away that were field hospitals. In some of the tunnels we found some bodies and some VC alive still on operating tables. Another few weeks went by with the same routines. We were all sick of the jungle and the whole country. The heat and the rains never stopped. I still had a tough time trying to sleep. I couldn't get Andy out of my mind, no matter how hard I tried. The pain from all the guys we lost was taking its toll.

CHAPTER 14

JIMMY "NIGHT FEVER"

A few more weeks dredged by and we were out on patrol. I started to feel sick. This time I mean really sick. The next thing I knew I was burning up with a fever. I was totally out of it when they coppered me back to Pleiku. They started to give me these ice baths to bring my fever down. I would reach for a blanket because I was freezing and they would pull it off me. More ice baths the bastards were trying to kill me. They tested me, but they found nothing. They then shipped me to Cam Ranh Bay to a larger and better equipped hospital. I was mostly out of it and I was hallucinating from the high fever. All crazy things, I was seeing bodies, explosions, weird colors and all sought of nightmares. The Doctors at Cam Ranh Bay finally found that I had malaria and started to treat me with Quinine. The night before they told me I had malaria I had a very weird dream, I think. I was kind of in a twilight like sleep when I heard a voice whispering in my ear, "It's no big thing Jimmy you are going to be fine. I miss you buddy, but you can't come to me, not yet. You will get out of here, don't worry. Thanks for being there for me. You were and always will be my brother. Getting shot was no big thing I am fine. I have been watching you. You're a great soldier and a better person. Take care of yourself, be careful out there when you go back. Be really careful in the village. I love you Jimmy please be safe." I opened my eyes and I saw Andy like smiling and backing away. Then it was like he just floated and slowly disappeared. It was freaky but I had been hallucinating so many times that I just thought it was just another bad night. The next morning the Quinine slowly started to kick in. I dismissed the visit from Andy as a dream, but there was something different about it. It was so real it stayed with me. I found out that Red was in the same hospital with Malaria. We both caught it at the same time. While we were recovering the guys had come in from the field and they visited with us. Me and Red pulled some favors and they brought our beds side by side. After the fever finally broke both of us were feeling a lot better. The nurses were great and the doctors took good care of us. The only problem was that we knew that as soon as we were recovered, they would send us back into the field. I said to Red, "Hey I have to be honest, I don't want to go back. I miss the guys and I want to be there for them, but I don't want to go out there anymore." Red smiled, "Dam right. I don't want to back out there either. I am spoiled now for sure. Pretty nurses, warm beds, good food, no way do I want to go back. We have to think of something to stay. We could say we are still sick. We can fake it." "No way will that work." We started to count the days we had left because now we were short timers. Two months and we are out of here. Just as they were ready to release us, we started to wander around the bases. There were Army, Navy and a large Air Force presence there. We spotted a poster for a painting detail and we volunteered for that. We were painting a few days. Are names were being called to be assigned back into the field. We ignored the calls and wandered around the basis. We wandered into an Air Force Base and made friends with a couple of guys there. They said there was no room in the barracks, but we could sleep on the floor and no one would say anything. That's what we did. We would have stayed anywhere to keep from going back out. We didn't have any leave, but we hitched a ride into, Cam Ranh Bay sin city. We were like wild men on the loose. We drank ourselves to the limits and were totally wasted. As we were sobering up a bit we were just walking the streets when two MP'S stopped us. They ask for our passes. Unfortunately, we didn't have any. Red tells the MP's we lost them. When that didn't work we tried everything to talk our way out. We told them what we have been through, but nothing worked. They put us in the jeep and escorted us back to Cam Ran Bay Base. The next day they put us on a plane and escorted us back to our base in Pleiku. The MP's writes us up this Article 15 and they bring us to our C.O (Commanding Officer). The big mouth all gung ho MP starts telling the C.O that we are AWOL. The C.O yells at the MP to slow down. "I'm a Captain and you're a Sargent so stop right now. I will deal with that matter. You both are excused, so leave my office now!" We smile at the MP's as they slowly walk out the door. The Captain looks at us and says, "Wipe that smile off your faces and get the hell out of here. I don't want to see either of you again. Do you understand?" We both reply, "Yes Sir" He then rips up the paper work, smiles as he tosses it in the garbage. The next day Red gets called in and his Father is very sick. The Army is letting him go home right away. We hug and I wish him the best. He says he sorry to leave me but his dad needs him. I understand, but I wish I was going home with him. After Red leaves, I bounce around doing everything I can to not let them find me. That hasn't work out for too long. They find me and send me back to the field and my unit. I rejoin the guys and it was good seeing them. We all hugged and caught up on everything that happened. I told them about me and Red's adventures at Cam Ranh Bay and Red going home. There were a lot of new greenies in our Company. Just a few of us were left from when we started. We were short timers and we just wanted to stay safe and get the hell out of this place. After seeing Red leave and be reunited with my buddies, I was in a daze. I still couldn't get Andy out of my head. That night in the hospital still was bothering me. I know I had the fever, but I saw him and I heard him. It was different then the dreams and the hallucinating, it was somehow very different. I tried to block it out and concentrate on my time left. I thought of going back to the real world, all my old buddies and Danny. I had mixed emotions on what it would be like, but I knew it was a million times better than being here.

CHAPTER 15

"LAST HOORAH"

The next morning my old buddy Sargent Willie tells me that Army Intelligence is saying there are VC held up in a village not too far from where we are. This is normally a search and destroy mission, but this one is search and capture. This was going to be a night mission of twelve men and an interpreter. Sargent Willie says that because of my expertise as a forward observer and in reading maps I would be one of the twelve. We all hated night patrols you couldn't see shit. I had to read the map with a red lens. That night the rain was coming down very hard as we moved out. I was with Gordan, Vogel, Gulli, Sonny and a few other grunts. The squad leader, Sargent Lambeau was a GI Joe type of guy from the boonies in Louisiana and an interpreter. I was towards the back with a grunt who was carrying the radio hidden in a sandbag. The radio would be a target for a sniper so we hid it as best we could. We tried to be as quick as possible as we went towards the village. The rain hitting our ponchos would intensify the sound. As we slopped through the mud, I couldn't help think about that night back at Cam Ranh Bay hospital and the whispering of Andy. He said "Be careful at the village." At that time, it made no sense, but now we are headed for a village with VC there, it sent a shiver through my whole body. As we approached the village I felt very tense. I was always tense, scared on any patrol, but this time it was worse. Look, we had a few weeks left and we all can get out of here in one piece. If we are lucky this could be our last patrol. Red is back home, Moo was sent back after being shot. The rest of us our time was almost up. Now is not the time to get shot. We approached the first hut and Sonny, Sargent Lambeau, Vogel, me and the interpreter enter it. There are two women there alone and we see no one else. The Interpreter asks the women where are the VC. They keep on repeating, "No VC. No VC. They left." The Sargent loses his patients and puts his weapon directly to their heads saying, "Show me where the VC went, now!" The two women make a sign to follow them. They lead us out of the hut and a short way down the road. They approach an entrance to the jungle and point that way. The Sargent tells the Interpreter to tell them to lead the way. They say, "No, you go." Again, the Sargent loses his patients and points his rifle, for them to lead the way. The two women then jump over a group of rocks and begin to run, the Sargent opens fire and the bullets rip them both apart. He pushes us back and shows us the mines they wanted to lead us onto and blow the shit out of us. It was sickening to watch. Kill or be killed, simple as that. Shoot first, take no chances they were all VC, women, kids, young men, you could never tell. We returned to the village the squad had a male villager in the second hut. We came over to the hut and entered.

We were all getting antsy now after the gunfire. We knew the VC could be closing in on us at any time. We entered the hut and the interpreter started to interrogate the villager. He kept on denying he was a VC. We told the Sargent to bring him back to camp to interrogate him. The Sargent agreed and told the Interrogator to tell the VC to come with us. He refused to move. The Sargent went over to him and grabbed him by the arm and pushed him towards the front. The VC stopped, reached into his back and pulled a pistol out. He fired point blank at the Sargent hitting twice in the chest before any of us could react. He fired again hitting Sonny in the stomach. I returned the fire and shot the VC twice in the chest. He fell to the ground. We checked the Sargent but he was gone. Sonny was wounded pretty badly so we wrapped him up and carried him out. I dragged the VC out of the hut. We rushed as fast as we could, but dragging the VC was a slow go. As we were making our way as far from the village as possible the VC starts to scream out. I tried to shut him up, but he wouldn't stop. We dragged him into the jungle and we hear all kinds of sounds coming from the village. There was no question, it was VC coming after us. I grab the radio and call in our status. The Captain says, "Shut him up, the hell with bringing him back." I went down on top of the VC and I grabbed his throat with both my hands and squeezed him as hard as I could. I looked into his eyes as he was dying and I felt nothing. I just watched him kill the Sargent and put two holes in Sonny. I was following my orders and I did what a soldier should do. I pushed him away and barked out to move out. We started to move out as fast as possible, but there were now bullets flying all around us. We returned fire and moved out. After we moved quite a distance from the village the jungle got deeper and darker. We could hardly see anything. The good news was even the VC couldn't see us. We waited for a long time and it seemed they gave up. I was the highest rank so I was now the squad leader. I ordered them to slowly move out and don't make a sound. We made our way through the jungle as I checked the map and plotted our course to get back to our camp. It was difficult carrying Sargent Lambeau and Sonny, it took two men each to carry them. As we approached an opening in the jungle I hesitated. We had to cross an opened field. I thought that this would be a good place to call in a chopper, to evacuate our wounded and dead. As the chopper got close, I called in for illumination, so they can find us. The chopper spots us and lands. It was a dangerous decision because the VC in the area would now know where we were but I was afraid Sonny wouldn't make it. We get Sonny and Lambeau on it and it takes off. As I lead the squad out, we get to the middle a blast of fire comes at us. I turn to my left and I see the flashes and the tracers of light leaving the VC rifles. I scream and open fire. I take out at least three of them. Then I feel a burst like someone kicked me in the face. I hit the ground and everything goes black.

CHAPTER 16

DANNY AND JIMMY "REUNITED"

A few years later, Ray, Sal and Robbie are all happily married. Wow! Life just never stops changing. It felt like yesterday we were all doing the clubs and hanging out. I just turned thirty years old and my daughters were growing up way too fast. Maria was teaching and her Mom was watching the kids. Our business was still doing great and we kept getting bigger. Robbie was a great partner and a better friend. He was a natural salesman and he loved it. After my dad died, there were some solid years of fun and family. All was good. I hadn't from Jimmy in years. I still wrote him all the time. I had no idea where he was or what he was up to. He just kind of disappeared. All the guys would take turns with house parties, summer barbeques and holidays. Sal and Ray each had one daughter and Robbie had a daughter and a son. When we would all get together, it was a madhouse, but we loved it. One day at work I get a phone call. I answer B and D motors, but all I hear is silence. I repeat hello a few times, but there is nothing. I hung up the phone. A few minutes later the phone rings again. I answer again and this time a very low voice, "Danny." I answer and ask who this is? "It's Jimmy." "Jimmy, where are you? I've been so worried, where are you? Are you okay? He answers, "Well thought of. I am back on Long Island."

"Where are you, still in the Army?" "I am in an Army hospital in Northport." "Hospital, are you sick?" "Listen Danny if you can come and see me, I will try to explain everything to you. Now is not the time. I need to get some rest, but if you make it out here I will fill you in." "Sure, should I bring the guys?" "No Danny not now. I just want to see you." "Okay Jimmy, no problem. I can come out on Saturday if that's okay?" Jimmy said, "Sure that would be great. I can't talk anymore now but I will see you on Saturday." He gave me the name and address and I hung up the phone. It was crazy. I haven't heard from Jimmy in so long. He sounded different. Hospital, that didn't sound good at all. He could just have some treatable sickness or maybe he was wounded. It could be so many things. I'm just going to wait and see what's wrong. I felt bad that maybe I should have gone there right away. I had a couple of big meetings on Thursday and Friday, so that's why I made it for Saturday. He did seem okay with that. Saturday couldn't come fast enough. Maria never met Jimmy but I told her so much about him it was like she knew him for years. She wanted to go with me, but she understood it was better I went alone. Northport was not far at all. We lived in Plainview, so it was less than a half hour drive. As I walked up to Jimmy's room, I just had this bad feeling. I wasn't sure what it was but I was very uneasy. I didn't know what to expect. It's been ten years since I last saw him. All those letters I sent him went unanswered. The ones he did answer he never really said anything. The mystery of where he was and what was he doing all these years made me feel strange. Jimmy was like a brother to me but I don't know what to expect now. I came into Jimmy's room and knocked softly. A young nurse came out and said, "Hi, you must be Danny? You could go right in, he has been waiting for you." The room was kind of dark and there was another bed but it was empty. I walked over to Jimmy. He was in a deep high-backed chair. He had his head turned looking out the window. He had a large blanket covering most of his body. I came closer and said, "Jimmy, hey, it's me, Danny." "I know it's you I've been waiting for you. It's great to hear your voice. It's been so damn long." Jimmy was talking but he did not turn to look at me. He continued to look out the window. I went a little closer, "Hey, you okay?" He said, "I guess so. I'm a little banged up and I was for a long time." As he spoke he slowly turned toward me and I could see his whole right side of his face was bandaged from his neck to over his head. I must have looked kind of shocked as I just kind of stared at him. I didn't know what to say. "Your head, were you in some kind of accident?" He gave me a little smile, saying, "You could say that. But the only accident is that I am still around. Don't let this bandage fool you. This happened many years ago. I just went through another operation. I lost count a long time ago. They call it reconstructive and mixed with some type of plastic surgery. Look Danny now that you're here I'm going to be straight with you. There is no reason not to. As you know I stopped writing you years ago. But open that drawer over there." I went over to a dresser and opened the top drawer. It was stuffed with all the letters I wrote to him. On top of the dresser was all kinds of books and notebooks. It was obvious that Jimmy did a ton of reading and writing. "Danny, I read every one of your letters. I read them over and over again. I know about Maria, your daughters and your dad dying. I am really sorry about your Dad. How's your Mom?" "She's okay, Jimmy, Thanks for asking." "Look Danny, I know you must be confused. Why did I stop writing? The answer is simple. I just couldn't bring myself to tell you what happened. I mean I've been through years of therapy and finally I can talk about it. I have wanted to call you for years. I just couldn't do it. I didn't know what to say." I still was confused, but I said, "Were you wounded while you were in the MP's?" "Danny, I was never an MP. I wasn't in Saigon, but in a hospital in Cam Ranh Bay. I was shipped from a hospital in Pleiku to Cam Ranh Bay and then to the States.

It's a real long story, but I don't think I can get into it now. The bottom line is that I was hit pretty hard. I had half my face blown off. My spine was damaged. I have been in one hospital after another. The Veterans Administration has been treating me really good. The doctors have been great. The nurses have been fantastic. You know it's not so bad." He swiveled around in the chair and I saw it was some kind of special chair and it had wheels. It hit me that it seems like he can't walk. I was kind of blown away and didn't know what to say. I just looked at him, saying, "Your face, are the operations going to fix it?" After I said that I realized what a stupid question and I felt awful. Jimmy sensed it and said, "Hey, I was pretty ugly before this so it's no big deal. Maybe when they're finished, I will look like a movie star." He was smiling so I relaxed. I said, "Is there anything I can do? Anything at all Jimmy I want to help." Jimmy smiled, "Yeah, I just want you back in my life. I can use a friend. Danny, I miss you. I miss not having you and the guys around. I just can't face the others. But you Danny I know I can talk to. Right now, I just need my best friend back." As Jimmy spoke, he started tearing up and so did I. I went closer to him and just gave him a hug. "Jimmy, you don't have to worry about anything. I will be here for you. I will come so many times you will be sick of me. And if you can ever get out of here you can come to stay with me. We are not just friends we are family. You will always have a home with me." Jimmy just broke down and cried. We were both crying like crazy when the cute nurse came into the room. She said she was sorry to interrupt but she needed to do some vitals on Jimmy and some meds. Jimmy said he needed to rest anyway, so maybe I could come back soon. I told him I will be there the next day. He nodded his head and I grabbed his hand, "Jimmy, I will be here tomorrow and as many days as I can. You just tell me what you need or want and it's done. I love you buddy and don't you forget it. We were always like brothers and always will be." Jimmy smiled through the tears and just shook my hand with both of his. "Thanks Danny, I wish I called you a lot sooner. I'm glad you came and I want you to know that this means a lot to me. Now go home to your wife and kids and give them a big kiss from me." I slowly took my hand away and said, "I will see you tomorrow."

  As I drove home, I knew Jimmy went through a lot, but I never thought it was this bad. Now it all made sense to him not answering my letters. He was fighting for his life in Viet Nam and then all these hospitals and operations. I wish I knew. I wish I could have been there for him. He must have been through a lot and I could see that was not going to be easy for him to tell me. I am not sure if he was capable of talking about it. I figured I wouldn't push him on it. When he is ready to tell me, he will. The only thing I can do is be there for him now. It was going to be hard not saying anything to Sal and Ray but I had to respect Jimmy's wishes. I went home and told Maria everything. I could never keep anything from her. I asked her not to say a word to anyone and she promised. I knew she wouldn't and I felt better just being able to talk about it. I filled Maria in on Jimmy's background. He was raised by his mom. He never knew his dad. He lived with his mom and his aunt. His mom died when Jimmy was very young. His aunt provided for him until he went into the service. I am not sure what ever happened to his aunt. I knew she moved away a few years ago. Maria wanted to come and meet Jimmy but I told her it was too soon. When the time comes I know she will love Jimmy.

The weeks flew by and I kept my promise to Jimmy. I visited with him three or four times a week. We would call each other on the phone a few times a week. His spirits seemed to be improving. He still wouldn't talk about the events in Viet Nam. What he really wanted was for me to do all the talking. He wanted to know everything. I did just that. As time went on he wanted to meet Maria. I brought Maria up to see him one Saturday afternoon. They got along and connected right away just like I thought. Jimmy felt at ease with her and loved to listen to her talk about me and the kids. He also liked the stories about the guys and their wives and kids. He still wouldn't agree to see them. I am not sure, but I think he was still embarrassed of his condition. He asked for many different kinds of books and magazines. He was doing a lot of writing, but would not tell us about what. I thought maybe it was about Viet Nam, but I was not sure. As the months went by I found out that Jimmy was also exposed to Agent Orange. He spoke about this a few times, but very little information on it. One day Jimmy was in a talkative mood for a change. He started to tell me about him and his buddies, breathing in this shit called Agent Orange. He said they were told that the Air Force would be spraying the jungles all around them. They were told that this Agent Orange would kill the heavy bush and dense jungle so that the Viet Cong couldn't hide. It would destroy their food and forced them out. It was going to save many soldiers' lives. It was safe, so we had nothing to worry about. They said the English used it before in the jungles and it will force the Viet Cong to come out in the open to fight. The operation code name was Operation Ranch Hand. The name Agent Orange came from the barrels it was shipped in. The barrels had an orange stripe around it. Jimmy said he did some research on it and he said it was TCDD and he found out it was extremely toxic and he worried if he was going to get sick from it. The Doctors were telling him the Government says it was safe and there was no proof that it would do any damage to those who were exposed. I wasn't aware of any of this so I just listened to him. Eventually I learned that this was some bad shit. There were birth defects in Viet Nam and many Vets were getting really sick from it. They even said it was causing some kind of cancer. There was also some brain damage that it was being blamed for. Around this time Jimmy was in good spirits but something about him was different. At first there were little things that he would refer to. He started talking a lot about Stevie and the night he was killed. He was also talking a lot about time travel and he was reading a lot about it. He was saying he thinks it's possible to go back in time. He said if we could go back we could save Stevie. I kind of laughed it off. I figured Jimmy had so much time on his hands, he was letting his imagination run wild. Hey, why not. He wasn't doing anybody any harm. He was just escaping into some crazy possibilities he could invent. One day out of the blue he asked me," Danny do you believe in spirits or ghosts. I'm not talking about the spooky stuff in horror films. I mean like that the dead can come visit you somehow." I just looked at him, saying, "I don't know Jimmy. I never really thought about it. Why do you ask that?" Jimmy put his head down saying, "When I was in Nam in the hospital I had a high fever. I was having all sought of nightmares and crazy dreams. Then one night my good buddy of mine, Andy, appeared right in front of me. He was killed just before I came down with Malaria. I know this is going to sound crazy but he was there. It was much different from the dreams he was real. I know he was. He told me I would be okay, but be careful when I go to the village. At the time I thought it was a dream and I didn't know what he was talking about. The village, I wasn't going to any village. Then after I was better and went back into the field I get this patrol and we have to go looking for VC in a village. That's when all the shit happened and I got wounded. As I was headed for the village I remembered his words and it freaked me out. Even now I can see him in front of me that night and warning me. Look, I know you are thinking it was a dream and a coincidence about the village, but Danny I'm telling you it was real." I didn't know how to answer that and said, "Hey, I don't know if it was real or not but if you feel it was real I believe you. Anything is possible, I do believe." Can you tell me what happened to Andy and what happened to you?" Jimmy shook his head up and down saying he could. After a couple of hours went by I listened to the horrors that Jimmy went through. Losing all his buddies and what he had to do to survive. He had the hardest time telling me about taking out the VC and I could never have an idea what it was like to take a life. He said that he fired on and called in many strikes against the VC and he knows he must have been responsible for many deaths and casualties. That is war and that is what he had to do. In all of those cases, he wasn't face to face to see the reality of dying. They were all from a distance and the results of his actions were not very clear. "Danny, when I looked at that VC who had just killed our Sargent and shot my buddy I felt nothing. I didn't have anger or sympathy I was just doing what I was told to do. As time went on I could see his face in my dreams. Now I am confused because I took his life. I watched him die and I felt nothing. Now I feel guilty for what I did. I realize I had no choice but it still sickens me. I should have never enlisted. I should never have gone. When my buddies Gulli, Maytag, Vogel, Rega and Gordan flew back to the States they stopped at a local bar to celebrate and have a drink together. They were going in all different directions to their homes. They went to a local bar while they were still in uniform and had a few drinks. They were enjoying being back and being safe. They would be seeing all their loved ones soon and the nightmare was over. They were feeling really good. Rega who always thought he was a lady's man decides to ask a local girl to dance. The bar was filled with young guys and girls. She was pretty and Rega said she also looked like a college girl. She was smiling and laughing with her friends. He approached her and asked if she would like to dance.

The next thing he knew she stops smiling, "Get away from me you are disgusting. I don't dance with baby killers. Get the hell out of here and crawl back in the hole you came from." Her friends joined in calling them baby killers and spit in his face. The other guys joined in and they kicked some college guy's asses pretty bad. That's when they all knew that they weren't heroes. They were not welcomed home as soldiers who fought to protect their country. No, we were not greeted at the airports with flowers instead with dirty looks and disgust. Like we were the enemies and the VC were defending their country. All the papers were showing us killing innocent villagers. Women and children being killed by drugged up US soldiers. Danny, it made us all sick. We never wanted to go over there and be part of any of that shit. We were doing what we had to do. We were trained and ordered to fight for our country. We were attacked by VNA, VC, women, kids and snipers every step of the way there could be a mine. It was not like fighting in World War Two where we were liberating countries. We weren't fighting off some mad dictator like Hitler to save the world. We were just doing what we were ordered to do. The rest was pure survival kill or be killed it was that simple. We had no choice. To every one of us over there we are changed forever. They stole our youth and our souls. They made us killers and we paid the toll. All the guys that died and were wounded over there were mostly just kids. We couldn't buy a drink in a bar here because we were too young. But we were old enough to go fight some bull shit war across the world that we didn't even know existed. We were sent into the jungle to fight ghosts that disappeared after they attacked. Our own country sprayed Agent Orange into our lungs and said it was to help us. Now we find out it's killing us slowly. We had to be part of a nightmare that will haunt us the rest of our lives. All this for what, did we kill Hitler, did we save the world? No, we just did what our country leaders told us to do. Our reward Danny is to come home to be spit at and looked upon as dirt. Those guys that fought over there deserve a lot better from the Government and the people. Hey, I'm sorry I said too much. I'm not feeling sorry for myself, I'm feeling sorry for this great country to let this happen." "Jimmy, I can't imagine what you guys went through. While you were going through all that horror, I was here and enjoying a good life. I'm sorry for that. Part of me feels I should have been there with you, but I was spared. I didn't know I would be assigned to such a safe place. I didn't ask for it. I honestly can say I do feel guilty, but down deep I didn't want to go either. Down deep I was happy to be here in the States and away from the danger. What can I say other then I am sorry that you had to go?" "Look Danny, I don't blame you one bit. If the situation was reversed, I would have done the same thing so don't feel guilty buddy, I understand and it is Okay." We needed to clear the air and I felt better about it. I always did feel guilty that Jimmy went and I didn't and by talking about it made me feel better.

CHAPTER 17

"SCIENCE FICTION"

As the days and weeks went by, we would talk more and more about the time Andy visited Jimmy. Jimmy seemed obsessed with the experience and he believes that Andy will appear again to him. Jimmy one day says, "What if you could go back in time and save Stevie? What if we could travel back and stop what happened? Would you do it?" "Of course, I would Jimmy but I don't think that is going to be possible" "Yeah, I know Danny but I have been doing a lot of reading and there are all kinds of things that have happened. There was this guy in the 1950's that was in clothing, wearing 19-century clothes and was killed by a car. The guy had ID on him since 1876 and he just vanished that year. Next thing he appears in the 1950's in NYC. I read about all kinds of time travelers and I think there could be some truth to it." "I don't know Jimmy, sounds kind of science fiction to me." He then tells me that his army buddy Donny Gulli is now a NYC detective. He has been visiting Jimmy on a regular basis. He says that Donny tells him all about his job. You think the guy didn't see enough in Viet Nam now he is dealing with the murders. Jimmy says he enjoys his visits and he likes the stories. Jimmy says they're not as good as time travel, but they are for real. We both laughed about it and I told Jimmy I would be back the day after tomorrow. All the way home, I was thinking of everything Jimmy went through. The Andy stuff and now his fascination with time travel seemed understandable. The visits from his army buddy was a good thing too.

A few weeks went by and Maria and I listen to many of Jimmy's stories especially about time travel. Also, Gulli's detective stories that Jimmy liked to pass on to us. Jimmy also wanted to hear all about the girls and everything about Maria, family and anything else she had to say. Month after month I visited with Jimmy, sometimes alone and sometimes with Maria. Maria befriends one of the nurses at the VA and she tells Maria there is no chance for Jimmy to ever walk again. The damage to lower his body was traumatic and can never be corrected. They will continue to do more plastic surgery on his face. After work on Friday I was beat but I had to stop and visit Jimmy before I went home. I picked up some pizza that Jimmy loved. He just finished his last bite and says, "You know I had this crazy thing happen last night. It was 3:00 in the morning I know the exact time because I looked at the radio clock when it started. I had a visitor appear in my room." "Let me guess, it was Andy." "No Danny it was not Andy. It was Stevie." I looked and smiled, "You're kidding, right?" "No, I'm not. He stood right where you are right now. I know what you're thinking. Jimmy is hallucinating again. If it isn't Andy it's time travel and now it's Stevie. I get it. I would think the same way. I know it sounds nuts, but he was here." "Jimmy, what did Stevie say?" "He said he needed our help." "Jimmy, you said our help? "Yes, Danny our help. He said that we could go back in time and change what happened to him that night." I just smiled and said, "I get it time travel." "I know how it sounds but I'm not crazy. Yeah, it's sought of time travel but Stevie says it's not. He can lead us through a portal that can take us back to that night. He would be our guide. He said that he has been in some type of limbo all these years. He said that somehow in a way he can't explain he can be a messenger that takes us back to that night and save him. He said that there are portals that will allow us to do this." I looked at Jimmy, shaking my head, "Jimmy this sound crazy. You hear what you are saying?" "I know Danny it is really crazy. I wouldn't believe anyone who told me what I just told you. The problem is that he was here and that is what he said. I think we should do some research on this to see if it's possible. Please trust me Danny I'm not crazy." "Okay Jimmy, I tell you what I will do. I will ask Maria to go to the library tomorrow and do all the research on this. She is way better at this stuff than me. She can find and research things because of her education much better than me. How's that sound?" "I'm okay with that but please tell her I'm not nuts?" I left Jimmy totally confused. I wasn't sure if I should speak with the doctor's or what to do. I was starting to fear that Jimmy was kind of losing it somehow. I went home and decided to tell Maria what he said. I trusted her opinion and see what she says. After I explained to Maria what Jimmy said, she said, "I don't know if he is hallucinating or just having some type of weird dreams? I think we should not try to alienate him by telling him we don't believe him. I will go to the library and do some research. This way we can talk to him with some knowledge about what he is saying. Also, maybe if we give this some time it will pass. I also could speak with Lori the nurse who I know over there and see what she thinks." "Okay honey, thanks. I will wait for what you can find out." Maria did her research over the next few days. After work and dinner two nights later, we sat down to talk. Maria said. "As crazy as this sounds, there are many different theories on what Jimmy said. One thing I think I learned was that just maybe anything is possible, when you think about all the modern devices, we enjoy today which seemed all but impossible many years ago. For instance, I took some of these quotes to show you." Maria handed me a notepad and I read the notes she had, "Heavier-than-air flying machines are impossible." (Lord Kelvin, president, Royal Society, 1895) "The telephone has too many shortcomings to be seriously considered as a means of communication. The device is inherently of no value to us." (Western Union internal memo, 1876) "Airplanes are interesting toys but of no military value." (Marshal Ferdinand Foch, French commander of Allied forces during the closing months of World War I, 1918) "The wireless music box has no imaginable commercial value. Who would pay for a message sent to nobody in particular?" (David Sarnoff's associates, in response to his urgings for investment in the radio in the 1920's) "Who the hell wants to hear actors talk?" (Harry M. Warner, Warner Brothers, 1927) "Everything that can be invented has been invented." (Charles H.

Duell, commissioner, US Office of Patents, 1899) Look, I don't know nor do I believe that time travel is possible but that it seems to be is that in time who knows. As I read there could be different ways to go back in time. Of course, all are just that theories so who knows. Then there are the religious beliefs on the subject. The ancient Greeks believed in time as cyclical- everything that was born was reborn, every event would occur again. Aristotle said, "What is eternal is circular and what is circular is eternal" There are so many different religious beliefs about Angels are being spirited-like messengers that are believed to travel and communicate with God and humanity. Angels, spirits and ghosts appear to be similar. It's the interpretation of the person that has the encounter who determines what name is given. Encounters with spirit beings have been recorded since the dawn of man and many people think that such spiritual entities are all around us." "So, what are you saying Maria you think Jimmy is for real and he actually was visited by Stevie who is now some kind of angel?" "No, I'm not saying that. I'm just telling you what I found, just as you asked me to. That's all. The rest I don't have a clue as to what Jimmy saw. Listen, it is more than likely he was just having a dream. In the state he is in the dream could have seemed more real than normal." "Hey, I'm sorry I appreciate what you have done. This whole thing with Jimmy is kind of freaking me out. I want to believe him and I want to help him but this visitation just seems crazy to me. I'm going to see Jimmy tomorrow and I will tell him what you have found out. The rest is up to him on how he deals with it." The next day I went and visited with Jimmy. He was in good spirits. We talked about a few different things and then he asked, "Did Maria find any information out?" "Yes, she did." I told Jimmy what Maria had told me. Jimmy said, "So you believe me?" "Yeah, Jimmy I do. The thing is I'm not sure what to believe. Stevie is a spirit a messenger an Angel I don't know what to think." "Look, I appreciate what Maria and you have done. I have been able to get some books from the library myself with some help of course. I have been reading up on all of it. I know how you must feel and I understand. I'm not going to drive you crazy with this.

CHAPTER 18

"MEMORIES"

It's been a few nights and I have had no visits so maybe I was just dreaming. It gives me something to do and I have the time, so I will just keep reading up on it." "Okay, jimmy sounds good. If you have any more visits from Stevie though, please you have to tell me. "Of course, who else am I going to tell?" We hugged and I left. Jimmy seemed like he had his act together and as far as I was concerned the whole subject was over. As time went on there were no more visits from Stevie or any other spirits with Jimmy. He seemed to be doing really well. Donny was a frequent visitor and Jimmy was absorbed by Donny's detective cases. I finally was able to get Jimmy to see the other guys. Sal and Ray were happy that Jimmy was back in their lives and so was Jimmy. We had some good gatherings at the hospital as we took turns about telling old stories from when we were young. One day we were all there visiting with Jimmy. Sal, Ray, Maria and I had Robbie there as well. Robbie bonded with jimmy right away. It was like he knew us all from the beginning. Jimmy says to Maria, "Did Danny ever tell you the time he pulled the fire alarm at school." I jumped in, "That's all right, we don't need to hear that story again." Maria said, "No way Danny, come on Jimmy let's hear it." Jimmy says, "Great story. Danny was the only one of us that went to catholic school. It was a street away from the public school we all went to. Danny's Mom was big into the local church so she made

Danny go to the catholic school. One day Sal, Ray and I were just out of school and we were hanging out talking. You know Danny you tell the rest." Maria smiled, "Yeah, Danny you tell it." "Okay for some stupid reason this stupid friend of mine dares me to pull this handle on the red box just outside the school. I had pulled one like it many times in a different location that was not real. I honestly thought that nothing would happen. This kid Mikey dares me to pull this one. I say okay. He just looks at me and says no way I will do it. So just to show him up I walk over to the box and pull the handle down. He goes crazy, saying, I'm nuts to have done that. He then runs off back to the school. I was laughing at what a jerk he was. I was convinced that nothing was going to happen. Now you have to realize I was just ten years old. Well to my surprise all hell breaks out. The fire department was only a few streets away from the school. In minutes all kinds of sirens were ringing and all these fire trucks came tearing down the road. I start to panic so I started to run home. I am running one way and there are police cars and fire trucks going the other way. I was in a panic. I ran all the way home, which was a few streets away and I go right past Sal, Ray and Jimmy. They yell out to me but I ignore them and just keep on running. I run all the way home and I go next store to my neighbor who would watch me from time to time. Mrs. Gisonne she was a real sweet older woman who was like an aunt to me. I told her I was sick and she told me to lay down on her couch. She put a blanket on me and I just laid there. I was so scared I couldn't move. About a half hour later I hear my Mom yelling at the door, "Where is he. Danny!" Mrs. Gisonne told my Mom that I was sick and I was laying down on the couch. Mom says, "He's not sick but he is going to feel sick now!" She came storming into the living room where I was, saying, "What did you do?" I said, "Nothing, Mom." "Get up." She screamed and pulled me by my ear and out the door. Mrs. Gisonne yelled, "Lucy what did he do?" She yelled back, "He pulled the fire alarm and evacuated the school and the church. I was setting up the altar when the alarm went off. Danny's friend came back to the school and told the principle Sister Edith what Danny did." As she spoke with Mrs. Gisonne she still had me by my ear. Then she dragged me through the streets and back to the school. As she dragged me we went by Sal, Ray and Jimmy. They had no idea at that time what I had done so they just watched me crying and they knew I was in big trouble. As my Mom dragged me back to school all I heard was all these kids yelling, "Hey Danny, there goes Danny, what did you this time Danny, Danny's is in trouble." I didn't stop hearing about that for years." Maria was laughing, "What did they do to you?" "Well at first I denied doing it and my Mom almost pulled my ear off. Then I confessed but I swore I didn't know that it was a real alarm. They gave me extra homework and I had to write a dozen letters of apology to the Priests, the Sisters, the Fire Department, and the Police Department." We all sat around and told stories from the past. We had Jimmy laughing and that was good to see. A few more weeks go by and all is well. The kids keep Maria busy and crazy. The business is going well so I had no complaints. Then as life always seems to do are even things out.

As it seems it always seems to happen at night. The dreaded phone call and something bad is happening. My Brother calls and it's my Mom. She was rushed to the hospital in a lot of pain. Maria and I rush to the hospital to see her. I meet my brother there and he fills me in. My Mom was having bad stomach pain and we were waiting for the doctor to give us an update. They were going to run all kinds of tests on her. My Mom meant the world to me and it was hard seeing her sick. She was the one who would always take care of us. The night slowly went bye as we waited for the results. Finally, one of the doctors comes out and tells us that it looks like she has stomach scar tissue from a previous operation. That could be causing the pain. They will run more tests in the day and let us know. We get to see my Mom and of course she says she is feeling better and not to worry she will be fine. We were all shot so we kissed her and tell her to get some sleep and we will be back later in the day. We all go home and try to get some rest. Maria's parents are watching the kids so we were okay with that. It was hard to sleep but after a while I was able to shut down and fall asleep. We go back to the hospital later that day and they tell us they want to operate on Mom to remove the scar tissue. They schedule her for the following day. That night I prayed all night long to please let her be okay. Maria was there for me and comforted me telling me she will be fine. The next day we get to the hospital and start the long wait for the operation to be over with. The hours pass slowly. Waiting is one of the hardest things for me it seems time stands still. Finally, one of the doctors that did the operation comes out and wants to talk to me and my brother. I have not been through this before so I am not sure what that means good or bad. Maria smiles and says to go he just wants to go over the results. I nod and follow my brother into a small conference room. The doctor says, "I am sorry but it is a lot worse than we thought. What is causing all the pain is cancer? Your Mom has generalized cancer and it has spread all through her body. It is terminal and there is nothing we can do for her but to keep her as comfortable as possible." My stomach sinks and my legs wobble as it was so sickening to hear what he had just said. I look at the doctor saying, "There has to be some treatment or operation. I don't understand you just can't do nothing. You have to be able to do something. That's why she is here. You surgeons operate remove the shit from her. That's what you should do." "I'm sorry it has spread too far it is impossible." He shakes his head and turns and leaves. I look at my brother and we just hug and cry together. I tried to call all around to see if there were any other course of action but there were none. No help was coming. I felt hopeless and lost. I couldn't help my Mom. There is not a thing I could do. We spent the next few weeks at the hospital trying to keep her from knowing anything. I looked into her eyes and I knew she knew. Her eyes told me that she knew what was going to happen. It took all I had not to hug her and cry like a baby. I tried to smile and said she will be fine. We talked about when she gets out we expect her to make some of her delicious meatballs and lasagna. She would just smile and say she couldn't wait. The following two weeks were pure agony. To see my Mom there in the hospital bed in pain was brutal. She couldn't eat anymore and she was going fast. It was hard to leave the hospital and it was hard going to the hospital knowing I had to see her like this. A few days later it was over she passed away at night.

  We made the arrangements for the wake and the funeral together with my brother but I was no help. He was the older brother and he took care of all the decisions. Maria and I stayed at my Mom's house, downstairs from my brother for the wake and the funeral. The last night I cried myself to sleep and about two thirty in the morning the bedroom light comes on. I jump up and ask Maria if she was alright. She says she is fine and asked me why I put the light on. I said, I didn't I thought she did. I just smiled and said, "My Mom's just playing games with me." Somehow, I felt it was a sign or something from her saying she alright. After the funeral, I tried my best to live a normal life. I visited with Jimmy and he told me how sorry he was. All my friends were at the funeral and tried their best to console me. One of them would call every day. My brother and I stayed close. Maria and the kids were there for me and that meant everything to me. A few weeks went by and I was doing okay. Then I had some waves of depression. I never felt that before. When my Dad died I was hit hard with sorrow but I had my Mom. Now that my Mom is gone, I felt all alone. I know I had my wife and my kids but I had no parents. My whole life they were there for me. It was so hard to realize I couldn't pick up the phone and call my Mom. I would never be able to talk to her. I could never hug her again. How could this be? That I would never see them anymore? I started to have these anxiety attacks. All of a sudden, I would start to shiver and shake. I went into a panic. I never experienced anything like this before. I was embarrassed to tell Maria or anyone what was happening to me. I went into like a shell. When it would hit me at home I would just lay down. I would sweat, shake, it was very unnerving. One day at work in the middle of the day it hit me hard. I was shaking and in a complete panic. I called my brother and I told him what was happening. He came down to my office right away. We sat outside in his car and talked for hours. I explained everything I was feeling. Thank God for my brother, he was able to calm me down. I needed to talk about it and he totally understood. He was now like my parents, he was my last link to my family. After that I tried everything to deal with what was happening. I told Maria and she dragged me to the doctor. He gave me these tranquilizers to take. I managed to take one and it made me worse. I hated taking any type of pills. I then went to the library and I took out as many books on anxiety and depression I could find. I read about the systems I had. This one book I had seemed to help me the most. It said to recognize what was happening and come to terms with it. It said to think of what was the worst thing that could happen from the anxiety and deal with it. So that's what I did. When the anxiety hit me, I would think about what is the worst thing that could happen. It wouldn't kill me. The worst thing was that maybe I would have some kind of nervous breakdown. I would have to go into some safe treatment place where I would be taken care of. Or maybe they would send me to my brothers to rest up. I couldn't work but Robbie could take care of the business. Maria would take care of the kids. So maybe things wouldn't be that bad. As I used this method to deal with the attacks it seemed to help. I then went on a vitamin kick on anything that was good for nerves. I read B-12 was good so I loaded up on them. As time passed, I started to recognize the anxiety as soon as it started. I would say to myself here it comes. I would almost challenge the attacks to bring it on. I know what it is and I can deal with it. Believe or not it worked. The attacks were lesser and lesser and not as severe. I think I used to make them worse when I started to panic. What happened was that I learned how to deal with it. A few months go by and the attacks were not as frequent. I felt that I had the anxiety under control. I was starting to feel better.

CHAPTER 19

"JUST A DREAM?"

I spent a full Saturday with Jimmy and I was decent. Maria was staying over at her Mom's house because she was not feeling well. She took the kids there and said she would spend the night. That night I went to bed feeling that I turned the corner to this anxiety problem and I felt it was time to start to enjoy my life again. I would spend more time with Maria and the kids. I went to bed and it was some time around three AM in the black of night I hear, "Danny wake up I need your help." I open my eyes slowly, "Danny please wake up." "Who, what, Maria is that you?" "No Danny it's me, Stevie." I pull myself up and slowly sit up, "Who's there if this is a joke it's not funny." I look around and there is just darkness. I reach for the light and turn it on but nothing happens. By the side of my bed, I feel a cool sensation and then, "Danny it's me Stevie. I need your help. I need for you to come with me. I need to change what happened." "What happened, who are you, what's going on?" "Listen Danny, it's me, Stevie. I know this sounds crazy, but it's really me. I need you to come with me. I have only a short time so please come with me." "Get away from me. I don't know what or who you are but Stevie is dead. Get the hell out of here I'm going to call the cops." I get up and make my way towards the bathroom and switch on the light. The bathroom and the hall adjoining the bedroom light up. I look around and see nothing. Damn it, I must be cracking up.

My anxiety attacks and now this dream, nightmare or whatever it was. I want to call Maria but what am I going to say. My dead friend Stevie just appeared to me. She is going to think I'm going crazy and maybe I am. The problem was it didn't feel like a dream it felt very real. I started to calm down as I sat on the bed. I started thinking about what Jimmy had told me. He said Stevie came to him in pretty much the same way. Can we both be going nuts or whatever Jimmy has now I'm getting. I was still kind of shaken but I decided to try to get some sleep. It was a tough night lying there almost afraid to shut my eyes because he might come back. After tossing around half the night I fell asleep. The next morning, I call Maria to see when she is coming home. Maria says, "I will be leaving in a few hours is everything okay, you sound a little strange?" "Yeah, I'm fine, just had a bad night. It's hard to sleep without you and the kids in the house." "Sorry Danny I will be home soon." I called work and spoke with Robbie all was good there. I showered and headed over to see Jimmy. I walked into his room "Hey buddy, how are you doing?" "Great, Danny just great." I looked at him saying, "What's up that sounded a little sarcastic?" "Hey I'm sorry just had a bad night that's all." "What kind of bad nights, lot of pain?" "No not that. It's hard to talk about." "What is it Jimmy? You can tell me anything you know that?" "If I tell you you're just going to think I'm losing my mind and I don't want to lose you." When he said those words, I could feel a chill go up and down my spine. I had this feeling he was going to tell me something I didn't want to hear. "Jimmy what happened?" "Last night Danny I had another crazy dream. It was Stevie again. He was in the room not a dream he was here. He said he needed help and if he couldn't count on me he was coming to you." As Jimmy said Stevie's name my legs were shaking. I must have turned white because Jimmy said, "What's the matter are you afraid of me? You must think I'm crazy now for sure." "No Jimmy not at all. The only thing that's crazy is what's going on. You're not going to believe this but Stevie came to me last night. I didn't know it at the time and thought it was a nightmare but this is too much of a coincidence that we both seen him. This is too crazy, I know this can't be real but what else can be going on. We can't be having the same dream, or could we?' Jimmy just looked at me saying, "You know I have read about things like this happening." "You mean ghosts appearing?" "Not really ghosts, but visitations from spirits." "Jimmy, that's the same thing, a spirit a ghost, what's the difference?" "Jimmy smiled, "Yeah, I guess you're right. I don't know what the heck is going on. What do we do about this?" "Nothing Jimmy we do nothing. You know that joint hallucinations are possible, like you planted in my mind and we both had the same dream." "Danny you really believe that?" "I don't know what to believe but it sounds better than Stevie floating around the both of us." "Let's just forget about it and see if it happens again. It's probably just a one-time thing and this dream or whatever it was will never happen again. Okay with you?" "Sure, Danny, you're right. Let's forget it." We both agreed although neither of us was too convinced but what other choice did we have. I left Jimmy and headed home. The next few nights were restless, but as time passed and a few weeks went by I seemed to settle down. I jumped back into work and the kids. I felt better about the whole Stevie thing it was obvious it was a dream, a stupid dream.

CHAPTER 20

"NIGHTMARES"

Maria was beat from work and it was my turn to put the girls to sleep. I kissed Lucia and Angie goodnight. And like every other night they both yelled out, "I love you Daddy." I never will get tired of hearing those beautiful words. I went into bed and softly kissed Maria goodnight but she was in a deep sleep. I was knocked out myself and fell asleep in a few minutes. I must have slept a few hours and then I hear something. I wake up and Maria is still asleep. I look around and see a soft light just outside of the room. I get up to see where it is coming from. It was like a cloudy soft pale light slowly moving down the stairs. I almost felt as I was in a trance as I just followed it down the stairs. It stopped by the front door and I see a figure in it. "Danny, it's me Stevie I need you to come with me now. I have a way of going back and you can save me. You can change the past and I can live. Come close to me and grab my hands with both your hands. Danny, please come to me now!" I'm shaking and don't know what to do. I start to move towards the light but something feels wrong I stop and back away. "Danny, no keep coming forward to me. Please Danny you can help save me. Please come with me." "No, you're not real this is a nightmare. Go away leave me alone." I start backing up and I reach for the wall light and push it on. The light comes on and I see nothing. "Danny are you alright? What are you doing down there?" I look up and it's Maria,

"I'm okay, I thought I heard something and I just was checking it out. Its fine honey, please go back to bed. I just need some water and I will be right up." "Hurry up you need some sleep." "I will be right up." I look all around the house and whatever that was it's gone. I'm not sure if I'm hallucinating or dreaming, but it seemed very real. I don't know what to do about it. I feel a big anxiety attack coming on so I quickly go up to bed to sweat it out. I can't sleep so I just shake and pray to let it pass. Just before the sun rises I fall asleep, just a few minutes later the alarm clock goes off. I tell Maria, I'm feeling a little sick and to call Robbie for me. I need to stay home and gets some rest. She gets the kids ready and takes care of everything. After she leaves, I sit up and I am not sure what I should do. All I know that I need some help. I can't go on having these dreams or whatever they are. I don't want to upset Jimmy because he has had no more of his dreams about Stevie. I have to do something. I decided to go to the V.A and see a psychologist. I needed help and I needed to talk about what happened. Fortunately, that same day doctor Spencer had a cancelation and agreed to see me. I sat down in his office saying, "I appreciate you seeing me like this without an appointment. I needed to talk to someone about what I have been going through." I started a little shaky trying to explain about the dreams. I went over my problems with anxiety and then worked into the dreams. Dr. Spencer was a good listener and he let me talk. After telling him about the first dream with Stevie, asking for my help, I then told him about this last one. "Dr. I know its sounds crazy, but it was so much more than a dream. It was so real that I could have touched him but something pulled me away. Almost like you almost touch something very hot and without touching it you pull away. It's hard to explain, but the bottom line it seemed very real." After listening to me Dr. Spencer says, "Danny our time is up right now but I want to help you." "Doc, I know you are going to blow me off but one other thing you should know." I told the Doctor about Jimmy and he had the same dream. "Look Doc, I know how all this sounds but it's the truth." Danny, I do want to help so I am going to clear my schedule for Wednesday. Why don't you come back then and I will spend a solid two hours or more if necessary to hear the complete story. How does that sound?"

"Okay, Doc, I will be back on Wednesday, thanks." The next two nights were uneventful. I said nothing to Maria or anybody else about Dr. Spencer and my visit. Wednesday came and I went to see the doctor. "Hi Danny come in and have a seat. Danny let's start at the beginning and tell me about Jimmy and Stevie and the dreams." I said okay and went right into it. I went back to how Stevie died and my relationship with him. "Danny you went through a traumatic experience and so did Jimmy. It is not that strange that you are having these dreams. Dreams can be very realistic. Lucid dreams are extremely realistic. They are not that common but they are realistic. Sigmund Freud said that dreams are forms of wish fulfillment. They are attempts by the unconscious to resolve a conflict of some sort. Because of the information in the unconscious is in an unruly and often disturbing form, a "censor" in the preconscious will not allow it to pass unaltered into the conscious. Freud said there are three types of: 1. dreams are direct prophecies received in the dream. 2. The foretelling of a future event; 3. The symbolic dream, which requires interpretation. In this case Danny I believe that you did encounter a disturbing and traumatic event with Stevie. He died in your arms. He was a close and dear friend. As in, what Freud says that is your unconscious of trying to resolve a wish fulfillment. In other words, you wish to go back and save Stevie." "Doc, what you're telling me I'm wishing to go back and save Stevie, that's why I'm having him come to me in this dream to lead me so I can save him. So even though it's so real you're telling me it is a dream." "Danny yes, it is a dream. It cannot be real, you know that. It's a dream." "How do I stop it from coming back? I don't want to go through this night after night." "There is no simple answer for that. I want to continue to see you and I believe in time I can help you. These issues that you have been experiencing have stretched over a long period of time. There is no magical or quick cure. We have to work together to resolve these issues." "Any suggestions if I do have another dream about Stevie?" "If it is the same dream and he asks you to grab his hands and go with him, hold onto his hands and you will see there will be nothing there. This might help you to get some kind of closure and realize that it is in fact just a dream." "Thanks Doc you have been helpful. I do feel better and it feels good to be assured it is a dream. I will take your advice and if I have that same dream again, I will reach out and grab him. Like you say there will be nothing there and I will know it's just a dream. I will continue to see you every week correct." "That's correct Danny. I will see you one week from today at the same time."

I left the office feeling better but still uneasy. I know that he said it was a dream and I know it had to be a dream. The problem was that it seemed so real. I wavered back and forth if I should tell Jimmy what happened. I decided to give a few days and see how I feel. Once again, it was difficult getting to sleep. It was also difficult not telling Maria. I shared everything with her but this was tough. She has been there for me, but I don't want her to think I'm losing my mind. The anxiety is one thing but this is a lot worse. I did in fact, let a few days go by and visited with Jimmy. It was a cloudy day as I entered the VA. "Hey Jimmy how you doing today?" "Okay Danny, I'm good. There is not too much new in my world what about you?" It was almost like Jimmy sensed something in me and he was feeling me out. I couldn't make up my mind if I should tell him about the dream. Jimmy had to deal with a lot and I'm the one who should be there for him. If he thinks I'm not too normal how can I help him. "I was thinking about what you said about your friend Andy that he came to you in like a dream. You told me you were sure it wasn't a dream but instead he was there. I know he had died in the field, but you were certain it was real that it wasn't a dream. How could you be sure that he was really there?" "Why are you asking me about this now?" "I'm sorry it's stupid to bring it up. Please just forget I asked." Jimmy looked at me saying, "No it's okay. I don't mind talking about it. Andy was there. I know I can't prove it and nobody would believe me but yes, he was there. I had many dreams and even hallucinated when I had the fever but his visit was different. It's very hard to explain but it was different. I felt him there. I knew it was him. How? I can't tell you, but I just know. Now tell me what is up with you. You didn't asked about this in a long time. Why now?" Jimmy could always read through me and I knew he sensed where I was going with this. "Jimmy, I had another dream about Stevie and this one seemed very real. I even went to see a shrink about it. He told me it was a dream, but I just can't let it go. I was asleep and something woke me up. It was a cloudy sort of light. I followed it down the stairs and then it was Stevie. He asked me to reach out and hold his hand. He was taking me back to that night to change what happened. He said I could save him and he could live. Look, I know this sounds crazy but I feel it was real. The doc says a dream. My brain says it had to be a dream but it seemed so damn real. I can't sleep because I'm worried he will come again. I haven't told Maria about any of this. I'm having anxiety again because of this. I don't know what to do." "What did the doc say to do?" "He said to confront the dream and grab hold of Stevie and then I would see that he wasn't really there. Then I would know for sure that it was a dream. He said this would give me proof and closure. Then it would clear up in time with more sessions with him." Jimmy nodded his head saying, "I think the doc is right. If Andy reappeared to me I would do what he is saying to do for you. Makes sense, if it is a dream, which it probably is, you would just wake up." "If is a dream, then I'm also sleep walking because I did end up downstairs. The doc said that could be too. Jimmy what about you telling me you had the same dream?" "I knew you were going to bring that up. That's a good question. I did have the same dream and I am not sure if it was real or not. I know it did feel real. I believed it was Stevie. You know this is going to sound weird but what if it was real. Maybe Stevie needs our help. Maybe he found a way to come back. You know there are many cases of visits. We talked about this before. What if we could go back somehow and change what happened. The timeline of our lives would not change much other than Stevie would be there with us. I read there are many different theories on this. There could many different timelines that we follow and there could be other dimensions that we all could be in." "Jimmy slows down listen to what you are saying. Now you think this is for real and Stevie can come back from the dead?" "No Danny, not come back, he would have never died." "Jimmy, we have to stop. This is getting too weird. I loved Stevie more than anyone and I wish he was here. I wish I could go back to that night and drag him out of there. He could have been here today, but I can't change the past. You can't do it and I can't do it. We both know that. The doc is right. It has to be wishful thinking triggering the dream. It can't be real it has to be a dream." "Danny, calm down, you're right. It has to be a dream. I think we both need some time to let this whole thing pass. We both always felt guilty about it and it makes sense, we both could have the same dream. Let's give a rest."

On the way home, I felt drained. I have had my share of heartache with losing my mom and my dad. Other than that, it's been a great life. I have a great wife wonderful kids, family and friends. My business has been strong and I have no complaints. Now this Stevie stuff is wearing me down. Part of me wishes the dream of Stevie stops and never happens again. There is a part of me that hopes it does happen again. If it happens, I want to do what Doctor Spencer says to do and reach out and put an end to this once and for all. A few more weeks go by and all is good again. No dreams and my anxiety have been under control. I feel good about controlling it with no medication. It's a Saturday night and we are having Robbie and his family over for dinner. I visited with Jimmy during the late afternoon and he is doing well. He is scheduled for one more and possibly his last operation on his face next week. We sat down after dinner; it was just me and Robbie. Maria was with Katie, Robbie's wife, in the kitchen. We talked about the business and the Army days. We were wondering how Sargent Tullo was doing. We lost touch with him and it's been a while since either of us had heard from him. The night went by and we walked them outside saying goodnight. It was a chilly October night as Maria held on to me as we waved them off. We walked back into the house and Maria said she wanted to check on the kids upstairs. They were asleep for a while but she needed to check on them. She asked me to pour her a glass of wine and she would be right down. There was an open bottle of red wine on the table and I poured her a half a glass. I picked it up and walked over to the living room couch. I put the glass down and went over to the sliding glass doors to shut the blinds. As I approach the door, I see a cloud white shadow outside the door. I open the door to see what it was. My stomach sank as I see Stevie standing in the middle of my patio. "Danny, I need you now. Please come with me. Just grab my hand and we can go back. You can change what happened and you can save me." I tried to process what was happening but I was a blank. The words came from my mouth without thought, "Stevie, why are you doing this to me. How can this be happening? You died, you can't be real." "Yes, I am Danny. Just trust me and come with me." I remember what the Doctor Spencer said and I quickly decide to take his advice. I take a deep breath and walk towards Stevie. He holds his hand out and I reach for it. We clutch each other's forearm and he pulls me towards him. "Stevie what's happening. I can't see anything." Then there was total silence. I felt I was in outer space just drifting in a silence I have never experienced before and total darkness as if I was blind. I didn't feel Stevie anymore. I tried to speak, but nothing came out it was black and silent. Then there was nothing, I was gone. I felt light headed like I had too much to drink but I knew I didn't. I was a little disorientated and Ray says, "Danny, are you okay?" I look at him and knew something was different but I couldn't figure out what it was. I just looked at Ray and Sal and said, "I'm fine. What's happening?" Sal said, "You know we're waiting for Stevie and then we said we're going to the diner. What's up with you? Hey, here comes Stevie now." As the music stopped Stevie walked over to us, arm and arm with his new love. Her name was Jennifer she was pretty and very friendly.

This was weird like this intro to Jennifer felt like I did this before. I looked at Stevie and told him to get her number because we were ready to go. He was cool and knew it was time, so he took Jennifer by the hand to a corner and they spoke a while. He started to write down her number. As he was writing down her number, two guys came from, what I have guessed the back door. One of them pulled Jennifer by the arm and away from Stevie. I knew right away this was not good. I had a cold wave go down my back as I just knew something bad was about to happen. I told Jimmy to get the car and get ready to pick us up so we get the hell out of here real fast. Jimmy grabbed Sal and they went to get the car. I was watching Stevie, waiting for him to do something stupid, but he didn't move. He just watched as Jennifer and this guy were in a heavy conversation. I told Ray to come with me and we would get Stevie out of here. Ray and I went over to Stevie and I told him to be cool and let's get out now.

Stevie smiled and said he was good. He just wanted to wait just to make sure Jennifer was okay with this guy. Stevie seemed calm, so I started to relax a bit and said I would wait with him. Ray went to the door to see if they were ready with the car. Jennifer waved at Stevie and mouthed to call her she is fine. Stevie smiled, nodded his head and said okay. We both turned and started for the door, thank God no problem. I guess my instincts were wrong, but I couldn't shake this feeling that something bad was going to happen. I took a deep breath and started to walk away with Stevie. As I started to feel relieved this guy yells out, "You better get the hell out of here you asshole." Stevie stops short and turns back at the jerk; he starts to walk towards this guy. I see where this is going so I get in front of Stevie and tell him no don't be stupid, just forget it and let's go. Stevie stops, looks me in the eye and smiles with that angelic look on his face and says, "You're right, let's go home." I take a deep breath once more and move away from Stevie towards the door. The rest happened so fast it was surreal. Stevie instead of following me turns back at the guy and goes right at him. I don't hesitate because somehow, I anticipated this was going to happen. Stevie gets right in the guy's face and punches him in the stomach and they both fall to the floor. As they both struggle, cursing at each other I see the guy reach into his pocket. I don't know how I saw him reach because it was happening so fast but I did. A second later I reach down to grab the gun but my arm gets pulled and I lose my balance. As I'm falling down, I hear a loud sound "Pop, pop" I feel a burn go into my stomach. I see Stevie's face and it was like he was smiling at me. The next thing there is nothing.

CHAPTER 21

"ANOTHER LIFE"

My head is pounding and I start hearing all these voices. "Danny, Danny" Over and over again, someone is calling me. Not just one voice, but there are a few different voices. I try to open my eyes but I just can't seem to get them to open. I start to shake my head back and forth, left to right. I hear, "He's coming around. He's moving. Danny, it's me. Honey it's me." Maria could that be my wife, maybe I'm alright, but I can't seem to open my eyes or move. Now I'm moving. "Wake up, it's your brother." "Give him some space he's starting to come out of it" I opened my eyes and looked around. There's my brother Alex, all my friends. "I'm so glad you're awake" I look at her but I'm not sure if I recognize her. Then a doctor comes over to me, "I'm Doctor Davis. You have been in a coma for three days, but you are fine. All your vitals are good. We will be running some tests, but so far all is good." "What happened to me?" "To me honestly, we do not really know. Your wife found you on the patio. You just passed out. She called 911 and they brought you here. "What caused me to go into a coma?" We are not sure that is why we will be continuing to run some tests. But for now, there is not much we can do. You will be fine and hopefully in the next day or so we will have some answers for you." "Thanks Doc" "We were all so worried about you. The boys send their love they are home with my sister Jayne. Why are you looking at me so strangely? Are you

Okay?"" "Pat, I think Danny needs some time to adjust. He just came out of a coma." "I know that Alex but I am his wife and I want to make sure he is alright. Maybe I should ask the Doctor about his condition." "Good Pat why you don't." I watched Pat walk away and I look at Alex, Sal, Ray and Robbie they all look the same but Pat I am confused about her. "Alex, you said Pat's my wife?" "Of course, Danny she's your wife." Something is just not right. I remember everyone just fine but Pat seems wrong. I can't seem to remember but there feels someone is missing. "Robbie when did I meet Pat, do you remember?" "Of course, I remember. She worked at Ft Hamilton when we were there." Just as I was about to ask a few more questions I have another visitor walk in. "Danny how are you feeling? I've been so worried about you." I can't believe my eyes as I watch Stevie walk over to me. "Stevie it can't be you, you were shot, is that you?" "No, I am someone else. Of course, it's me. What happened, did you lose your memory or something?" "Hey Stevie watch what you say he just woke up." As my brother lectured Stevie I wondered if I have gone crazy. Stevie has been dead for years. I say, "I don't understand Stevie you were shot and killed in the club." Stevie laughed, "I don't think so. If it wasn't for you, take the bullet for me and saving my life I would have been dead. What's going on Danny you haven't brought that night up in years?" Alex says, "I am sure Danny is very confused he has been in a coma for days. I think we should all clear out and let him get some rest. I am sure all this confusion, he is feeling will be fine after some rest." With that everyone agrees and they walk out and say they will be back tomorrow. I look at Stevie and he just smiles and turns away. My brother is the only one left in the room. "Danny you will be fine, you just need some time. You have had a traumatic event, but it will all work out. I will be back tomorrow" "No wait" As I hold on to my brother's arm, "Not yet. I know I have been through a lot but Stevie and Pat something is way out of whack. I know Stevie died and I don't even remember Pat. It's like Stevie is a ghost and Pat is a stranger." My brother looks at me and answers, "I don't know why you feel the way you do. I will ask the doctor what he thinks. It could be the coma has wiped some of your memory out. Stevie never died, you saved him and took a bullet in your stomach.

Lift up your top and look at the scar." I lifted up my hospital top and did in fact see a long scar in the middle of my stomach. "You see, that's where you took the bullet. You were lucky it didn't hit any organ or any vital just a clean wound. I didn't even keep out of the Army. You were a hero and saved Stevie, he's the one that the ass hole shot at, not you. I'm sure this memory thing has to do with the coma. This makes a lot of sense that this is a side effect." I look at him and say, "I guess your right but it seems so weird to me. Stevie alive it's hard to get that. It seems so clear to me that he was the one that was shot. I remember holding him in my arms and he was bleeding all over me. I remember his funeral. I don't understand how this can be." Just then Pat comes back to the room saying, "I just spoke with Josh and Ryan and they said they miss their Daddy." I don't know what to say to her because I don't know who Josh and Ryan are. The way she is looking at me is making me very uneasy, so I say, "I'm sorry, but I am tired and I think I need to get some sleep." "We will leave and come back in the morning." She nods her head and turns and walks away. My brother does the same. I just lay there totally confused. There are so many questions that I have and I don't know who to ask. They all seem so sure everything is normal but to me it's not. Stevie died. I know he did. Pat's now my wife and I have two boys. The problem is I don't think I even know her and the boys, I have no idea who they are. I have to speak to the doctor hopefully he could help me out on this. I close my eyes and fall asleep in minutes. Next thing I know there's Doctor Davis standing in front of me. "Danny, we are going to run a test on your brain to see if there is any damage. I don't believe there is but we have to be sure." "Doc I am confused. Things don't seem right to me. My brother, my friends, are all the same but my wife, it's like I don't know her. I can't remember my sons it's like I never had sons. There are other things that seem very wrong." "Danny you were in a coma and sometimes events happen that cannot be explained. What you are feeling could just be a temporary memory loss. We should know more after the tests. For now, just relax and after the results we can talk." "Doc, do what you have to." After the tests were done, they wheeled me back to the room. Waiting for me was Pat. She was tall and a little on the heavy side. She had light brown short hair. She was an average looking, but certainly did not look like she was my wife. Until the tests come back, I just thought it was best to along with whatever she had to say. "How are you feeling today? I hope better than yesterday?" "I'm feeling better thanks." I can't stay long I have to get back to the house for the boys. Jayne has to go soon so I have to be there." "No problem. Give my thanks to Jayne." Whoever she is I thought to myself. "I wanted to hear the results of the tests they ran on you but I'm not sure when they will have the results." "That's okay Pat please take care of the boys." "Good I will. I will call you later. If you hear anything at all, call me at home. Your phone is now hooked up." "Great I will." As I watched her leave I knew I didn't have a clue what the phone number was and I really didn't care. As I lay there I started thinking of everything that has happened since I woke up from the coma. Before the coma the last thing I could remember, I was out on my patio. A place I felt I knew and was my home. I couldn't see it, but I knew it was home. After that and before standing on the patio I am blank. Then something hit me, Jimmy. I need to speak with him maybe he can help. I know he has been in the VA and in a wheel chair. I can see him clearly. Then I remembered his number. I pick up the phone and call the number I think it's the right number. The phone rings for the third time then I hear, "Hello" "Jimmy its Danny." "Hey how are you feeling? I have been worried about you. Sal and Ray told me what happened, are you doing alright? "I'm fine, I think. They did a bunch of test this morning and I have not heard from them yet. I do feel good but my memory is all screwed up. Jimmy, Stevie is alive?" "Yeah, why do you ask that?" "This is one of the problems I have been having. I remember he was shot and died in the club back when we were kids." "Danny you saved him. You don't remember that?" "No Jimmy. I remember he died. I couldn't save him." "Danny, I don't know what to say. It was so long ago and there are times the memory of that night is blurry to me. The bottom line though is that he lived you were shot saving him. That's the way I seem to remember it." "You don't sound so sure Jimmy?" "I'm sure, but like I said it's been so long ago it's a little foggy to me."

Early the next morning Doctor, Davis visited with me, "How are you feeling today?" "Pretty good Doc." "Well, we have all your test results back and the good news they are all negative. No damage, no tumors all clear. If you don't have any other issues we can release you later today." "Doc, what about the reason I blacked out?" "I do not like saying this but the truth we have no idea what happened and why it happened. I know hearing that from your Doctor is unsettling but it is the truth." Doctor Davis was about forty years old, six feet tall, dark hair with a touch of gray. He was straight forward but he was also comforting and seemed very capable. I looked at him, saying, "This is all very strange. I black out for no reason. I go into a coma for three days. My wife, I don't think I even met before. I have two boys I can't even remember seeing and a few other disturbing things I won't even mention. My tests are all good and you're telling me there is no answer for any of this. I don't what to say. I'm happy there is no brain damage but all the rest leaves me confused and I don't what to do from here." "Danny, I would say that in time your memory should come back and clear all of this up. I can also recommend a psychologist that might be able to help you." "That's fine Doc, I'm already seeing one over at the VA. When I tell him, what has happened, I'm sure he will recommend me to an institution somewhere." "I'm sorry Danny but we have done all we can do. If you have any other symptoms at all, come back and we will take care of it. I will get the paperwork started for your release and you can call your wife to come pick you up." "Thanks Doc, I do appreciate your help." Now what do I do? My head is spinning trying to decide where I go from here. Call my wife who I don't even know. Go home to where? I have no idea where I live anymore. How could this be? I'm like blank on so many things but others are normal. Like Jimmy, Sal, Ray, Robbie and my brother Alex are all normal. But then there is Pat my wife, Kids, and the strangest of all is Stevie. He's dead damn it. I know he died, but then how can he have been just here yesterday. Plus, Jimmy and everyone else is okay with him being alive. At this point I don't seem to have many choices. I guess I will call Pat my wife and tell her to pick me up. It's time I meet my kids. I pick up the phone and I dial the number that was written down on a list of numbers I should have. I call Pat and she says that's great that I'm coming home. She will be here in a half an hour. I get dressed and sit on a chair just looking out the window. I try hard to remember what happened before I blacked out. I feel Robbie was there somehow. I will call him later and see what he says about that night. Pat comes in with two young boys. The boys come running right to me, "Daddy, we missed you." The oldest is Josh, who is ten and Ryan is seven. They are, nice looking, blond hair, blue eyes and fair skinned. They are all over me but I know I have never seen them before in my life. At least that's the way I feel right now. They know me as their Dad and I'm blank. Maybe the Doc is right it's a temporary memory loss and all this will clear up. That does make the most sense. I need to go along with all of this and see what happens. Pat takes me home. We pull up in the driveway of a nice size ranch. The development is large with similar house all around. I get out of the car and start walking up the driveway, "Hey buddy welcome home. We were all worried about you. If there is anything I can do, you know I'm right next door." Pat responds, "Thanks Charlie, but I think we will be alright." Charlie who the heck is Charlie? Well, it's obvious he is my next-door neighbor, but I never saw him before either. We go in the house and I know or I think I know I never have been in this house before. The only thing I could think of was getting some rest. Pat leads me into the bedroom and I lay down. "Thanks, I think I just need to rest a bit." She says that's a good idea and closes the door. I close my eyes and take a deep breath and try hard to settle down. I was feeling kind of drained and in a few minutes, I fell asleep. As I am sleeping, I see glimpses of images flashing across my mind. I see a dark-haired girl young smiling and I'm holding her hand. I see a club in the background with a sign lit up, but I can't make out the name. I then see images of a wedding. I could see a beautiful dark-haired girl standing beside me looking at me whispering, "I love you." I see myself in a house that somehow, I know that is my home. I can see two beautiful little girls sleeping in their beds that I just kissed goodnight. Then a cold chill up and down my back and then I see a face. It's coming at me. I know that face and he is smiling at me, it's Stevie. "Danny, wake up are you alright?" I open my eyes and I see Pat. "I don't know I was dreaming I think." "You were having a nightmare because you were yelling go away get away from me. Can I get you anything?" "No thanks, I just need a little time." I went to the bathroom and washed my face. A few minutes later, Pat comes back in and says, "Stevie is on the phone and he wants to speak to you." I slowly walk over to the phone, "Hello." "Hey there he is. How are you feeling?" "I'm fine." "I just want to let you know you can take as long as you need before you come back to work. I got everything under control. Robbie says to say hello." "Where are you Stevie?" "I'm in the office where else would I be on a Tuesday?" I hesitate and then say, "Is Robbie selling any cars?" "You bet he is. Business is great so don't you worry about nothing. Call me if you need anything." "Yeah, I will, thanks." I hang up the phone. Stevie is at the store. I don't know what to think. All I know it's all wrong. I don't belong here, Stevie shouldn't be alive. And I know I have another life that I should be living.

The next morning, I go visit Jimmy. As I walk into his room everything seems very familiar. I know I have visited him here many times. "Jimmy, I needed to talk with you. I get this feeling I have another life somehow. I know this sounds crazy, but Pat is not my wife. Josh and Ryan are not my kids. I think I remember meeting another girl in a club. I think she is my wife and I have two little girls." "Wow Danny, you have to slow down. Everything you're saying does sound crazy. First of all, you never could have met anyone in a club. After you were shot you said and kept your word that you never would go back into a club or a bar ever again. You can never have met anyone in a club. I know Pat is your wife and those boys are your kids. All this has to be from the coma. You have had some kind of memory loss and also some hallucinations that are getting you confused. I know you have seen Doctor Spencer and I think it's important you go see him. I'm sure he can help you and this will all pass." "Jimmy, what about Stevie?" "What about him?" "Forgetting the fact that I think he died, do you see anything strange about him?" "No not really. The one thing I know is that he is still bitter about Jennifer. I mean, that's pretty strange considering it's been so long ago and her ending up with the guy that shot you. Not to mention that he was shooting at Stevie before you got in the way. If that's what you mean, yes, I do think that is strange." "Jimmy, he doesn't talk about her with me but he does with you? You haven't mentioned anything about that to me, how come?" "I didn't think you wanted to hear anything about her or that night. I didn't want to bring up old wounds. When Stevie starts talking about her he gets really worked up. I mean you can see it in his eyes." I looked at Jimmy saying, "This coma thing has really left me a mess. I know it could be a memory loss, somehow but Stevie gets to me. When he looks at me it's like he knows something about me. He even gives this creepy grin like he has something only he knows. Once again, I can't explain it, but to me he is not the Stevie we grew up with." "Danny why don't you talk to him about how you feel and see if you can clear it up. You know my Army buddy Gulli he is a NYC detective? He is coming to see me this afternoon. He is now a homicide detective and I like listening to the cases he works on." I cringe a bit saying, "That murder crap would freak me out. Doesn't bother you?" "No, I get into it. If I wasn't stuck in this chair I would have loved to be a cop. He has been working on some special case that is what he says is a cold case that has now been reopened. That's the one case he has told be nothing about but today he said he would. I'm like a wheel chair detective when he gives me the details. It's really cool." "Jimmy, you enjoy your murder stories, but I got to go back to work. I have to come to terms that this will all work out once I get my memory back. For now, I'm going to try to accept the life I have and hopefully it will all come back to me." I made my exit and left Jimmy. What I told Jimmy I believe that is what I have to do. I'm going to work and hope all this works itself out.

CHAPTER 22

"SUSPICION"

"Here he is, the big dick, Gulli. It's good to see you. It's been a while." "Sorry Jimmy, I've been tied up in this case that I told you about and it's sucking up all my time. You're looking good Jimmy, my man. Have these nurses been taking good care of you?" "I have no complaints. I just try to make the best of everyday and I'm still grateful I made it back." "I know what you mean I feel the same. I try not to think about Nam and all the shit that we went through. There are times I wake up screaming. I don't have too many nights like that thank God for that. There are days I drift away into a sad trance as some of the guys that we left over there come back to me. That's why I bury myself in the job. I can't go back and get the bastards that took our buddies, but I can get the criminals that do the damage here." "Rullo, you said you would tell me about the case you are working on now." "I know I did. I'm not supposed to give any information on any case but this stays only with you. You can't say a word to anyone. I could lose my job if anyone found out." "Of course, I would never say a word, I promise." "Jimmy, I trust you. Like I told you this is about a cold case that started about 9 years ago. There was a murder of a young woman. She was twenty-one, very attractive. She was coming home from the city after working late. She was found by a young kid walking his dog the next morning in a lot, off of Cross Way Blvd in Howard Beach, Queens.

She was strangled with a rope. There was no sign of a struggle. There was nothing missing and there was no sign of any sexual abuse. We never found the killer. Two years later there was another murder of a young woman twenty-two years old and also very attractive. She was found early the next morning in Central Park. She was also strangled with no signs of robbery or sexual abuse. This case too was never solved. Nine months after that there was a third murder the same circumstances young, twenty, pretty, strangled no apparent motive and no suspects. Sure, looks like we have a serial killer on the loose. The investigation went on for years and nothing. No more murders until last year, the same M.O, young, attractive women strangled and found in Eisenhower Park. Then last month a young woman twenty-two was found on the side of the road off Ocean Parkway in Lido Beach. This is the case I have been assigned to. I'm on a special task force a joint effort with the NYPD, Nassau and Suffolk Counties PD. No leads no motives just a cold blank canvass. The amazing part is that we have been able to keep the connection apart from the new murders and the old ones. The press has been light on it. It's only a matter of time till some reporter or a leak will get out. Then we will have a full serial killer panic on our hands.

Here's the kicker in all the murders the victims all have been strangled with a rope and all of the victims were similar in appearance." "What do you mean by appearance, did they all look alike?" "They all were approximately the same age they were all very attractive they all had long brown hair, thin, brown eyes. They could all be from the same family that's how close they looked alike to each other. They were not related nor did they know each other. There are no apparent connections other than the way they looked and the way they were murdered. Most of the time they were coming home from work or just happened to be out and alone when they were murdered. There are no clubs, drinking, drugs, jealous boyfriends anything to go on. We have had some leads but they all go nowhere. We should have something but there are never any witnesses, no connections at all." Jimmy just listened and then said, "Wow that's brutal. This has to be so frustrating. No wonder why you have been so engrossed in this case. I wish you catch this asshole. Do you think he will kill again?"

"The way it looks, yes. We are sure it's the same guy. The pattern is there, it's almost for sure he will kill again. We have no DNA like he wears a body suit or something. He hits and disappears. There is no rhyme or pattern that we can put together to predict anything with this killer. After Rullo leaves Jimmy rolls over to the window and looks out at the afternoon sun h. He can't help to think about what Rullo said, "They all look alike long dark hair, brown eyes, thin, attractive around twenty-one years old." Jimmy shakes his head "No way just a coincidence for sure.

CHAPTER 23

DANNY "ALTERNATE UNIVERSE"

I head into work trying to see if everything is the way it should be nor at least the way I remembered them to be. I opened a small used car dealership along with Robbie. We both loved cars and after the Army we didn't have many options to make a living. The one thing neither of us wanted to do was work in an office and punch a clock. We had a few bucks saved and we decided to give the car business a shot. We rented a small corner lot out on the northeast part of Long Island. It was a small town but it was a working blue-collar middle-class area. The attractive part the rent was cheap. It was on a corner off the main road and it had a small garage and small office. It was and old gas station that was vacated a long time ago. The owner was happy just to get it rented. We picked up a few used cars from the auction. We went over them well and cleaned them up. We hung some signs distributed some flyers and we were in business. It was a tough start up but we did manage to sell a couple of cars. We reinvested every dollar we made and bought more cars. Robbie had a good feel for what would sell and we went with that. It was a small neighborhood and we made a lot of friends. They recommended us as reliable and honest. That went a long way and our sales started to rise. After a couple of years, we were able to take over the lot next store to us. We saved enough and the sales were good so we got a bank loan and bought the property. All our plans went really well and the business was solid. I had a great friendship with Robbie so it was great to have him as my partner. I drove up to the store it was mid-afternoon. I went around the side entrance and into my office. I looked around and everything looked normal. I went around to my desk and sat down. On the left side of my desk is a large framed picture of my two boys. I stared at the picture for a long time but it was the same as I have felt since the coma. They're two cute kids but it's like they belong to someone else and not mine. There is a slight knock on the door and I see Robbie, "Hey, there he is. How are you feeling? I didn't think you would be in today." "I thought it was for the best that I come in and try to get back to normal. Robbie sit down a minute I want to ask you a few questions. We were both in the Army together and stationed at Fort Hamilton, right?" "Of course, why do you ask that?" "I'm not sure that everything that I know or remember are the way things are now. Stay with me for a while. I remember Sargent Tullo was our Sarge at the base. He was married and had kids. I remember dating Ronnie and Sandy from the office. After I stopped seeing Ronnie she married Dave. We went to the wedding and Sargent Tullo had a girlfriend a blonde named Ann and his wife was Bee. They had a blow out at the wedding. Our Captain was Monroe and he was always after the Sarge. How am I doing with this, am I right?" "Yes of course your memory is fine." "Okay then here is where it gets weird. I have no memory of Pat. I don't remember meeting her at all. I thought of remembering meeting another girl and I think it was at a club and you were there. Does any of this mean anything to you?" "No Danny. You never went to any clubs. You told me once that you got into a fight in a club and you were shot. Since that incident you never went or never would go to any bar or club again. After you broke up with Sue you dated Pat. You met her at your cousin's house, she was the daughter of his neighbor Ed. You don't remember any of this?" "No. It's driving me crazy. Pat is like a stranger and so are the boys." I was just about to ask Robbie another question but the door opens, "Look at this my partner are all back together. How are you feeling Danny, you look good?" I just froze, I didn't know what to say. Stevie was now my partner. I just sat there and stared at him. I can't understand him even being alive. I remembered him dying in my arms years ago in the club. "Danny, what's up? You're looking at me like you're seeing a ghost or something?" "No, it's just I'm still foggy from the coma I guess." "No problem I understand. You have been through a lot. I told you to stay home till you feel yourself. I and the Robster here has everything under control. Don't we Rob?" Robbie looked a little intimidated by Stevie and just said, "Yes, no problem." "I told you Danny we have it all under control. Go home spend some time with the kids and the rest. Do what I say okay? I have to meet someone so I will be back in an hour or so. Go home buddy." "Sure Stevie. I will see you soon." I watch Stevie walk out of the room and I turn to Robbie saying, "When did Stevie join the business I don't remember him as a partner?" "He came in a few years after we started up. To be honest, I wasn't too crazy about the idea. Things were going well and I didn't think we needed anybody else. You explained to me that we needed two people here all the time. There were times when we needed a day off or a sick day or even a vacation. Plus, you told me that you always watched over Stevie and I would be doing you a favor to let him partner with us. He did have some money to add to our expansion, so I went along with it. It was an adjustment having him here and he can be a headache sometimes but I learned how to deal with him. Look Danny he is not my friend like you are and if it wasn't for you I would not have anything to do with him. You asked me and for you Danny I agreed to let him in. If you really want to know the truth, I never completely trusted him. I don't mean about money. I don't think he would ever steal, but he seems to have two sides to him.

    Like he can be a nice guy and then he could be dark and strange. Listen, he's okay and I'm fine with him but being you asked I'm telling you how I really feel." "Thanks Robbie I appreciate that you did what I asked. The problem is that now I don't ever remember asking to bring him in. Up until this point I believed that Stevie was killed at the club. I don't want to upset you, it's my memory, and it's all screwed up from the coma. If you don't mind, I'm just going to stay here in my office and spend some time alone and try to work things out." Robbie stood up and grabbed my hand saying, "Whatever you need to do is fine with me. I'm just happy to have you back here. Whatever I can do just let me know." I closed my eyes and let my mind drift into a blank state. I was hoping that somehow, I would find a way to make sense of everything that has happened. I tried to mentally go back to the night where all of this started. For some reason it was still a blank but the one thing is that it's always Stevie that comes to mind. I get the feeling that Stevie is the only one who knows something about that night. I decide it's time I have a talk with Stevie. Stevie is due back in the office so I decide no matter how long it takes I will wait for him. I search through my desk looking for I don't know what but anything that can help me remember. I find the usual bills and office supplies and nothing else. With time on my hands I pick up the phone and give Jimmy a call. "Hey, Jimmy, how are you doing? I'm at the office and I just needed to talk to you. I am waiting to see Stevie. For some reason I get this feeling that he knows something about what happened to me. I can't seem to know why I feel this way but I do." "I'm glad you called because I was just thinking of you. I told you about my buddy Gulli the detective. He visited with me after you left and he told me about the case he is working on.

 The problem is that I gave him my word that I won't talk about it but I need to tell you. It's really a big coincidence but I just can't let it go. You know how I told you before that Stevie gets all worked up when he starts to talk about Jennifer. He gets this look in his eyes and real intense. I always thought that it was pretty strange after all these years. Every so often out of nowhere he will start talking about her and the asshole she ended up with. I mean, come on get over it. It was a lifetime ago. I tell him to just forget it and then he goes off on how much he hates them both. I mean he has been with a lot of women since Jennifer so why does he keep bringing her up. After a while he normally just laughs and says that he knows it's stupid and he will not bring her up anymore. But every third or fourth visit from him, he goes off again. I kind of just shrug it off and say that's just Stevie being Stevie. After Gulli told me about his case he is working on I got this ugly feeling that it could be connected with Stevie." I said to Jimmy, "What about the case that he is working on?" "I'm not supposed to talk about it." "Then why did you start? It's obvious you want to tell me. Just tell me and I promise I will not say a word to anyone about it." Gulli told me he is working on a cold case that just turned hot. There has been a string of murders spanning over ten years. The thing is that every one of the murders the victims are all around twenty years old. They were all thin with long brown hair, brown eyes and very attractive. Does that ring a bell to you?" I shake my head and without thinking I say, "Jennifer?" Jimmy says, "That's the first thing that came into my mind too. It has to be a stupid coincidence, I'm sure, but it did strike a chord. I don't believe for one second that Stevie would ever hurt anyone. I just thought it was strange that all these girls looked alike and they all fit Jennifer's description.

Of course, none of this makes any sense because if Stevie did want some kind of revenge why not her? Why would he harm ones that looked like her when he could go after the one that hurt him? Hey, this whole conversation is stupid. We know Stevie since we were kids and he never hurt anybody. Just talking about him like this is wrong." "You're right, but the problem I have is that in my mind Stevie died at the club. I can't get that out of my head. According to the way I feel is that he can't be here. The Stevie I knew died and this Stevie seems different. I can't really explain it but he is not the same. I'm not saying he is involved in any of these murders but I know he is not the same as I remember him. He looks like Stevie but." "But what Danny?" I look up and Stevie is at the front of the door. "Hey Stevie, I didn't know you were there." I turn back to the phone and say, "I have to go I will call you later." "You should have told Jimmy I said hello. If you and Jimmy wants to know something about me, why don't you just ask me? I have nothing to hide. Ever since you have come out of the hospital you have been acting strange. Now I hear you and Jimmy talking about me and about Jennifer. Tell me what's going on?" I scratched my head and tried to think of what I should say. "You're right. I have been different since the coma. My memory is all out of whack. I mean I don't even remember my kids or my wife Pat. It's like they are strangers to me. The last memory I had about you is that I remember you getting shot in the club. Stevie, I saw you die in my arms. Now you're back and evidently you have always been here and you never died. I have been looking at you very strangely because I can't get used to the fact that you're alive." Stevie smiled and said, "Wow! That is really screwed up. As you can see I am here right in front of you so I could never have died. That night you saved my life and you took a bullet to protect me. Danny, I will never forget that.

For some reason I think that the coma has messed up your memory and your mind. I think you need to let the doctors know how you are feeling. I'm no doctor, but it does sound to me like you have some kind of post shock symptoms and stress. I'm your friend Danny and if I can help you in any way just let me know. All I can tell you is that Pat is your wife and the boys are your kids. I never died and it's obvious that all your problems are from the coma. The one thing I don't understand is what all this has to do with me and Jennifer. I haven't seen her in a million years, so why are you and Jimmy talking about her?" I looked down and my mind was racing on what I should say to Stevie. He seems normal now and I am second guessing myself on everything that has been going on. I figured I might as well tell him the truth and get it over with. "Here is the deal. Jimmy told me that his buddy from the Army is a detective and he is working this case. He told me he is not supposed to tell anyone about it but he did tell me. I gave Jimmy my word that I wouldn't say a word about it to anyone. The one thing I can tell you that the case happens to be about five women that all look like Jennifer. I mean we haven't seen them but they fit her description. They all had long dark hair, brown eyes, thin, attractive and all around twenty years old. That is why we were talking about how they all sound like they resemble Jennifer. That's it, just a coincidence that Jimmy had to tell me about." Stevie looked at me saying, "This makes no sense. First of all, that describes Jennifer the way she looked maybe fifteen years ago. That description also could fit about another million girls in NY alone. When I came in I heard you talk about me. What does all of this have to do with me? Let me guess, they were all raped and you guys think I had something to do with it. Because they all look like Jennifer I am some kind of pervert and go around raping girls who resemble Jennifer. Is that what you guys think of me?"

"No Stevie not at all. It was just a coincidence, that's all. We talked about you because we know that you still get worked up about her." "What makes you say that? You don't even remember I am alive, so how do you know that I get worked up about her?" Stevie's tone changed dramatically from soft and soothing to edgy and aggressive. I was getting very uncomfortable and I was trying to get out of this conversation. "Stevie this all bullshit and I'm sorry I brought it up. We were just talking, more gossiping like we were old women. I am sorry that we talked about you. The whole thing is stupid. Let's just drop it. Stevie's expression didn't change. He stared at me saying, "What really happened to these girls you were talking about?" "I don't know Jimmy couldn't say." "Jimmy knows what happened but he couldn't tell you because he promised his buddy?" "No. I don't think he told him. Look Stevie I don't know. It doesn't matter anyway. It has nothing to do with you. This all because of the description that he gave Jimmy. That's what reminded us of Jennifer. Anytime we think of her, of course we are going to think of you. That's all there is too it. No big deal." I took a deep breath as I watched Stevie's reaction. He stared at me for the longest time with a very unnerving look. Then his faced changed and he gave me a big smile saying, "You're right this is all a bunch of bullshit. Let's forget it. I will go see Jimmy soon and I will tell him the same thing. It's all forgotten already. Hey the main thing is we get you all better. Need to get your memory back and get your head straight, right buddy?" "Yeah Stevie you got that right." Stevie smiled and relaxed saying, "We should call Sal and Ray and plan a dinner or something. Just the guys like old times. We should all get together and shoot the shit like we used to do. Let's go to a nice Italian restaurant have a couple of drinks and talk about the old days.

What do you say Danny how's that sound?" "Sounds great, I will call Ray and Sal and set it up." "Great. Let me know what they say and when we are going to go. I'm looking forward to it. I'm going to head out so I'll see you tomorrow." "Yeah, see you tomorrow." I watched Stevie walk out the door and I started to relax. That was one strange conversation. He went from the old Stevie to someone I didn't even know is a split second. I'm not sure what to think about him. The one thing I do know is that he made me feel really uneasy. At one point I felt like he could be dangerous. Maybe I should take him up on the dinner with the guys. I could see if it's just me or Sal and Ray feel the same way. The more I thought about it the better it felt. I'm not sure of anything anymore. Is Pat really my wife? Do I have two boys? That night at the club it was me that was shot? Stevie didn't die that night and he has been my partner for all these years. What has happened to me? It has to be because of that dam coma, it did something to me. I can't remember any of this but yet there are things that seem normal. Jimmy seems to be the way I remember. He served in Viet Nam, he was badly wounded. I have been visiting him for years. Robbie is my partner, we were in the Army together. Maybe Sal and Ray could help me out of this. I called Sal and Ray and set up a dinner at Mamma Mia's restaurant by the airport. I called Stevie and he said that it sounds great. I called Robbie and told him to come and he said he will be there. Friday night meeting the guys for dinner, just like old times. I pull up to the restaurant a few minutes after seven. I see Stevie, Sal, Robbie and Ray talking and laughing at the front door. I walk up to the door and they all greet me with a big hug. Even Stevie is all smiles and it all feels just like it always was with us. We get seated at a table and order a round of drinks. The drinks are served and Sal says, "A toast to Danny. Thank God that he is Okay and to all of us being together again, salute!" We all bang glasses and drink. The restaurant is your typical Italian restaurant.

 The tables are all filled with a mixture of office workers and local patrons. There is a pretty loud party going on in an adjoining room with about twenty-five family members. We start taking turns with the normal questions on how is all the families and the Kids doing. I watch Stevie closely and I can't see anything different about him. He seems like the same old Stevie, smiling, drinking and just having a good time. After eating the salads Ray says, "Danny what about the time we got stuck in the Hamptons. Robbie doesn't know all the crazy things Ray did when we were young. He had a few nerds for friends which he called his pets. He never bothered them, they just would make him crazy, crazy in a funny way. He blamed this kid Stanley Kravitz for everything that would happen. Stanley was a real nerd who would write tickets for lateness, dress code violations and all sought of stupid school rules. Ray was one of his favorite targets. Ray would never hurt Stanley but he would go out of his way to annoy Stanley. Ray was a crazy driver and he liked to stupid things basically just for laughs. Unless you knew Ray well like we did the other kids thought he might be a little nuts. Come on Danny Tell Robbie the story about the Hamptons." I said, "Come on, no one wants to hear that again." Robbie says, "I never heard it. Come on Danny tell me what happened?" All the guys join in urging me to tell the story. "Alright, if I can remember it, I will tell it. Robbie like Sal said when we were kids Ray was a total wild man. I mean he did some real crazy things. We all decided to take a trip out to the Hamptons. Ray says he will drive. Now back then we were just seventeen and Ray didn't have his own car. He used his Mom's Chevy Biscayne. It was great with all of us because none of us had any money. Ray's Mom always had a full tank of gas. We had just graduated from High School and it was the beginning of the summer.

 Ray was a crazy ass driver. He would drive on lawns, sidewalks and anything else he could think of to make us go crazy. He would love to drive backwards for long periods of time. Especially late at night when we all had a few too many drinks. How we didn't kill ourselves back then I will never know. We would go to this bar in the old part of Huntington and drink all night. We would take the old winding roads back home and go through a pretty expensive area. They were big houses with big manicured lawns. Ray would drive and of course most of the time he was still feeling no pain from the booze. For some reason Ray would go up on this huge lawn and drive all over it. The house lights would come on and then he would drive off and go flying down the road. We all would take turns yelling at him, but he would just laugh. I'm telling you he must have done these five or six times this one month. Back then I had just started to work in Manhattan and I took the Long Island Railroad from Plainview into Penn Station That Monday I was on the Railroad and on my way to Penn Station. I have my eyes shut and I was still half asleep. There were these two guys sitting right in back of me. It was quite so I could hear every word they were saying. One guy says to the other that Friday night that son of a bitch did it again. This asshole drives all over my lawn. I called the cops this time. If I ever catch him I will personally break his head. The other guy asks if the cops caught him. He says no but I'm going to be waiting from now on. He always does it on Fridays. I'll get the bastard next time, I will get him. As I hear this guy telling the story I wouldn't dare turn around and see what he looked like. I just slowly slipped as far down in the seat as I could. I realized the stop before mine was Huntington so there was no doubt he was talking about us. I knew it was a pretty stupid thing to do, but I heard the anger in this guy's voice I was really scared. I called Ray as soon as I could and he swore he wouldn't do it again. Now we laugh about it, but it was a stupid thing to do. Wasn't it Ray?"

Ray smiled and shook his head in agreement. We all agreed it was crazy, but we all knew we did laugh about it and didn't try to stop him. We were all to blame. Robbie smiled and said, "What about the Hamptons?" "Okay back to that. Like I was saying we decided to go out east and have some fun. Once again, we had very little money between us, but Ray had the car and the gas. We drove out towards the Hamptons and Ray was doing his thing. He was driving crazy. He called it the Weeble-wobbles and he would steer the car hard to the left and quickly hard to the right. We would be rocking back and forth like a ride at an amusement park. Well, he kept on doing this on the two-lane road Montauk Highway. While we were laughing and having a good time we hear a police siren. Oh, crap there was a cop car following us. We all yelled at Ray to pull over which he did do. The cop comes out of his car and over to Ray. Ray rolls down the window. The cop asks Ray what the hell does he think he is doing driving like that. Ray goes off on some crazy story that he was trying to avoid hitting flying ants. The cop listens patiently as he keeps talking about flying ants all over the road. Finally, the cop has heard enough and tells Ray to get out of the car. He gets out and the cop was trying to see if he was drinking. It was late morning and we didn't have anything to drink Ray sticks to his story about these flying ants and how he had to do Weeble-wobbles to avoid them. We were all getting pretty silly in the car listening to him. We were trying to hold off on the laughing, but it was hard. The cop asks for his license and registration. Ray stars going through the glove compartment and all he has is tons of Chinese menus and all kinds of garbage. Of course, Ray doesn't have his license with him because he left his wallet home. There is no registration either. The inspection sticker expired to make things worse. Ray now starts telling the cop that he had his license when he left the house but he thinks Stanley Kravitz stole his wallet.

He tells the cop that Stanley came over his house when he was getting ready to leave. Stanley wanted to come with him out the Hamptons. Ray said no. Stanley then got mad and pushed him against the car. Ray said that's when Stanley lifted his wallet. He told the cop that he should go and arrest Stanley right away before he leaves town with his money. The cop once again listened to Ray's incredible story. I think he actually started to enjoy Ray's craziness. I am sure he didn't believe anything he was saying. The cop says to Ray what about the expired inspection. Ray said oh that's his mother's fault. It's her car and he has nothing to do with that. He told the cop when he gets home he will tell her that she better get the inspection done right away. The cop asked if Stanley took the registration too. Ray said no that was his dog Buster's fault and he ate the registration last night because his sister took it out of the car. He said she bought Buster dog biscuits and put them in the glove compartment. She must have mixed in the registration with the dog biscuits. With that the cop said he heard enough and was impounding the car. Plus, Ray had to see the judge because he was driving without a license. He gave us all a ride into town where we had to wait in the courthouse for the judge. We waited for two hours and finally they called Ray into the judge's chambers. Ray stuck with his story that they should be after Stanley. He was a criminal and Ray did nothing wrong. The cop never told the judge about the flying ants so he did give Ray a break on that. The judge gave Ray a fine of fifty dollars and he had to send in a copy of his license within ten days. Ray or any of us had any money to pay the fine that's why the judge agreed to have him send in the money. Now we were stuck in East Hampton with no car. Our only way home was to take the bus. We found the bus station and it was right in front of a small Italian restaurant.

We all were starved but we had only a few dollars each and we had to pay for the bus to get home. The smell of the food was driving us all crazy so we decided we would get a little bite and share it. We sat down and the waitress said that they had a special on spaghetti and meatballs. We couldn't resist. We ate like it was our last meal and it was great. Nothing like spaghetti and meatballs when you are starving. After we chipped in and paid the bill along with the tip we came to the unfortunate reality that we had just spent all of our money. The bus was due in about five minutes and we had no money for the fare. Ray said it was all his fault and he would talk to the driver and get us home. The bus pulled in and Ray led us onto the bus. He told the bus driver that we had no money because this guy named Stanley Kravitz stole all our money. We just reported him to the cops and they would be arresting him soon, but we had no money to get home. The bus driver was a cool guy and we all knew he didn't believe Ray but he said he would let us ride home. He gave us a voucher that we had to mail in to the bus company. He told us that if we didn't mail it in they would take it from his pay. We all thanked him and sat in the back of the bus. We all were knocked out and slept the entire trip home. We got off the bus and we all shook the bus driver hand to thank him. That Monday we sent all the money into the bus company. Ray had a lot of explaining to do to his Mom and Dad on what happened to the car. The next time we saw Ray he said they were good with it and they made arrangements to pick up the car and pay for all the fees." Robbie laughed, saying, "Ray, where did you come up with all those stories and what the hell are flying ants?" Ray said' "I just said the first thing that came into my head and that was it."

We all shared a good laugh reminiscing. Stevie joined in and told Robbie how these guys were always there for him. He had some tough times growing up but he always had us to be there for him. He also said how important Jimmy was to him. How inseparable, we all were back then. How every one of us was so worried about Jimmy when he went to Viet Nam? He also said he felt guilty that only

Jimmy went to Viet Nam. We are more like brothers then friends. Listening to Stevie and seeing him with all of us made me feel guilty of doubting him. Stevie seemed to be the same friend that I have always known. We continued to talk on and on about old times. We laughed most of the night. We realized that we were the only ones left in the restaurant so it was time to call it a night. We all hugged and said this is something we should do a lot more often. I agreed with that and it felt so good to be with my friends again. I got back in my car and my mind started to wonder. I sat there for a long time just thinking things through. If tonight felt so normal and Stevie seemed just as normal, then it must be me. Everything is the way it is because it's my life. Pat and the boys have to be my family and the coma has messed up my mind. The only thing for me to do was to go home and try to start all over again. Hopefully my memory will come all back and everything will fall into place.

CHAPTER 24

"TWO DIFFERENT WORLDS"

The next few weeks go by and nothing has changed. I'm starting to feel more comfortable with my life. I keep busy with Josh and Ryan taking them to their games. Josh is a pretty good baseball player. Ryan's not as good but he enjoys the game. Pat is a good cook and has been patient with me. The intimacy is still not there, but she is very understanding and seems optimistic it all will work out. I can't say I'm happy with this life but it is okay. I still get pangs that it's not my life but I'm trying hard to make it work. The Doctors tell me it could take a long time for my memory to come back. They also warn me that there is a good possibility it might never come back. There is no way of telling. Other than that, my health is good and I don't need any further treatments. I visit Jimmy a few times a week and all is good with him. The business is good and I have no problem with Robbie or Stevie. Ever since the dinner Stevie seems like the Stevie of old. I stopped asking questions about Stevie and decided to let it go. It was early December and the house was freezing. I get out of bed to check on the oil burner in the basement. It was freezing down in the basement as I turned on the light. I walk over to the burner and check if it's running. The burner is not running at all so I know something is wrong. About the only thing I know is to hit the restart red button. I hit the button and the burner kicks in. I turn to go back towards the stairs and I feel a little light headed. Then in a flash I see a different house. A house that looks very familiar to me. The flash stops and then another flash, this time it is two young girls running towards me. They are calling me Daddy. I see them clearly, they're beautiful. They are hugging me and kissing me. I can see myself clearly. Then I see a dark-haired girl crying and running towards me. She is saying, "Danny I was so worried about you. Are you alright? Danny, I love you." I run to her and hug and kiss her, saying, "I missed you too. I love so much. Maria, I never want to be a part again." Just in a flash they are gone. I'm standing, holding onto a work table and balance myself.

What was that; what has just happened? I know they were my family. Somehow, I knew it was my wife Maria and my daughters. How can this be? Now I'm confused again. This life with Pat that I was trying to accept is clearly not right. It has felt wrong ever since I woke up in the hospital. This vision I have just seen I know that that is my family. I felt disorientated so I went back upstairs to bed. I lie in bed and pray hard and long, "Please God bring me back to my real life. I know that is where I belong. This is not my life, not my family. Please Lord, let me go home. Please let me go home. I know I was in a coma, but I also know that what I have just seen downstairs is my real life. I know that now I know it. After a while I fall asleep. The next thing that happens is that I'm lying in bed and the sun is shining in my face. Maria says, "Hey, wake up sleepy head we have a big day ahead of us." I look at her not knowing what to say. I must have a strange look on my face because she says, "What's with that face. You look like you've seen a ghost or something. Come on Babe we got to get a move on. The kids are finishing breakfast and they are so excited they will be running up here any second." "Without thinking, I say, "Where are we going?" "Yeah right like you don't know it's Lucia's birthday. Come on fool, you have to pick up the cake. I have a million things to do so get up." Just looking at Maria and it all came rushing back to me. Yes, it's Sofia's birthday and standing in front of me is my beautiful wife Maria. I jump up and grab her throw her on the bed. I kiss her all over and say, "I love you! I love you!" "I love you too, but let go of me we have a party to do." I reply, "Yes we do. Angie my beautiful daughter Angie and Lucia my sweet Lucia I missed them so bad." Maria just smiles, "What are you talking about they just got out of bed and went down for breakfast. You are whacky today Danny, now cut the bull and let's get going. My Mom will be here any minute to help set up for the party." "Your Mom, yes, your Mom is coming, great that's great." "Wow, now I know you're screwy today. I'm very happy that you feel so good about my Mom coming. Now for the last time let's go." I jump out of bed and run down the stairs yelling, "Lucia, where's my birthday girl."

Lucia sees me coming and comes running to me, "Daddy, it's my birthday." I give her a big hug and then Angie comes charging and jumps on top of me, "Daddy, I love you too." "I love both of you so much I could just eat you up." I have a million questions on how can this be? Am I dreaming or worse am I going crazy. Could my prayers have been answered and I am where I should be but how? How could I just be back or is this whole experience been some kind of delusion? I wanted to get Maria and ask what is going on but I don't want anything to change right now. I certainly don't want her to think I am nuts. If I am Okay then I just want to be with my family and ask the questions later. I decide to play it my ear and see what happens. The rest of the day was pure happiness. The house was filled with relatives, neighbors and friends. Everything was exactly like it should be. Robbie with his family, Maria's Mom and dad, Sal and all the rest. Then a big surprise Ray brought Jimmy from the hospital for the day. Everything was happening so fast I didn't have time to talk to Maria or anyone about the biggest question in my mind. What the hell is going on? One minute I am with a different family and they all tell me it is all normal. The next thing I know now I'm back with my real family and this is all normal. I have to be losing my mind for sure. I was reluctant to ask anyone about it because I didn't want to ruin Lucia's birthday. The last thing I wanted was a scene where Lucia's dad has gone nuts. The only thing I could do was go along with it all. To be honest, it was wonderful to be back with Maria and the girls I just tried to forget all the rest and enjoy the day. About midway through the party I was able to get a moment with Maria. I pulled her over to the corner by the garage and said, "Honey, I love you so much and I'm so happy to be here. I never want anything to ever change. I have such a great life with you and the girls I want it to last forever.

I just need to ask you, have you noticed anything different about me recently?" Maria smiled, "Only this morning you were a little strange. Are you feeling alright?" "Yes, I'm fine, but has everything with us been normal. I mean the last few weeks have everything been normal?" "Danny you're starting to get me worried. After last week when you felt you did blank out. The entire tests were negative and they said it could have been dehydration. Don't you remember this?" "Yes of course I do. I don't know what it is but I'm fine." Why are you asking these strange questions? Are you sick or something? Are you keeping something from me?" "No, not at all. It's just I had a few crazy dreams lately. I had a lot of dreams about Stevie. Do you know anything about Stevie?" Maria looked at me a little baffled, saying, "Stevie, you mean your friend that was killed? The only thing I know about him is what you told me. I know you were very close to him and it had to be traumatic what you have gone through. Why are you asking about him after so many years? I was relieved that Maria said that Stevie was dead. Now I know everything is the way it has always been. I could see I was upsetting Maria, so I quickly said, "Babe its nothing. I had a few dreams about him and it kind of upset me. I guess it's normal to have flash backs on such a bad experience and loss like that. I'm sorry I brought it up. It was stupid of me and bad timing. Please, let's forget it. I just wanted to make sure that the dreams haven't affected the way I have been with you and the girls. Now let's get back to the party. We have a birthday cake to do." Maria smiled, "Sure, as long as you are okay and we are good, right?" "It was just a dream and it bothered me a bit but it's all good now. As far as us, we are not good, we are fantastic. I couldn't be happier." I took Maria by the hand and we went back to the party. The rest of the day was perfect. Everyone was happy. Lucia was the little princess and was in heaven opening all her presents. Angie was a touch jealous but we made her feel special too. Towards the end of the party I couldn't resist to question Jimmy about Stevie. I sat next to Jimmy, "How's everything been going at the hospital, are they taking good care of you?" "You know they do Danny. I have my good days and then some bad ones, but the nurses have been great. You know I have one more reconstruction surgery coming up and I think that will do it." "I know that will go fine. Jimmy, I did want to ask you about Stevie do you ever dream or think about him much anymore?" "Sure, I think of him now and then. Last night I was dreaming about him. It was a little weird, but that was about it. Look he was our close friend and we will never forget him." "What do you mean the dream was weird?" "Well I'm not sure. He was like floating around me smiling. He seemed to be saying something to me but I can't remember what it was. That was it. I can't remember anything else about the dream. Why do you ask?" "I don't know, just curious, that's all." "Jimmy, can you remember anything he was saying," "Not really, but it sounded like he will be back, but I'm not sure if that was what he was saying. It was very strange. What's this all about Danny?" "It's just nothing that I was thinking about Stevie lately that's it, no big deal." I didn't want to get into it with Jimmy anymore. I was tired of everybody thinking I was crazy. I could see Jimmy would not have the answers anyway. I freaked Maria out a little so I decided I wasn't going to do the same for Jimmy. The party came to an end and all our friends and family had left. The girls were putting on their pajamas as I was helping Maria clean up. She was finishing a few of the last of the dishes. I was standing behind her by the dining room entrance watching her. I still couldn't make any sense of what has been happening. It was so hard to believe that I am back with my wife and kids. It feels so good but yet so strange. I don't want ever to go back to that other life, but I still have no idea how that was at all possible. To have another life with a strange family how is that even possible.

Could I have imagined or dreamt all of that. That Stevie was alive and I had such a different life. What are my choices going to a shrink and tell them this incredible story? Tell Maria I think I had another family. I mean this is so strange. The only thing that makes any sense is that I have had some weird dream like experience. I know it was so real but how can that be. I am not going to worry Maria with any of this and I'm not going to some shrink. As long as I have my wife and kids back, I'm going to accept it. This is my life and I have to forget the sick events that I have been through. It had to be some kind of nightmare, but thank God it's over. That's all that counts, it's over. Maria is standing right in front of me so this is reality. Just to make sure I go up to Maria turn her around and give her a huge kiss. I hug her so tight she actually lost her breath. "Wow! What's that all about?" "That is my way of saying I love you." "Well, let's go up to put the kids to bed and then I'll show you how much I love you." I give a huge smile, "That's a deal." We go up to the girl's room and I go over to Sofia in her bed and sit next to her. "Well princess did you have a good birthday?" "Oh yes, Daddy I had a great birthday. I love all my presents. I love you Daddy." A few tears roll down my eyes from sheer happiness. "I love you so much princess, but it's time for bed. Even birthday girls have to sleep." I kiss her goodnight and go over to Angie saying, "How's my other princess doing. Don't forget when your birthday comes we will have a big party just for you. You were such a good girl there will be some big presents for you on your birthday." "That's great Daddy. I love you this much." Angie spreads her hands as far as they go and has the biggest smile possible. "Well, I love you from the moon to all the stars and back to the house. Now you get some sleep and we will have a big bunch of pancakes waiting for you in the morning. Okay, sweetie?" "You bet Daddy. Goodnight." I walk out of the room and both the girls yell out, "Night Daddy, I love you." I blow them kisses and turn out the lights. I went into our bedroom and I just throw myself onto the bed. A few seconds later Maria joins me in bed and we made sweet love. It felt as good as any time in my life. I know we have made love many times, but this felt like heaven. I held her in my arms and wouldn't let go. After a while she fell asleep in my arms. I was so happy I was back that I could scream out in joy. As I held her in my arms I realized I was afraid to fall asleep. What if I wake up and I'm back in that other world. No, I could not bear to lose my wife and kids again. If I have to go without sleep the rest of my life I will. About an hour or so later, my eyes started to close. The next thing I know it is morning. I lift myself up and realize there is no Maria. Oh no it can't be and just as I start to panic in comes Sofia and Angie. They both jump on top of me laughing and giggling like crazy. I ask the girls, "Where's Mommy?" "She's making pancakes silly." I pick them both up off of the bed and put them down on the floor saying, "Go tell Mommy, I will be right down." I watch them run off and I go into the bathroom. I wash my face and look in the mirror. I'm thinking this is it. This is my life and I'm not thinking about the other stuff anymore. I'm going to go downstairs and have a great breakfast with my wife and kids. I'm going to live my life from now on and enjoy every second of it. I will pray every day that I don't ever go back to that other life.

CHAPTER 25

"EVIL"

The next day after the party I go to work where everything in his mind is the way it should be. My only partner is Robbie and all the pictures of Maria and the kids are in their place. I walk into my office and take a deep breath thinking, "This is right. This is my life and the way it always was and should be. The other life had to be some kind of nightmare. The more I think about what happened, it probably has something to do with last week when I blanked out. It must have screwed me up somehow. At this point now, I am going to just try to forget all the craziness and enjoy my life the way it is. No more questions just let it go and move on. That is exactly what I have done. A week goes by and all is good. Late one afternoon I'm sitting in my chair and I shut my eyes. It was quiet and I dozed off into a soft nap. "Danny, it's me, your buddy Stevie. I miss you Danny I need you to come back." I open my eyes and its Stevie, smiling and he is right in front of me. "I have you to thank Danny. You're the one who saved me and brought me back. I need you over here in this life with me. It's because of your buddy that I am having all this fun. I need you to be here so you can be part of my sweet revenge. You know what I'm talking about. I have been quenching my thirst on the appetizers, but the main course is coming. You have to be there so you can witness all of it. I want to thank you because of you it is all possible. I know you like being here with your beautiful family, but that does not work for me. I want you with me, now! You created me Danny and the world that I exist in. Come back with me and enjoy the show. You can't resist me or that wonderful wife and sweet daughters will pay for your unwillingness to join me. So just relax and sleep I will do the rest.

I wake up and head right to the bathroom just in time. I am as sick to my stomach as I ever have been. What the hell has happened? What did I eat for lunch that must be it or maybe one of those stomach flu's? I wash my face and walk back to the bedroom. Wait a second the bedroom? I was just in my office, I don't remember going home. I look around and I just freeze with panic. This is not my bedroom. I walk over to the dresser, "Oh no. This can't be possible not again. I pick up the frame in front of me and its Pat and the two boys. That's it I have lost my mind for sure. I flop on the bed and my mind is racing. This can't be happening to me. Please don't let this happen. I feel sick and run back to the bathroom just in time again. What the hell am I going to do now? I try to remember what happened and then it hit me. Stevie has done this. That evil bastard, it has to be him. This is no dream its real. I don't know how it is possible, but I'm not crazy. It was he who came to me. He is orchestrating this right from the beginning. He is the devil. He made me go back and save him. That was real. He has led me to a different life with him back in it. He is evil. He is the one that killed those girls and the main course has to be Jennifer. It is his screwed-up world he has sucked me back in.

Subconsciously I didn't fight him because he threatened Maria and the girls. That was no dream. It's that evil son of a bitch. I have no clue how this could be happening. None of it seems at all possible, but yet it is. I have been in denial and had to deal with the memory lapse. Now it is clear. This is a nightmare, but the nightmare is real. Now what do I do from here. For the first time in a long time I'm feeling in control. I feel sick but I know I'm right. He is evil and has somehow, someway the power to cross over my world into my life and pull me into his. He has been playing with me for all of this time. Now I have to play along with him and figure out how to stop him for good. If I go to the police with this story I will be held for psychiatric evaluation. The cops are not going to be of any help. Go to Jimmy but what could he do even if he did believe me about Stevie. I sat on the bed for about an hour and I realized I was back home after I prayed. I can sit here and pray all day, but I had the feeling that won't do it. I decided to go to my church and see a priest. Maybe I get lucky and the priest could help me. It was the best I could come up with so I washed up and headed to church. St Pius X is a pretty modern church in Plainview. I walked up to the front door and it was open. I walked into the church and it was quiet as churches usually are when there is nothing going on. I walked up to the alter, "Hello, anybody here" "A short elderly women who I was pretty sure was a sister but not in the traditional garb answered, "Shush stop making so much noise this a church you know. "Sorry Sister I was trying to see if I can see one of the priests." "Do you have an appointment?" "Sorry I don't but it is very important." "You need to make an appointment to see one the priests. That is how we do it here." "I understand and I am sorry but it is very important and I needed to come right away." She looked me up and down, "What is so important that it cannot wait, did you kill somebody?" "No, Sister nothing like that." Just then I heard from the back of my "Sister Mary it's alright I will speak with the gentleman." The sister shot me a pretty nasty look and turned to the priest, "Fine Father Francis." As she walked away in disgust mumbling, "" I guess now we do not need appointments anymore." Father Francis smiled, "How can I help you." "Well, it's kind of a long story. Do you have the time and if so, is there a place we can talk?" "Of course, follow me." I followed the priest up passed the altar and into a small room. There was a desk and a couple of chairs. He pointed to a chair, "Please sit and tell me what is on your mind." "Father, please don't think I'm crazy but what I am going to tell you will sound very strange to say the least. It all started when I was young." I told Father Francis the whole story from the beginning. From when Stevie was killed and right up to the present. I did not leave anything out. The two families, the visitation from Stevie after he was killed and he brings me back over here to a different life or world. I don't know what to call it.

Father Francis listened to every word I said. Then he shook his head, "That is a very interesting story. I will be honest with you your story is hard to believe. That being said I have heard many different stories about evil, reincarnation, demonic visitations, but nothing as interesting as the story you just told me. You seem very rational and very sincere so I have no reason not to believe you. If your story is as you say it is I have to admit I can be no help to you. This is way out of my training and knowledge to be of any guidance. I can offer you my prayers and encourage you to do the same. Prayer is very powerful and can work miracles." "Thanks Father, I am sorry to bother you with this, but I am lost and didn't know where to turn to. I thank you for your time and I appreciate your prayers." "Before you go Danny there is one other option I should mention. There is a priest that I know of. His name is Father Thomas. He is an elderly priest who has been all over the world. He has even spent time at the Vatican. He has a reputation for being involved in many events that have just about crossed the line. He has been held in high regard at times and then has been cast off. If there is anybody who could be of any help to you I would say it would be Father Thomas. He is visiting at St Isadore's in Riverhead. He is a guest there and he has family in the area. I can call him and see if he would see you if you like." "Thank you Father Francis I would appreciate that very much. Will he contact me?" "Yes, I am sure he will." I gave my number to Father Francis thanked him and left.

I was not sure where or what I should do next. I then decided to go see Jimmy. I walked up to Jimmy's room. As I'm walking in, Jimmy's friend the detective was just leaving. We exchange hellos and I enter the room. "Hey Jimmy how you doing?" "Better now that you're here. It's always good seeing my best buddy. What brings you in today? You miss me?" "Yeah, I always miss you. Have you missed me? Have I been around lately?" "That's a strange question. You have some memory problems or something?" "No, not really, but I did have something I wanted to talk about. Your detective buddy have any new stories for you today?" "Yeah, he was in a talkative mood today. He was telling me about the murders he has been working on. You know I'm not supposed to tell anyone about what he says." "I know you told me that a few times, but this time I think it will fit in with what I want to talk to you about. Look Jimmy anything you tell me I swear I will never repeat a word of it to anyone. It's just that I think I should know what he has told you. When you tell me then I will tell you how and why I need to know. Can you trust me?" "Of course, I can. Okay, I will. To be honest, I have been dying to tell you anyway. The first three girls this nut job killed were your basic strangulation murders. He said they were spread over so many years that the serial killer label never got connected with the press. The last two were picked up because they were closer together but so far, all five have not been connected. Gulli said he has put them all together because he was assigned the cold cases and the new ones. He says they match. The problem is there is no DNA, no prints, no anything about the killer. It's like the killer is a ghost. Gulli says he has never come across a case like this. No evidence, no witness, no leads. He is frustrated. What's even worse is the last two have been much uglier. He wouldn't go into the details but he said they were brutal. He just couldn't tell me, but it was very disturbing. Also, the pattern of the murderer is that he is progressing each time in the way he kills. He says it's horrible. They have buried as much information as possible because they don't want to start a panic.

That is why I can't say anything. Me and Gulli went through a lot in Nam and he knows he can trust me. I know I can trust you. Any leak could cause a panic and his job. How is me telling you about the murders have anything to do with what you have to say?" "Jimmy you know me a long time and I'm pretty sure you know I'm not crazy. What I'm going to tell you now you might have some doubts about my mental state. I hope you have some time for me because this might take a while." "Don't worry about that I'm all yours so take your time and tell me everything." Once again just like as I told Father Francis I told Jimmy the whole story. Two lives, two worlds, two families, the visitations from Stevie my meeting with Father Francis. Up to the point that now I think that Stevie is a killer. "I know all this is a lot to take in but I'm not hallucinating and I am not nuts. "He is evil. He threatened my wife and kids. He told me he wanted me in this world so I can watch the show. He said it was his revenge ant the rest were appetizers to the main course. What else could that mean? Now you tell me about all these girls murdered and each one looks like Jennifer did back then. It's bizarre and it's sounds impossible but in a sick way now it all makes sense. He tricked me in traveling back in time to save him but I didn't save the Stevie we knew. I helped bring back a dark evil version of Stevie and all he wants is revenge on Jennifer. I would also guess he wants to kill both of them, the jerk, Carlo who killed him and Jennifer for ending up with his killer." Jimmy just stared at me and for the longest time said nothing. Then he finally spoke, "Man, that's a hell of a story and I don't know what to say. I do believe everything you say, but it's so hard to comprehend. You actually traveled back in time and changed the past that changed the future. That would mean there are two separate worlds or timelines that still exist. We can cross from one to the other. You're saying you have gone back and forth. This is unbelievable, but, in a way, it does answer a lot of other questions. How come I don't know anything about the other life you have. I am in both worlds that you have been in is that right?" "Yeah, you certainly are and we are the same friends in each one. Everything else is pretty much the same.

Except in one world I have Maria and my beautiful daughters and the other I have a wife named Pat and two boys I don't even know. The first world or life I met Maria in a club in the second life I never met her because I was wounded and swore I would never enter a bar or club again. I never went to the Page Two that night and I never met the women I dearly love. In one world all is good, no Stevie, no murders that I ever heard about and the other there is Stevie and these horrendous murders. My next question is simple am I crazy and there is no other life or am I in the wrong life and I am guilty of bringing a murderer into it?" "Danny all this so insane, I thought Viet Nam was a nightmare and now this. I don't believe you are crazy. I did have some weird dreams about Stevie. It was just the other night he came to me smiling and I thought he said, 'That he will be back'." "That happened to you too?'" "Yeah, the other night he had this weird smile and that's all I remember." "Jimmy the same exact thing that happened to me in the other world or life and you told me about it. Okay, let's suppose that this is real. That Stevie is evil and all this has happened, what do we do about it?" Jimmy was as puzzled as I was about, what to do now. He then replied, "I could speak to my buddy and tell him about Stevie. I'm not sure if I should tell him the rest of the story, but I could lead him to Stevie. The fact about all the girls resembling his girlfriend Jennifer could be enough for him to check Stevie out." "That makes a lot of sense but one thing is a problem. That still leaves me in this life and that is not what I want. It still leaves five innocent girls dead. Even if they lock Stevie up that does not change what has happened." "Danny, what other choices do we have?" "There is one. You know I told you about Father Francis, who told me about Father Thomas. What if I go see him before we do anything with your buddy?

I know it sounds crazy, but if all of this is real that means I did go back in time and changed events that happened. Well, what if I could do it again and this time unchanged them. Put them back into the way they should have been. I don't save Stevie, he does get shot and he dies. That would mean Stevie never came back. The girls would have never been killed and I would be still with Maria." "You actually think that is possible? Do you think this priest can actually help you to do that?" "I don't know. I know it's a long shot, but the outcome is a hell of a lot better than the other." "Danny the problem is the time factor, what if he is ready to get Jennifer. How much time do we have to try this, like you say, a long shot idea?" "That's true. I will go to see him right away. If it is a dead end, I will call you immediately, then you can call the detective." Just as I finish the last sentence I hear, "Well how's this for timing. My two best friends are here. I make one trip and I get to see both of you." "Hey Stevie, must be my lucky day both you guys visiting with me." Stevie stared at Jimmy, "Did I interrupt anything important? You guys seemed in some kind of intense subject. I could come back later if you need your privacy." I smiled at Stevie, "Don't be ridiculous we were just bullshitting no big deal. I'm glad to see you. Sit down." Jimmy joined in, "This is great the three of us together like old times, right Stevie?" Stevie did not smile, "Just like old times, not really. I get the feeling both of you have been talking about these murders and the girls that looked like Jennifer. That really bothers me. The two friends that I grew up with seem to think that I could have been involved in something like that. I happened to hear you mention my name and your detective friend in the same sentence. That makes me feel like both of you don't believe me. I told you Jimmy I had nothing to do with any sicko shit like that. It pisses me off that you could even think of such a thing.

Jennifer was a piece of shit for hooking up with that asshole. You know the one Danny, the guy that tried to kill me and shot you. It does get me mad when I think of them, but that's it. That doesn't mean that I'm some psycho killer going around strangling Jennifer look alike." As Stevie spoke his anger and intensity were unnerving both I and Jimmy. "Hey Stevie, slows down, we don't think anything like that. I told you before that it was just a coincidence about the resemblance to Jennifer that's it. Me and Danny would never think that about you." I jumped in, "Jimmy is telling the truth. You're a friend we know you since we were kids. Come on Stevie let's stop all this. We know that you would never do anything like that." Stevie started to relax, "You're right I should know better than that. With everything we've been through together the one thing is for sure is that no way any of us would go to the cops to rat any of us out. Not where we come from, that never happens." I tried to get the conversation over with as soon as I could. "Of course, Stevie, we will always be friends and all this is garbage. Come on, let's talk about better things than this." They all smiled and agreed with me. The next half hour went by with normal small talk. The first opportunity I got, I jumped on, "Look guys, I have to get out of here. I promised the boys I would help them with their homework." Jimmy responded, "No problem Danny, take care and keep in touch" "Of course Jimmy, I will call you tomorrow." I Turned to Stevie, "I'll see you at the store tomorrow." Stevie just glanced at me with a strange, eerie look, "Yeah, see you tomorrow." I walked out the door and could feel my body start to unwind. That was one strange experience with a guy I thought I knew. That thing in there is not the Stevie I knew. That was the one thing I was sure of. I started walking towards the car breathing in the fresh air and I felt so relieved just to get away from him.

CHAPTER 26

"NOT SO FRIENDLY"

Back in the room, Stevie asked Jimmy, "Tell me about your detective friend and what has he told you about these murders?" Jimmy replied, "Come on Stevie I don't want to talk about that crap again." Stevie smiled, "Okay I get it. I tell you what, let me take you for a walk around the grounds. Let's get some fresh air. It's a beautiful day out." "I don't think I feel like going outside now. Besides, it's getting late and my dinner will be here soon." "Jimmy, it's only 4:30 you have over an hour. Come on, I'm taking you out for some air." Jimmy didn't have a choice as Stevie wheeled him down the corridor passed the nurses station and into the elevator. They came down to the first floor and out the front door. It was a mild late September day around seventy-two degrees, sunny and a slight breeze. Stevie pushed Jimmy up the path towards the walkway that went around the hospital. The area surrounding the hospital had steep hills that look down into the Long Island Sound. The harbor had many boats coming in and out. Stevie continued to push Jimmy up the hills towards the path that overlooked the Long Island Sound.

As I walked to the car I stopped, "Dam, Stevie said the girls were strangled how could he have known that. I don't think Jimmy told him." I just had this bad feeling come over me and I needed to go back and see if Jimmy was okay. I hurried back to the hospital and as I came up to the front entrance, one of Jimmy's nurses Karen was walking out, "Hey you going to see Jimmy, He's not in his room. He went with his friend they were going up the path towards the Sound." "Thanks, I will go find them." I turn and head up to the walking path up the hill. "Stevie, I don't feel like going too much further, how about we go back to my room." "You know there are a lot of things that I don't feel like doing either, but sometimes they have to be done." Jimmy shook his head and didn't respond to Stevie. He had a bad feeling about the way this was going, so he tried hard not to get Stevie agitated. "How about we go and get a beer before my dinner how does that sound?" "Yeah, that sounds good, after we finish our little stroll around the grounds. You know Jimmy sometimes it pays not to turn your back on a friend. No matter what the situation is. There is a bond that friends share and when that bond is broken the friendship kind of ends. It is hard for me to understand why you would want to speak to your detective buddy about me. We go back a long way together. When I overhear you say you are going to speak to the cops about me it is very upsetting." As Stevie continued to push Jimmy up the path Stevie's tone was much more threatening than before. Jimmy started to look around for any possible help, but there no one else around. They were approaching the overlook that looks down at the rocky inlet of the Sound. Jimmy looked down and started to feel the fear building inside of him. He was not sure what Stevie was thinking but it certainly didn't feel like he was being with a friend out for a stroll. His mind was racing as he looked up at Stevie, "I'm not sure what you heard me say about you but you couldn't have heard the whole story. I was telling Danny that if it was anyone else that my civic duty would be to talk to my buddy about the coincidence of the murdered girls looking like Jennifer. I also told Danny that because it was your old girlfriend that I wouldn't ever say anything to him. For two reasons, one, it's ridiculous that you could have had anything to do with those girls. Second, I would never rat out a friend, especially you or Danny to a cop for any reason. The thing is I know you would never do anything to hurt anyone Stevie. Believe me you must have heard a small part of our conversation." Jimmy held his breath waiting for Stevie's reaction. As Jimmy waited for him to reply they came up to a small bench by the fence overlooking the Sound. Stevie pushed the wheelchair to the edge of the fence. There was a little gate that led to a downward path leading to the bottom of the hill and the inlet. It was an extreme steep climb down and it was probably used for some type of maintenance. There were pipes running down the side of the hill. The path was very narrow, maybe for one person. The rest were all rocks and weeds lining the path all the way down. There was a small padlock on the gate. Stevie in one quick kicking motion kicked the lock with the heel of his booth and the rusted lock snapped off. The gate swung open. Jimmy squeezed the two sides of his chair, "Stevie, what the hell are you doing?" Stevie's eyes were wide open and his look was evil like he was possessed, "I'm not sure what I'm doing. I was thinking that if a friend like you would turn on me and go to the cops then he should be pushed off this cliff and go smashing down to the bottom. His head would be smashed into those rocks and then drown in the water. That's what I'm thinking. Because if a friend turns out to be a rat and blows the whistle on a buddy, then that's what that piece of shit deserves." "Stevie stop please. I'm not a rat and I would never talk to the cops or my friend or anybody. You have to believe me. Stevie, think about what you're doing. The nurses saw you take me out and they would know that you killed me. The gate was locked it could never be an accident." "That's right, it couldn't be an accident. They would get me for murder and maybe tie me into those whores that were killed just for the hell of it. What would happen to me? I don't know, does New York have the death penalty? Wouldn't that be something? I could be killed. Maybe that's not so bad. It's not like I've never been there before." Stevie pushed Jimmy through the gate and to the edge of the cliff.

    I followed the path up the hill and around the back of the hospital. I'm sure that Stevie would not hurt Jimmy but I just had to make sure everything was okay. I was walking as fast as I could. I felt so uneasy that I forced myself into a run. The uphill was a slow go as I was not in the best of shape. I tried keeping calm, but I wanted to get to them as soon as I could. I reached the top of the hill and coming straight at me was Stevie. He was smiling and then laughing. I didn't know what he was up to and why he was laughing so I yelled, "Where the hell is Jimmy. Where is he?" Stevie continued laughing putting his head down. I grabbed him by the shirt and lifted him upward screaming, "Where is Jimmy?" Stevie pushed my hands away, "Take your hands off me. What's your problem? You are as screwed up as Jimmy. Both of you think I'm some sicko, so I thought I would have some fun." He turned and walked by a tree and behind the tree was Jimmy. I ran to Jimmy, "Are you alright?" Jimmy took a deep breath, "Yeah I'm just great." Stevie came between us, "You two are unbelievable. You really bought into the whole show. I tried to tell you that I am not a killer. I'm not a psycho and my two best friends' think I am makes me sick. I gave Jimmy little theatrics to play along with the psycho thing. Tell him Jimmy. I really got you believing it. Tell him!" "Yeah Danny, he scared the shit out of me. He took me to the cliff and said he was going to throw me over the edge." I turned to Stevie, "What the hell is wrong with you? Why would you do that?" Stevie gave me his eerie sarcastic grin, "It was a joke asshole. Jimmy deserved it for not trusting me. Both of you were talking behind my back. You think I'm some kind of an idiot. I think you needed to see a psycho in action. It was all a payback joke for thinking that I would hurt anyone, so both of you loosen up. We're friends, we grew up together and we always bust each other balls. Just a joke that's all it was. Just like the old days, right?" Jimmy quickly relied, "Your right Stevie. I should have realized you were screwing around. But you should have known we would never think that you were a psycho, either. Let's forget this whole thing and get me back. I don't want to be late for my dinner." Jimmy gave me a look and I knew right away what he was doing.

 I went right along with it. With a big smile I turned to Stevie, "Come on you sick freak let's get Jimmy back. No more sick stunts for a while okay. Stevie gave a real smile, "Now that's the kind of talk that can get you in trouble, shit head." We walked back down the hill and all I could think about is Stevie is a sick bastard. I know Jimmy was down playing it because he knows Stevie is a psycho. Now the problem is what to do about it. The one thing I should do is go to see that priest as soon as I can get out of here. I know he probably will think I'm crazy and blow me off. It's just that what are my choices? We can go to the cops and tell them about Stevie and they begin to investigate him. That would mean the freak would know it was us and he would more than likely try to kill both of us. The best scenario is they lock him up but the poor girls are still dead. If he gets to Jennifer before the cops get him she could end up dead too. No matter what I'm still stuck in this life without my real wife and kids. The way this has all played out it seems now that I believe that it was not some kind of a dream. I did go back in time and release the freak and he has been killing ever since he has returned. If I did in fact do it than why can't it be done again? I can't believe I am thinking all this is real but what else could it be. If this is one big nightmare than maybe the priest could wake me up and put it all to an end. We came back to the hospital and back into Jimmy's room. You could feel the tension in the air and just to break the tension I spoke, "How about we all get together next Friday. I will call Ray and Sal for one of our guys night dinner. How does that sound?" Stevie responded, "Sounds good. Let me know what time and I can pick up Jimmy and meet you at the restaurant." "Sounds good to me" Jimmy added. "I will call the guys and Robbie too. I'm going to head home. We will talk tomorrow." Stevie said he was heading out too. Jimmy smiled, "Talk to you tomorrow." I walked out first ahead of Stevie and went directly into the men's room. I waited in a stall for a good ten minutes before coming out. I went to a window overlooking the parking lot to make sure Stevie's car was gone.

CHAPTER 27

"BELIEVE"

I went back to see Jimmy. Soon as I walked in Jimmy nodded his head, "I knew you would be back. You waited for him to leave. I'm glad you came back. That psycho scarred the shit out of me. He threatens me, takes me to the edge and then just like that he says it was all a joke. He goes from a sinister sicko to laughing in a heartbeat. He is evil I'm sure." I ask Jimmy to tell me exactly what happened. Jimmy told me everything. "Danny, I say I call Gulli up right now and tell him everything. I hope he locks the nut job up and throws away the key." I shake my head, "I know how you feel but I think we should hold off just another day or so. Jimmy I just want to have enough time to go see Father Thomas and see what he has to say. I promise if he can't help we tell your buddy the whole story. I just want to have one shot at making all this hell that I caused right. I know its way out there but it's my only chance to get the life back for those girls and myself. Jimmy twenty-four to forty-eight hours that's it. Please Jimmy I need to do this." "Alright Danny I will hold off but if that nut job comes at me again I'm going to stick him with a knife." Jimmy had a steak knife in his hands. He wiped it off and put into his pocket. "Let's pray he doesn't go after Jennifer in the next day or two. I think I should try to call her and tell her to make sure she stays away from Stevie no matter what." I agreed, "You have her number?" "I can get it from my cop buddy, remember. I will say it's an old girlfriend that I'm trying to reconnect to. I'm lonely in here and it's worth a try." I looked at Jimmy and smiled, "Be careful. Stevie can know nothing. Don't leave this room with him. Don't let him get to close." "I was in the service remember?" If I wasn't stuck in this wheel chair I would beat the hell out of him and put him out of his misery." "I know you would Jimmy but it is what it is. We have to be cool just a couple of days. I will go right now to find the priest. I will call you as soon as I can and let you know what he says." We shook hands and I gave Jimmy a big hug and walked out.

    I walked out to my car and my mind was racing. Going to see this priest is crazy but I don't know what else I can do. It is my only shot at getting my life back and saving those girls. I start the car and pull out of the parking lot. I head to the Long Island Expressway. I drive for over an hour and finally get to Riverhead. I follow the map and directions that I had. I pull up to St Isadore's Church. I get lucky right away because I meet a young priest coming out of the church. I smile, "Excuse me Father I'm looking for a Father Thomas. Do you know where I can find him? He seems surprised and smiles, "Father Thomas, sure he is in the rectory across the street." He was a little hard to understand because of his accent. St Isadore's is a polish church and the priest was probably visiting and sounded like he was polish. "Is it okay if I go over and see if I can see him?" "Yes of course. Come follow me and I will take you to him." I thank the priest and follow him across the street and to the entrance of the rectory. It was across the street from a polish hall. The priest tells me to wait in a small seating area which I do. Ten minutes later the same priest comes back and asks me to follow him. I follow the priest into a small office and take a seat. He leaves and tells me that Father Thomas will be right with me. A few minutes later Father Thomas comes in. He was medium height with thinning grey hair. He had a friendly round face and wore thin rimmed round glasses down around the tip of his nose. He was in a black sweater as he came and shook my hand, "Welcome I'm Father Thomas. What brings you to see me? I don't have many visitors and to be honest you're the first in a very long time." "Father I was recommended to you by Father Francis at St Pius in Plainview." Father Thomas looked confused, "I'm not sure but I don't think I know Father Francis." "Well he knew of you and he recommended I see you.

I know what I'm going to tell you is going to seem like I am nuts but I'm pretty sure I'm not. To be honest I don't even know where to begin." Father Thomas smiled, "Well start from the beginning. I have all the time you want so don't rush tell me everything." "Alright Father here goes." I then started from the beginning when I was shot all the way through today with Stevie and Jimmy at the hospital. I don't think I left anything out from the visit from my dead friend Stevie to an alternate life. I went through the murders of the girls who looked like Jennifer. After I was done I waited to hear what he thought and what shrink that he would tell me to go see. I couldn't take the silence as he seemed to be in some kind of deep thought, "Father do you think I'm crazy?" He then looked at me shaking his head, "Your story is a strange one but do I think you're crazy, no I do not. Daniel you don't mind if I call you Daniel?" "No, my Mom was the last one to call me Daniel so it's kind of nice." "Daniel, I have been around a long time. In my time as a priest I have gone into situations that many people told me I was crazy to get involved with. I have been judged to be a visionary, to a demon, to a mental patient. I have been called to the Vatican, had an ordinance with the Pope. I have been exiled and put out to pasture. I know what it is like to go through something as strange as you have experienced." "Father are you saying you believe me?" "Yes Daniel, I believe you. There are unexplainable encounters of all kinds that I have been personally involved with or have been told by parties I believed. Messengers of good and evil, Alternate universe, time travel, near death experiences, out of body occurrence, past life progressions, and so many more it challengers your sanity and your beliefs. As a priest I believe in one God and as a catholic one religion. As an opened minded spiritualist, I recognize all of these unexplainable events as possibilities. I have devoted my life to research and to find the answers. To debunk the lies and to investigate the possibilities of truth, I have had rewards and penalties. Most of all it has been the people that I try to help deal with all of these experiences. They have felt that they are alone and helpless. Daniel, is your story much different than the ones that

I have dealt with, the answer is no, it is not. Now we have to do something about your problem. As I see it there are many issues to deal with, one, being to save the poor girls that were murdered. Two, to get you back to the life you belong in. Three, too send this evil entity back where it belongs. To do all of this we need help. The only one that I know of that can help us is a monk, Brother Aidan. The problem though, he is located in the UK. He resides in a small village and monastery in North Umbria. It is on the northeastern part of England. There is no way to contact him, so the only way to see him is to go there. The monastery has no phones, no contact with the outside world. You have to realize they choose to live a life of separation of the modern world. They have no more sanction or ties to any church. They have cut all ties with the Vatican and all organized religions. The monastery itself is a fortress of privacy. They are surrounded by high walls and have one entrance. No one ever goes in or out. They have their own medical staff and grow their own food. They do not allow visitors." "Father, then how are we suppose too see this monk?" "I can visit him. I have been part of them and go back a long way with them. They know me and I will be granted entrance and permitted to visit with Brother Aidan. This is the one reason I was sent out to pasture by the Vatican because of my dealings with them." "So where do we go from here Father?" "To the airport, I can pack a bag and be ready in minutes. What about you?" "I can go now too. I can pick up whatever I need on the way. I have an American Express card and if we are successful I won't even have to pay the bill because I won't be in this world anymore." "What about your wife?" "Which one, the one in this life or the one I want to get back to?" "Understood Daniel, I will get my bag and off we go to England." "Is it okay to use your phone?" "Of course, please sit at the desk. Take as long as you need." I picked up the phone and called Jimmy. "Jimmy, I know this is going to sound crazy but I'm leaving for England as soon as today or as fast as I can get on a flight. I'm going with Father Thomas and we are going to get help to get rid of Stevie." "What are you going to do get a contract on him by a catholic priest hitman?" "Not quite wise guy but close. There is this monk that Father Thomas says can help. Please don't ask because.

I don't know how but it's my only hope. Before I go I wanted to see if you have reached Jennifer and warned her about Stevie?" "I tried Danny but there is no way to reach her. My buddy got me her phone number and I called but there was a recording that she is on a vacation. She won't check her messages until she gets back. That's the message she left on the machine." "Okay then maybe that's the best thing. She is out of town and in no danger, great. I will call you as soon as I can. Take care of yourself and keep a close eye on the sicko. Don't go on any outings with him." "Don't worry, I went once and that was enough. You be careful and let me know right away. If this is all bullshit then I will call Gulli and have the nut locked up." "That's a deal as soon as I know I will call you. At least I don't have the pressure of him getting to Jennifer. We caught a break she is away. Take care and I will call you." "You too Danny be safe." "I'm ready Daniel all packed." "Okay let's go Father."

CHAPTER 28

"PURE EVIL"

Jennifer picked up the towel and dried herself off. She jumped up on the porch step and opened the screen door. It was a warm Indian summer day in the mountains. The cabin sat just a few yards from the lake. It was Jennifer's parent's cabin. They had it for many years and she spent many family vacations there. It was just a few miles up in the mountains from the town of Roscoe NY. She jumped on the couch where Carlo was napping. "Wake up lazy, you're missing a beautiful day out there. We have all night to sleep." "Sorry Babe, I didn't realize I slept so long. I was out fishing while you were still sleeping, so cut me some slack." Jennifer was still extremely young looking for her being in her late thirties. Her long brown hair and thin body was perfect for her young-looking beautiful face. She could easily pass for twenty-five. As she walked away from the couch Carlo had to admire her in a small white bikini. She had natural olive skin darkened from her summer tan that still looked golden on her. Carlo yelled out as she walked away, "You know you are one fine looking women sweetheart. You still have the body of a twenty-year-old and no sign you ever popped out two kids." "Tell me something I don't know handsome." "It's hard to believe we've been married for ten years. I owe you so much, Babe. You straightened out my life. I was a mess. I know I was such an ass back then. I had that crap in my stupid head that I was going to be a wise guy. I had that connection to the mob and it was like I had to be this tough guy to prove myself. But after doing time in prison I knew I didn't want to be that guy anymore. Then you came back in my life and I knew that all I wanted was you and a new life. Thanks to you and your Dad helping me and giving me a chance to work in his company changed my life. You know how much I love you and the kids it's like living a dream. You know I'm so sorry for that night. I never wanted for that gun to go off. I was trying to scare the shit out of them. I never wanted to hurt anyone. It was a mistake, a stupid mistake. It was all acting that's what I was doing. I was trying to build this reputation and impress the guys.

    I wanted to make it into the mob. I was crazy about you from the first time I saw you. I just didn't know how to handle it. I was a jerk and I deserved the sentence. I was lucky the jury believed me. It was really an accident, I swear it.' "Honey calm down please. We have been over this a thousand times. I believe you. I know it was an accident. If I didn't believe you, I would never have married you. I would never let you be the Father to my children. Come on stop punishing yourself. It was a long time ago. It's time you let it go. Now wash up and start the barbeque I'm starving. We have a few more days then we have to go home. We pick up the kids from my parents and it's back to work." "Hey don't rush it we still have four more days up here. Come hear Jen I want to give you a big kiss." "No way, I know your big kiss. I told you I'm starving now start the fire."

    Before Stevie went up to the house, he reached into the mail box but there was no mail. He walked up to the front of the house and he got lucky the welcome mat said, "The Nelsons" Stevie knocked on the door of 2 Jupiter Street. "Hi Mrs. Nelson I'm looking for Carlo and Jennifer. I know they're not home and I was hoping you could tell me where they are." The heavy-set women around sixty years old smiled and replied, "Oh, they're on vacation." "Yes, I know they told me that. They also gave me their address but I had my wallet stolen and it was in my wallet." "Oh, I'm so sorry. I really don't feel right about giving out their address. I know they were looking forward to spending a few days alone. You know away from the kids and all." "Of course, I know that. You see they told me that when I spoke to them last week. I have just a short amount of time. I don't live around here. I'm from San Francisco and I am here on business. I haven't seen them since the wedding. I was with Carlo in the service. We were inseparable back then. I moved to San Francisco and I haven't been able to get to see them. This is an opportunity that I don't want to miss out on. I only have a day and they knew I was coming. They did tell me I can contact you and you would know where they were. Just in case if anything went wrong. It's a good thing they told me about you because of me losing the address." "I didn't know Carlo was in the service. He never mentioned it to me or my husband." "Yes, I know he never wants to talk about it. That's the way he is. I hate to be a pain but you think you can give me their address now. I only have until tomorrow to see them. Then it's off back home and work." "Well I guess it would be all right being that they knew you were coming. I will go get it." "Thanks, your very kind. I'm sure they will thank you when they come home." "Come in and I will be right back." Stevie stepped into the house and waited. He heard a voice yell out. "What you can't give out their address. How do you know who he is?" "He said he was in the service with Carlo." "Carlo was never in the service he was in jail. He told me that and made me promise I wouldn't tell anyone, even you." "Then who is he and what should I tell him?" Stevie was listening to the conversation as he came through the living room. He realized the husband was a lot smarter than the wife and he was not going to get the address. Mr. Nelson was not pleased with his wife as he snapped at her, "I will get rid of him." As he walked through the kitchen and entered the living room Stevie grabbed him around the neck. With one hand over Mr. Nelson's mouth he swiftly took him to the floor. Stevie took his nylon choker and wrapped sound Mr. Nelson's throat. He firmly squeezed the life out of the innocent victim. He then dragged his body behind the couch. He then went into the kitchen. Mrs. Nelson had her back to Stevie as she was watching her favorite daytime soap General Hospital. She had the volume loud because she didn't want to hear her husband get nasty with the nice young man at the door.

Stevie without any hesitation struck the women in the back of the head knocking her into the wall. He then wrapped the choker around her neck and took her life with no remorse. He dragged her body under the table and left her there. He then went to a message board and smiled. He ripped a note from the board with Jennifer's address in Roscoe NY. By the note was a picture of Jennifer, Carlo and their two sons with the family dog. Stevie smiled saying out loud, "I hope the dog finds a good home." With a sinister smile he puts the picture and the note in his pocket. He calmly walks out the door and locks it. He gets into his car and heads to find a gas station. He needs to get a map for upstate NY.

CHAPTER 29

"DO THE RIGHT THING"

I walked towards the luggage store at Kennedy Airport. I was not a big shopper but I needed some clothes and toiletries. I shifted the shopping bag from one hand to the other as I went into the store. It didn't take long to pick out a small suitcase. I paid with my American Express card and smiled. I really hoped I would not have to deal with this bill. The shops at the airport were convenient but the prices were ridiculous. I found a bench and pulled the tags off the luggage. I emptied the shopping bag into the case and stuffed it closed. Maria would have fainted if she seen me pack this case. I then went to the small coffee shop where I left Father Thomas. I sat next to him and we talked for a few minutes. Father Thomas stopped talking and I could see he was dosing off so I shut up and let him nap. The announcement was loud and clear "Now boarding flight 210 to Heathrow. It's hard to believe that I'm sitting here waiting to board a flight to the UK. Not only am I going to England but I am traveling with an Eighty-Five-year-old priest who I just met. Believe me this makes no sense. All I can think about is why am I doing this? My life was as good as I dreamed it would ever be. I had a great wife, two beautiful girls, my business was doing well enough and I'm flying to England in the middle of the night with a stranger. I should be just putting down my book shutting the light kissing my wife and falling asleep in my soft safe bed. I should blame my mom God rest her soul for preaching to me over and over again "Do the right thing." Well not just my mom because my dad said the same thing "Danny just do the right thing and you will be happy." Well my dad is with my mom in heaven, I hope. If they were here I wonder what they would say if I told them what I'm about to do. It's just another day in never land since this craziness started. Well if I was going to change my mind this would be the time to do it. They just announced our boarding and I knew this was it. I nudged Father Thomas who was in a peaceful nap and said, "We are boarding Father, wake up." He looked at me and smiled "Good, I think I will have a nice nap on the plane." We picked up our carry on and made our way on to the plane. We walked towards the back and sat two across with Father Thomas by the window. I like to stretch my legs so the aisle seat works for me. As the plane was taxing onto the runway I knew this was it and there was no turning back now. I'm not a great flyer so this was not what I really would prefer to be doing right now. Father Thomas was already asleep as I dug my nails into the arm rests as we started to surge forward. In a few minutes we were airborne. Once we were at cruising speed and the unfasten seat belt sign came on I was able to exhale a bit and was beginning to settle down. I needed to go over the plans again so I tapped Father Thomas and then nudged him a few times before he finally opened his eyes. "Father I'm sorry to bother you but I need to talk." "Yes, Daniel what is on your mind" "Look Father I want to be honest I'm scared." "About what Daniel" "Everything that I'm going to have to do, the more I think about it, the crazier it sounds. We are going to meet a monk who was kind of kicked out of the church. He is in a Monastery that no one knows exists. This is a monk who is going to give me the way to go back and fix this whole mess. I mean I could just go to the police and tell them what I know and let them do what they do." "Daniel, yes you could and if that is what you want to do I will understand and accept your decision. Justice would be served but there are the five women who died, that would never change." "I know Father but this whole thing is just bizarre, it can't be done. I really think it is impossible?" "But Daniel you already have done it." "Yeah, I know, well I think I know but I don't know how, this whole thing is crazy. If someone came to me with this story I would laugh in their face and think they went off the deep end. Why do you believe me Father?" "I believed you from the first time you told me. I believed you then and I believe you now. I know this is hard to believe but I have seen a lot in my life time. I know when someone is lying or hallucinating or just telling the truth. In your case I knew you were truthful." We continued to talk and Father Thomas went over all the things that he has been through. Later in the flight Father Thomas was in a good sound sleep. I couldn't sleep at all. I did manage to eat a small airline meal so at least my appetite is still good. I started to feel more confident so I ordered a cup of coffee. The stewardess brought over the cup smiled and handed it to me. The cup was filled to the top and boiling hot. As she walked away I tried to take sip and it was hard just getting the cup up to my mouth without spilling it. It was so hot it burnt, so I held back and waited. Just then the announcement for everyone to get back to their seats and buckle up. We are going through some turbulence. I look toward the stewardess and she is now sitting down and buckling up. Great, I have this full cup of hot coffee and the plane starts bucking and bouncing all over the place. I look around trying to figure out where I could dump some of the coffee out but there is no way to do it. So now the cup is shaking and spilling, so I start blow down on it to cool it off and get a few sips in. After the turbulence stops I have a burnt lip and coffee all over my pants. This is going to be a real fun trip that's for sure. About an hour later after I was able to read a few pages of my paperback Father Thomas woke up. "How are you doing Daniel?" "Fine Father but I would like to ask you a few questions If that's okay?" "Sure, Daniel what would you like to know." This monk Brother Aiden you said he does some kind of channeling. He will hook me up with some kind of angel messenger and it will take me back to that night. We go through some kind of portal and I can change what happened. Just like Stevie brought me back to save him. This messenger will do the same but this time I am not going to save Stevie. Then all the girls will be alive and I will wake up back with Maria in the world that I belong. Is that right?" "Yes, Daniel that is pretty much the plan if all goes well." "Father you said if all goes well. What if it does not go well what can happen?"

"To be honest Daniel I do not know. This is not something I have ever witnessed before." "Father, you said that you have seen and heard all types of events like this before." "Well I have heard of messengers and portals many times. Your situation is different and I am not sure how this will work. I am hoping that Brother Aiden will have the answers." I rock back in my seat and my mind is racing, he doesn't know, he is hoping Brother Aiden has the answers. Dam I'm in big trouble. This whole idea is now looking like a total waste. Father Thomas sensed my loss of faith in him and the plan. He looked at me and in a soothing voice, Daniel do not despair you need to have faith. I know there are alternate realities and I want to see you return to where you belong. I want to see this evil returned to the darkness where he came. I know Brother Aiden he will feel the same. When he hears your story, he will know what to do. We will not let you down. You will see, have faith my son, have faith." "Thank you Father I am sorry. I do believe in you and I will have faith that this is going to work, it has to." We touched down and came to a smooth stop, not bad at all. I do like landing that is my favorite part of the flight. When the wheels hit the ground and we slow down I feel like I'm at peace and my feet are on the ground. There is something not normal with that big monster of a plane flying and staying up in the air. It's still a miracle to me. We get our luggage and walk to the bus stop. I purchase the tickets to Edinburgh Scotland. The ticket agent told me it was the fastest way to North Umbria. This was a direct bus to Edinburgh with just a few rest stops and a lunch stop. The other bus routes went through all the small towns and had many stops. This route would take about ten to twelve hours. Then we can get a bus from Edinburgh to North Umbria which is about seventy miles. We get on the bus and I pick a seat towards the back and sit by the window. Father Thomas has made this trip before and he is ready for a nice long nap. We head up pretty much in the center of England heading north. As we drive on I hear a couple sitting in front of me talking. They have to be husband and wife because she is doing all the talking. By their accent I am sure they are from the USA. She has this guide book on her lap and she is telling him about all the sightseeing spots listed. At least I have a tour director to listen to. As we drive on I fall asleep off and on. I wake up and she is telling her husband that we just past Nottingham to the right. I think to myself wow Robin Hood, this is pretty cool. A while later she says that Liverpool is towards the left. Nice the Beatles were from there. From their conversation they are visiting relatives in Scotland. When they get there their relatives will take them by car to all the attractions throughout the UK. Sounds like a great trip for them and I wouldn't mind trading places with them. I would love to be making this trip with Maria. Visiting this entire beautiful county instead of with Father Thomas heading to the tip of nowhere. We finally stop for lunch in some small village not too far from Manchester, I think. I wake Father Thomas up and he says he is starving. I agree I am too. We get off the bus and it's a mad rush to the bathrooms for everybody. After we take care of business we walk through a small shopping village. The stores are all Tudor style designed and they do look old but updated. We walk in the middle of the shopping village and there is a nice inviting eatery that looks perfect. We agree and enter the shop. There is a front desk with a register and on the back wall is a show case full of all types of tea pots. They were all made of what looked like ceramic to me. The fun thing about them they were all Winnie the Pooh characters. Winnie and all his friends were the big design. I never saw so many types of tea pots in my life. I had no idea that Winnie the Pooh was an English creation. The chubby lady with a heavy accent told us that A. A. Milne was the English author of the original book written in 1926 titled "Winnie the Pooh." Prior to his book he first included a poem about Winnie the Pooh in the children's verse book "When We Were Very Young" written in 1924. It felt good to take a break from what my life has become and where I was going. To enjoy a little English history and learn about one of my favorite characters. I always loved Winnie the Pooh and so did Lucia and Angelina my beautiful daughters that I missed so much. I always thought Winnie was a Disney thing, so I learned something new. Maybe if I can ever make it back to my Maria and the girls I can take a nice vacation here. I thanked the lady for the information and walked over to the line. It was cafeteria style and I picked out a couple of great looking sandwiches. The seating was these big wooden tables with big high back chairs. All the condiments were on the table and we were joined by a number of fellow travelers. The cool thing about this place is they allowed dogs in there. As I am eating I am looking at this brown lab with big brown eyes under the table next to me. He has his head resting on the chair seat staring at me. I couldn't take it so I asked if it's okay to give him a little of my chunk of ham from my sandwich. The two ladies smiled saying, "He will love it and thankyou that is very sweet of you." They had the greatest British accent I ever heard. My new buddy sat next to me and we shared my lunch. After lunch I patted my new friend and said goodbye. We walked back to the car. It had just stopped raining and the sun was breaking through. I looked back and up at the sky. I had to stop and stare at the most beautiful rainbow I had ever seen. The colors were so bright it was awesome. I turned to Father Thomas who was smiling up at the rainbow, "Maybe that's a good sign Father what do you think?" "I believe it is Daniel, a very good sign." We went back to the bus stop and waited for all the others to come back. While waiting for the others the couple that was sitting in front of us was now standing right next to us. She smiled, "Hi, I'm Mary Spencer and this is my husband John. We are on vacation and we are traveling to meet family in Edinburg. This is so exciting and the country is beautiful. Have you been here before?" I smiled, "No my first time. My name is Danny and this is Father Thomas. Father Thomas has been here a few times." "Nice to meet you both, are you here for business?" "Yeah, a business meeting." "In Edinburg?" "No in North Umbria." "Oh, I'm not sure if I ever heard of that town. We are from Toledo Ohio. This is our first time out of the country." Thank goodness the driver called out for us to board and I could get out of this conversation. They were nice people but I needed time to think about what was going to happen. I was not in a very talkative mood. We boarded the bus and took our seats. I leaned towards Father Thomas, "Father what if the Brother is not there?" "He will be there." "When was the last time you had any contact with him?" "Must be about ten years." My stomach turned and I was dazed, "Ten years! How do you know that he is even alive? "Trust me Daniel he is very much alive and he will be there. Have faith Daniel." I put my head back on the high seat and closed my eyes. What have I got myself into? I'm not sure if Father Thomas is senile or crazy or what. Ten years since he had contact. Have faith that's it. That is his answer to all my concerns. What are my choices to go back home and do what? I really don't have a choice. This is my only option, continue to go on and follow Father Thomas and do what he says. I'm going to need a lot of faith and a miracle too. A few minutes go by and the weariness hits me hard. I feel exhausted so I shut my eyes and fall asleep. After a long trip we start to enter Edinburgh Scotland. My new tourist buddy Mary turns back to me all excited, "Did you know up in the highlands there is the Loch Ness Monster. We are going to go up and see if we can see it." I smile politely, "That sounds like fun. I hope you get to see it." "Yes, it's so exciting. We're going to all the castles too." I nod and smile thinking please turn around. She does that and goes back to her book of attractions. Father Thomas says to me, "Daniel they have the best scotch in the world here. You have to try some with me. There is this one bottle of scotch Glengoyne it sells for thousands of dollars." "Well I do have my American Express card but I think I will pass on that." Father Thomas laughed and nodded. We drive into the heart of Edinburgh I can't help but be impressed with the architecture. There are so many churches with high steeples. I am looking at one now that looks like its ten stories high with multiple peaks. There is this big clock in the center of the peak. The background beyond the church is a high sky overlooking the North Sea. The architecture is heavy gothic to me. As we continue driving my buddy Mary pops her head around again, "Look there it is. See that statue of the dog on the pedestal? See it? As she spoke the bus came to a stop for the traffic light. I looked across the road and I did see it. A bronze statue of a mid-size dog looks like a Scottish terrier I would guess. Mary whips her head around, "That's Greyfriars Bobby. I read all about him. He was the constable's dog. They were inseparable but unfortunately the constable died. The dog followed the casket from the funeral home to the cemetery. The dog lay on the grave and wouldn't move. The town's people tried to get him away but he wouldn't leave. They gave up and they took turns feeding him at the cemetery. The dog stayed there until he finally died lying on his masters grave." As she finished her story she was crying and so was I. Her husband put his arm around her and turned to me, "We have a dog and we miss him." I wiped the tears from my eyes and responded, "I know how you feel. I love dogs too and that is a sad story." Father Thomas reached over and comforted me. The bus pulled into the depot and I followed Mary and John off the bus. We gathered our luggage and Mary came over to me and gave me a hug, "Have a wonderful trip. I hope your meeting is successful and you are able to return home safely to your wife and children." I was a little startled by her comments but hugged her back, "Have a great time and enjoy your visit." I shook John's hand and wished him a safe trip. Father Thomas did the same as they walked off. I turned to Father Thomas, "Did you hear what she said to me?" "What did she say?" "She said for me to have a safe trip home and back to my wife and kids. I never told her that I had a wife and kids." "I guess she assumed you did Daniel." "I guess your right but it was the way she said it. It was like she knew." Just another bit of strangeness on this journey. I grabbed my luggage and we walked a few blocks to our hotel. The hotel was an old four-story building with a brick front. The Roxburghe hotel on Charlotte Court. It was just what you would think a hotel should look like in Scotland. Old but updated heavy dark wood furniture all around. We washed up and walked over to a restaurant a block away. It was a traditional Scottish pub. All dark wood tables and a long shined mahogany bar. We took a small table by the window. The walls were decorated with all kinds of framed pictures of the area through the years. The pub was over one hundred years old. We ordered a couple of pints of the local beer and two servings of shepherd's pie. We went back to the room and had a good night's sleep. The next morning, we boarded the bus to North Umbria.

CHAPTER 30

"PSYCHO"

Jimmy is sitting at the window reading as he does just about every day at this time. He hears a gentle knock at his door. "Jimmy how are you doing today?" "Oh, shit here come's trouble. Good to see you Gulli. I thought you forgot about me. Come sit down I know you must be tired from eating all those donuts." "Funny Jimmy good cop humor but not very original." Jimmy and Gulli talked for about a half hour. Mostly small talk. Jimmy brought him up to date on all his medical reports. Gulli started teasing Jimmy a bit about the nurses, "Hey you getting any action from any of these cute nurses I see come in and out?" "No most of them are married or living with someone." "Yeah, Jimmy I'm sorry I have not been around lately but I have been crazed with this serial killer. You know the one. I don't know if you heard there was this double homicide in Hicksville the other night." "Yeah I read about that. Who would want to kill an old couple like that? This world is screwed up. Probably some druggie, right?" "I'm not on that case but it doesn't look like a robbery because there was nothing missing. There was cash in the guy's wallet. There was jewelry upstairs and electronics all over the house." "You know Gulli the world is falling a part there too many nuts out there." Gulli looked at Jimmy with a strange look and Jimmy sensed it. "Why you looking at me like that. There is something else what is it?" "You know I'm not supposed to talk about this and this isn't even my case.

The crazy thing is that the victims lived at two Jupiter Street." Jimmy made a face "So?" "Jimmy, Jennifer lives at four Jupiter St directly next store." Jimmy rocked back in his chair, "Holy shit that is crazy." Jimmy was sick to his stomach and he knew that could not be a coincidence. But why would Stevie kill her neighbors? He knows he promised Danny he wouldn't say anything to Gulli about Stevie until he heard from Danny. Jimmy didn't say anything and after a few minutes Gulli spoke, "You told me that your friend Stevie still spoke about his old girlfriend Jennifer. This happens to be her neighbors. Jimmy do you think your friend could have anything to do with this?" Jimmy realized this has gone on too long. It was obvious Stevie was out of control. He couldn't think of any reason why Stevie would kill her neighbors but dam they were Jennifer's neighbors. Jimmy had no choice he had to tell Gulli the truth. There was nothing else he could do. He realized that if Stevie is arrested maybe Danny will never get his life back but he couldn't let this go on. He also realized as soon as he tells Gulli and they start investigating Stevie he could be putting his own life in danger. The only thing he could think of was to tell the truth. "Gulli I have some information that I should have told you. Stevie did seem obsessed with Jennifer. When he heard me and Danny talking about his connection to her, and possibly talking to you about it, he was pissed. He took me for a walk and I really thought he was going to push me off the cliff at the overlook. He threatened me and said a rat deserved to die. Then he pulls me back from the edge and tells me it was all a joke. He said he would never hurt me or anyone. Gulli I think he is a psycho and so does Danny. There are some other strange things about him but I can't tell you. You will think I lost it for sure. I think he could be your killer. He referred to those girls as whores in a fit of rage. Then he said he was kidding. He is dangerous I know it. If he thinks you are investigating him he is going to know it came from me and Danny. I think he will come after us." "Do you know where he is now?" "No. You could try where he works but he is hardly ever there anymore. Is there any way you can lock him up on what you have so far?" "No but I can build a case. I need to investigate and it will take time. Do you think this Jennifer is in danger?" "Absolutely yes. I think he is building up to her. I have no idea why he killed her neighbors but the others were warm ups for his big kill. They all looked like her." "Jimmy You wanted Jennifer's phone number. Your story was bullshit. You wanted to warn her, didn't you? Did you reach her?" "No, she had a message on her machine that she was on vacation." "That's its Jimmy, that's why he killed the neighbors. He wanted to know where she went on vacation. He is stalking her and he is ready for the kill. Somehow, he guessed that they were close friends and they would know where she went. He didn't want to leave any trail so he killed them. Now he knows where they are." "Gulli I'm sorry I should have told you the truth. Danny and I were buying some time but I see now that was a mistake. There is a lot more to the story but I don't think now is the time." "No, it's not Jimmy. I need to find Jennifer right away and get her safe. I have a lot of work to do so I have to go now. Be careful and I will have a guard assigned to you until we get this guy." "Thanks, Gulli keep me informed please." "You got it Jimmy, I promise."

CHAPTER 31

"BROTHER AIDEN"

Father Thomas and I stepped off the bus and took our luggage as we watched the bus pull away. It was a very cool day and a cool wind blowing that added to the fall chill. Father Thomas said there is a car service not too far from where we are. I followed him down a winding walkway into a small town. The walkway was cobblestone and it was bordered by deep green hedges. I followed Father Thomas into a small coffee shop. He suggested I have a seat and a coffee and he would be right back. I ordered a coffee and a scone along with a few jelly donuts. I was sure Father Thomas would join me. I enjoyed the donuts stuffed with fresh jelly. The scones were really dry so I stayed with the jelly donuts. They had to be just baked because they were so soft and warm. After a while Father Thomas came back and sat next to me. He ordered a tea and ate a scone. He didn't say a word he just ate. I looked at him, "So what's next?" He wiped his mouth and responded, "Our driver will be here in ten minutes and he will take us to the monastery. Everything will work out fine Daniel, no reason to worry." I smiled and finished my donut. The driver pulled up in front of the shop and we went out to meet him. The driver was a middle-aged stocky Scott with a heavy Scottish accent. He smiled at Father Thomas and took our luggage and put them in the trunk. The road was rough and definitely not a main route. We were the only car on the road. There were many spots where we drove through carved out mountains that were only passable by one car at a time. We continued to drive by streams along the narrow winding road. After an hour of silence and a bone jarring ride we came to a stop in the middle of nowhere. The driver gets out and opens the trunk takes out our luggage and places them on the ground. We get out of the car and I look around and see nothing but deep dark forest. The driver shakes Father Thomas's hand and they embrace and he gets back in his car and drives off. I turn to Father Thomas with a look of confusion, "Father I didn't pay him?" "No need Daniel. He is an old friend of mine and he would never charge me. It's a long story Daniel and maybe another time I will tell you." Father Thomas picks up his bag and starts to walk straight to the middle of the forest. "Father there is nothing here. Are you sure you have the right location? "Quite sure Daniel, just follow me we do not have far to go." I shook my head and followed him into the middle of a dense forest. We made our way through a deep setting of very tall trees and an eerie silence. I didn't seem to hear any wildlife just a still quiet that engulfed the area. There was no real path we were following. We just walked around the trees in what seemed to be a pretty straight line. After a while of following Father Thomas, we came to a brightness that was in front of us. The walk through the forest was dark and it was clear that we were coming to an opening. We walked out of the forest and there was an open field of green grass and shrubs. As my eyes readjusted to the daylight I could see a large stone wall not too far in the distance. Beyond the wall was a mountain covered with green grass. At the top of the mountain was the monastery. As we walked closer, the wall was massive. It must have been sixty or seventy feet high or more. It was all stone blocks more like a forte then a monastery. There seem not to be any way to enter it but Father Thomas did not hesitate and continued to walk. We walked along the wall for a few hundred feet and then the wall turned to the left. I didn't know what to say so I just followed in silence. We continued to walk around the bend of the wall and then suddenly Father Thomas stopped. I looked to see if there was any door but there was nothing. "There's no door now what Father?" "Be patient Daniel you will see." What a mess I have gotten into. I'm standing here in the middle of nowhere waiting for I don't know what? Is he thinking the wall is just magically going to open? I have doubts about everything that I am doing. I am just about ready to go off on the good Father Thomas when from the top of the wall I see this thing coming down. "What the hell is that?" Father Thomas smiles, "That is our elevator up to the monastery." "What?" I watch this basket come down lowered by some kind of pulley system. It descends and slowly lands a few feet from where we are standing. Father Thomas opens this little half door and says, "Come now Daniel we are going up." I look at this basket that looks like something from Eighty Days around the World movie. A wicker basket attached to a rope with rollers attached. "You're kidding right Father?" "No Daniel, this is the only way in or out. Don't worry I have done this many times it is perfectly safe." Well I don't have too many options so I step into the basket. Father Thomas shuts the door and upward we go. First is bucks up and I have to hold on to the side to keep my balance. The basket slowly continues to rise. It takes a few minutes and then we reach the top of the wall. At the top there are two monks waiting for us. They reach out to give us a hand and we step onto the monastery stone floor. "Quite the modern lift you have here." The two monks look right past me and greet Father Thomas with some kind of silent head barb. They pick up our luggage and we follow them. As I looked out to the west the castle sat at the tip of the North Sea. We followed the monks around the perimeter of the monastery and then down a steep stairway. We then entered a very large wooden door that opened into a large room. The room was enclosed with white stone or cement like walls. The floor was wood planks. There was a stone fire place against the far wall. There many long dark wood tables with wooden benches for seating around the tables.

 To me it was some type of ancient cafeteria for a lack of a better description. On the tables there were mettle pitchers filled to my surprise with red wine. The monks left and Father Thomas and I sat at one of the tables. Father Thomas took a tin cup and poured some wine. "Would you like some Daniel?" I'm not a wine drinker but under the circumstances I thought why not it might help. "Yes, thank you Father." We sat and drank the wine which was not bad at all. One of the monks came back a short time after and approached Father Thomas. "He will see you now. Please follow me." These monks are not the warmest hosts you might find but I followed Father Thomas and the Monk. We went through a few narrow corridors and then down a small wooden stairway. We continued to walk through dark cold stone corridors to a small thin wooden door. The monk led us through the doorway one by one. It was very narrow and you had to turn sideways to fit through. It's a good thing we were all on the thin side or else we wouldn't fit through the opening. Once through we went down a stairway that descended for what seemed forever. It was dark and lit only with candle globes attached to the walls. We followed the monk all the way down and then onto a walkway that led into a larger cavernous room. There was a round stone well in the middle of the room. We walked around the well and I tried to look into it to see what it was. It was filled with bubbling water almost like a pot of boiling water. There was a light fog that seems to rise from the well water. If these weren't monks I would be a little worried that they would be getting ready to make a Danny stew or something. We continued to walk into a narrow hallway. As we bent around the hallway we entered a small room. There was a wooden desk and behind the desk a wall of very old looking books. The books were on wooden shelves that wrapped around most of the walls. Once again, the only lighting was candles and torches all around. I always thought candle light was very romantic but this was quite the opposite. There were no religious art or statues of any kind. There was a large stone fire place that simmered with what look like coal. There were a few high back wooden chairs that faced the desk. There was one high back chair behind the desk. The monk pointed to the chairs and I followed Father Thomas's lead and we both sat down. The monk then turned and left the room. I looked at Father Thomas and in a very soft voice I said, "Is this the only way you get to visit with him?" "Well there was a time that he was a little more accessible but over the years he has become more and more reclusive." Just then Brother Aiden entered the room. He was very thin with thin grey hair and a short grey beard. He had a pointed nose and wore small round glasses.

He looked to be about five feet six or seven. It was hard to tell his age but I would guess in his late eighties. He walked right to Father Thomas and smiled, "It is good to see you my old friend it's been too long. How have you been?" "I have been good Brother. I thank you for seeing me and my friend Daniel." "There is no need to thank me Father you are always welcome here. We go back a long time together and you are my dearest friend." "Thank you Brother and you are mine. We come here though under some very disturbing events that has fallen onto Daniel." "Well then I will sit and please tell me what has occurred and how can I be of help." "Daniel has come to me with a situation that can only be explained by a dark messenger visitation. That is why I come to you Brother. Because of the extraordinary encounters that Daniel has been troubled with I think it is best if he tells you himself. Daniel please tell Brother Aiden everything that has happened right from the beginning." "Sure Father. I have told Father Thomas everything that has been happening. Thankfully he believes me and I hope you do too Brother. I have doubted myself and my own mental health but to me it is all too real. It started back many years ago. I was with my friends out for a fun night." I went on and told the Brother all that has happened right up to me being here now. It was a long story and Brother Aiden was a great listener. Father Thomas nodded along with me as he seemed to be confirming my story. After the completion of all the events that led up to this meeting I stopped. "Brother, I know this all sounds crazy but it is the way it has happened. This thing that was once my friend is some evil monster that has killed and will continue to do so. I unknowingly brought him back and now I am to blame for all of this. What has happened blows my mind.

There are two separate worlds that I have seemed to cross over too. It is all so confusing but here is where Father Thomas seems to believe you are the only one that can help me." Brother Aiden sat back in his chair and seemed to drift off for some time. He then looked at me, "Daniel, I believe you. I agree this evil that exists must be stopped. You could go to the police and I am sure they will do the rest." "No Brother that's not why I came here. I know I could go to the police but that will not change what has happened. All those poor people will still be dead. I will still be stuck in a place I don't belong. What I want is a way to go back and change the events of that night. To rectify the mistake, I made and let Stevie die. That's the only way to make this all right." "Daniel you did what a friend should do. You saved Stevie from being killed. You did nothing wrong." "Yes, I understand that but I can't change his coming to me in some evil spirit form and tricking me into helping him comeback. I can't change that can I?" "No, you cannot change that it is not possible." "Brother then there is only one other way. I need to go back and change that night. Is that possible?" Brother Aiden then asked if I would excuse him. He wanted a few minutes with Father Thomas alone. I agreed and they walked out of the room. Brother Aiden then spoke, "Father does Daniel have any idea what he is asking for?" "I'm not sure. The one thing I know he is willing and he is determined." Brother Aiden hesitated for a moment and then responded, "He does seem willing so I will explain the possible consequences and the danger." They both agreed and reentered the room. Brother Aiden sat down behind his desk, "Daniel tell me exactly what you want me to do." I look over at Father Thomas and he nods his approval. "I am not sure. What I want to happen is for me to go back in time and change the events of that night. I need to stop myself from saving Stevie so he dies. If he died then and I didn't save him that means all the girls will still be alive, right?" Brother Aiden replied, "I do not know the answer to that. No one knows the answer." "Brother, I don't understand I thought that Father Thomas said you have done things like this before. He said that you could connect me with a good messenger or angels that can take me back. Please tell me that this is possible." "Daniel, I believe everything is possible. It is the outcome I do not know. There is so much that we do not understand. I have helped set in motion many different types of events. In most of these cases I never truly know the results. Can one pass from one dimension to another? I believe the answer is yes. Do angels exist and can they act as messengers and guides I say yes. Can you go back and alter the events of that night I believe so. Can I help you to achieve such an event, yes, I believe I can? The results of the event, that is the question that I do not have the answer to.

Please understand that if we are successful in getting you back to that night there are no guarantees that the result will be the one you desire. Anything can happen to you and Stevie or anybody else that is there. Once these events are changed the effect is unknown. Although your motive will be well valid, changing the past could introduce a new chain of events. It could have consequences so drastically different that the new history time-line could be a disaster. Do you really want to go ahead and take on the responsibility for such a change in history? Your first such change to history turned out to be devastating. We have no idea what this change will do. Any benefit from altering the past might be wiped out by any small change in this time-line." "I understand Brother but I don' see any other way. I was tricked into helping Stevie and now I want to fix that. I feel responsible for all those innocent people that have died because of this monster. The monster that I helped bring back. I can't see living in a world that this has occurred. My life is in another dimension somewhere. I have a wife and two daughters that I love. Between the deaths and the loss of my family I have nothing here. I have no choice but to try and go back and make this right. No matter the consequences I am willing to take that gamble. In my mind Brother I have nothing to lose because all has been already lost. I will do whatever it takes to get it done." "It also could be your life that you risk and the lives of many others. We are dealing with a dark entity that has been helped by an evil force. The evil may be waiting for you. We have no idea what will unfold once we start. You do understand this Daniel" "Yes I do." Then because of the significance of what this monster can or will do I say we proceed immediately." "I am ready Brother where do we begin?" Follow me and we will start. I followed Brother Aiden and Father Thomas into the large area with the well that we passed through before. The room was hazy with fog and very dark. There was a bluish cloud that hung over the well. I held Father Thomas's arm back and asked him, "Father, will you be here with me?" Yes Daniel, I will be with you all the way. Don't worry, put your faith in God and Brother Aiden and no harm will come to you." I smiled at Father Thomas and whispered, "Thank you." Brother Aiden told me to sit on the edge of the well. "Daniel I will explain the process to you. At any time if you change your mind you can stop. I will understand so do not worry. There will be a point of no return when we get there I will warn you. Once past that point there is no turning back. Do you understand?" "Yes, I do." "Daniel, I believe that you have entered an alternate universe from where you started. These worlds start off equal. They are perfect copies of each other. When you went back in time you entered the parallel world and from that time the two worlds start to be different. The future of the world you visited changed and moved in a different direction. You were then part of that new world the one we are both in now. I do not know how Stevie with the help of a dark messenger was able to bring you back. I will try to do to bring you back. First, I will put you in a deep sense of concentration. Your responsibility is to concentrate on that night and that night only. You must visualize yourself walking into that club the exact same way you did twenty years ago. You cannot drift and let any other thoughts enter your mind at any time. This is most important do you understand?" "Yes" "The harder you concentrate the better your chances in being successful. I must warn you that this might not work originally or not at all. I will transcend into a trance like state and summon an angel to be your guide. Angels are spirit-like messenger who can travel between God and humanity and they do not originate from this world. I will help you disconnect your body and soul into an outer body experience. You will be then in a spirit state and the angel will lead you back to that night. Once there, your spirit will enter your body in that time-line and you will have your chance to change the events. At that point you will be on your own. The angel will have fulfilled its mission and leave. Once you act the time-line will change and you will be part of that world. No matter what the results are, you will be part of that world. There will be no reversing the chain of events that follow. Once you successfully reach the new time-line it is likely that time passes differently. What you experience as past, present and the future in our physical world might occur simultaneously in this world. Time might stand still. You will be entering a dimension filled with unknowns. There is a possibility that this will not work and you might not be able to change the events. There is a chance you will not be able to return to any of these worlds. Like I said before you will be entering a world of unknowns. Do you have any questions?" "Does this mean I don't have to pay my American Express Card bill?" "Brother Aiden looked at Father Thomas and they both laughed. They shook their heads in bewilderment over my remark. "It's amazing you can find humor at a time like this." I smiled at Brother Aiden, "Nervous habit I guess." "Then if you are ready we will begin?" "Okay, Brother I am ready." I took a deep breath and began to wait for my instructions. "Daniel, I will pour some of this water on to you and this help relax you. Then I want you to start to concentrate on that night just like I told you before." Brother Aiden poured a cup of water from the well on my head. The water was warm and soothing. It felt like silk waves running down my head. I concentrated hard on walking into the club. I concentrated harder and harder. I pictured myself walking over to Stevie and telling him it's time to leave.

I could see Jimmy by my side. It wasn't a vivid picture, but I tried as hard as I could to stay focused on it. Brother Aiden poured another cup of water on me and I felt like I was going into a semi sleep. I continued to focus on that scene. Brother Aiden started to hum slowly and chanting, "Quo Vadis Angelus Nuntius." He repeated this over and over again along with some other words that I could not make out. I was trying to focus on that night but hearing him chant was breaking my concentration. I did know Angelus was Latin for Angel. I tried to push out his voice and return my focus on that night I was starting to get back to a high state of concentration. After a few minutes I was totally back to that night. Harder and harder I zeroed in on that club. Then there was silence total silence. I heard nothing at all. I felt like I was drifting into a deep sleep. I was in total silence and at peace. I had the sensation I was floating and I slowly opened my eyes. I was looking down at Father Thomas and Brother Aiden. I also was looking down at my own body. I wasn't sure if I was dreaming or this was for real. It seemed like I was watching a movie by myself in a scene. I heard Brother Aiden's voice, "Now Daniel the time is coming." At the same time, I felt a cold presence surround me. The Angel it must be the Angel. I couldn't see anything but I felt it. Then out of the foggy haze I saw it. A dark shadow approached a low howling voice surrounded me, "No!! You will die. You will die! Go back or die!" My head started to pound and I felt a panic rush through me. I felt numb and then black. "Daniel, wake up. How do you feel?" I slowly opened my eyes and I saw Father Thomas standing in front of me. I was in bed in a small room. "Father what happened?" "As Brother Aiden warned you what could happen. You were visited by a dark entity that does not want you to interfere with the evil that is happening." "Did you see it Father?" "No, but by what happened to you and your state of panic it was obvious what happened. This is not the first time that we have been witness to a dark encounter. The process was at a critical state and an Angel was coming, but the dark messenger was also summoned." "How is that possible? Brother Aiden was chanting for an Angel, wasn't he?" "Yes, but he was like he told you all of this is filled with unknowns. He told you there could be danger. This force that has returned in Stevie is very dangerous. There is an evil force that wants him protected to continue his evil ways. Once your state was broken you started to panic and you passed out." 'Father, I was like out of my body I was some kind of spirit and I was looking down at you and Brother Aiden. I could see my own body by the well. At that point I was okay, but then I saw a dark shadow approach me and I heard it said no and I will die. It scared the heck out of me. The next thing I know is I see you looking over me. I guess I screwed everything up. I'm sorry." "No need to apologize Daniel. You were frightened and it broke your concentration. You were lucky you were not harmed." "Father does this mean I can't go back?" "I'm not sure. I am waiting for Brother Aiden to join us. Hopefully he will know what we can do next." The next few minutes went by as I drank some water and sat up. Brother Aiden then came in the room, "How are you." "I'm good Brother. I'm so sorry for messing it all up." "It is quite understandable what happened to you. This evil that interfered with us is very intimidating. I believe its intentions were just that to scare you back before the Angel came. I believe that once the Angel arrived the dark entity would have dispersed." "Bother you mean that if I went ahead that thing wouldn't have hurt me?" "I believe that is correct but I cannot be sure. There is only one way to find out." "That would be that I have to go through with it. I can't back down and panic. I have to stay focused and wait for the Angel to come no matter what." Brother Aiden glanced at Father Thomas and then spoke, "Yes. I believe that is the case. The problem is that this process is unpredictable and we do not know exactly what will happen. If you want to leave and go to your police and stop this monster now, I can arrange for your transportation immediately."

    I sat back into the bed putting my hands-on top of my head. I did not want to stop now. After all that I have gone through it seemed horrible to stop now. The problem is that I'm not sure if I could handle that evil thing. I'm not sure how I will react the second time. Brother Aiden interrupted my silence, "Daniel please thinks this over. Time is our enemy too, but you have to be willing to face this evil. I believe you will be able to hold out until the Angel arrives. Once the Angel is with you I do believe you will be safe. Safe until you arrive back at the club then you will be on your own. Take some time and I will come back for your decision." I asked Father Thomas to stay as Brother Aiden left the room. "Father I want to go ahead and try this again. The problem is, I'm scared. I don't see any other way out of this unless I go forward and fix it myself. I have a lot of faith in you Father and I want your honest opinion. Do you think I can safely get through this?" I stared at Father Thomas, waiting for his answer, "Daniel this is a very difficult decision that you will have to make. I cannot say one way or another on what you should do. I do believe that if we go to the police we can stop Stevie from doing any more damage. This would solve just part of your problem but you will be safe. You will still have a life with friends and family that care about you. That of course would not help the poor victims or return you to your wife and children. If you go ahead with this process, you will be facing great danger. I have been involved with dealings of this dark entity before. I have seen firsthand it destroy people in one way or another. I also have seen people like you fight off the demons and have a new life. This process that Brother Aiden will do is one that I have not truly experienced before. I do believe in Brother Aiden and he has told me of many events that he has been a part of. I do trust him and I do believe he is capable of summoning an Angel to help you succeed. You have not only to decide to go through with this, but also to be ready for anything you might have to deal with. You will have to reach a state of mind that you are ready and willing to do so no matter the consequences. If you think you can do that then I believe it can be done. I believe you will be safe in getting back there, but then the results are a total mystery. You have to decide, not me, but you and you alone." Father, I understand and I will need a few minutes to make my decision. Thank you, Father." Father Thomas left the room. I sat there and began to deal with what could happen, that evil approaching, threatening and dealing with the fear. If I choose to stay here and do nothing I don't think I could live with myself. I wish this whole thing never happened. I was so happy with my little piece of heaven. I want to get that back so bad. I miss Maria so much it hurts. My precious daughters, I want to hug and hold them and never let go. I haven't had enough time to even think about them with all this craziness happening. Those poor girls killed by the monster. That innocent couple murdered for no reason. Just as I was in deep thought Brother Aiden along with Father Thomas enters the room. Brother Aiden spoke, "Sorry Daniel but I hope you have made your decision time is running out." "I have Brother I want to do it. I will deal with anything that comes my way. I am definitely ready." Both Brother Aiden and Father Thomas nodded in agreement and I followed them out of the room. We walked through the halls and entered the great room again. I sat by the well and Brother Aiden once again explained the procedure. "Daniel, are you sure you are ready?" "Yes, Brother I am." "Fine, Daniel now takes a few deep breaths and relax. Now focus and concentrate on the night that it all started. The harder you concentrate the better the results. Just relax and concentrate." I felt the warm, soothing water running through my head as I concentrated on that night. I started to visualize the club. I began to focus in on Stevie. I felt another cup of water flowing over me and I was drifting away. Softly in the background, I heard Brother Aiden chanting as I drifted off. I now was once again suspended over the well looking down at myself. What an incredible feeling I'm actually out of my body I'm floating and I feel no fear. I close my eyes and regain my focus on the night and the club. I can see Stevie more clearly now. As I'm visualizing, I feel a cold wave approaching. I start to feel tense as I think I know what's coming. The coldness increases as I heard the low howling voice just like the last time. "No!! Stop or die. Stop or Die!" I feel my hands begin to shake as I slowly get up the courage to open my eyes and look. I see the dark cloud closing in on me with a face. At first, it's hard to make out but then it starts to become clearer. The face, it's Stevie's face in the shadow and he is now reaching out towards me with looks like claws extending from his sides. I hold my breath and pray as hard as I could." Please give me the strength to hold on. Please God help me." I feel his cold claws touch my face and finger by finger wrap around my throat. I can feel the claws digging into my skin and I hear, "I warned you, but now you must die!" I know this is it so I pray to God to save my soul.

CHAPTER 32

"CABIN IN THE WOODS"

Jimmy picked up the phone, "Gulli what's going on?" "I caught a break and I was able to get the location of Jennifer's cabin. Jennifer and her husband have been up there a few days. I cannot get a warrant on Stevie we just don't have enough for a case. We have victims, but no prints, no witnesses linking him to them. Just your information and that is not enough. I'm headed to the cabin anyway because I want to warn them about Stevie. I'm sure Stevie is headed up there as well. He more than likely got the address from Jennifer's neighbors before he killed them. Hopefully I can catch him before he try's anything.

There is no phone up there and no neighbors. It's very isolated and a perfect set up for him. I'm also worried about you Jimmy. He probably knows you and Danny are the only ones who can link him to the murders. Danny is out of the country, but you are vulnerable. If he takes care of Jennifer and Carlo the only ones left are you and Danny." "Don't worry Gulli I will not let the psycho get close to me. I will be ready. Just hurry doesn't let him take any more lives. You know Gulli I had a thing for Jennifer myself. When Stevie met Jennifer, I was attracted to her. You know the guy rule Stevie seen her first so she was off limits. After the shooting, she was definitely off limits but I still wanted to ask her out. I just couldn't do it to Stevie. Then I was drafted and the rest is history. The bottom line is that I wish things went differently because she is a sweetheart. She stayed with Carlo through all the tough times and straightened him out. I never told anyone, especially Stevie but she called me when she found out I was back. She never came to see me but she would call from time to time to keep in touch. I kind of think she had a little something for me too. Well, that's something I will never really know." "Wow, Jimmy I didn't know we were playing true confessions now." "Screw you Gulli." "I'm just busting them on you Jimmy lightens up. I'm pulling onto Route 17 now. I'm guessing about another two-hour drive to their cabin." "Are you going to arrest him if you get there before he does anything?" "I'm not sure what my plan is. I'm on my own on this. I have no just cause to do much but question him. I'm hoping he does something stupid and I can blow him away. Save the tax payers money and send him where he belongs, in the ground." "Be really careful, he is evil and very dangerous." "Jimmy I'm the cop remember. I know how to take care of business. After this is all over I will mention to Jennifer if she wants to dump Carlo you will be ready to move in on her." "Don't you say a word to anyone about what I told you?" "Man, you need to get out more Jimmy you are losing your sense of humor." "Maybe you're right but there has not much to laugh about recently. I haven't heard anything from Danny since he left and I'm worried about him. This crap with Stevie the whole dam thing is depressing." "Yeah, I hear you, just keep the faith Jimmy and hang in there. When I'm done, I will call you and give you some good news. I got to speed up and try to get there as soon as possible. You take care and I will call you." "Gulli be careful." Stevie pulled into a gas station next store to the Roscoe diner. He gassed up the car and then pulled off to the side. He looked at the map but these small roads leading to the cabin was difficult to follow. He decided to go inside the diner. He sat at the counter and ordered a coffee. A young waitress wearing a name tag that reads Amy, smiled, and served him the coffee. "Excuse me, Amy, maybe you can help me. I'm looking for my good friends who have a cabin up here. I have the address but I'm not sure how to get there." Stevie took out the address and showed it to the waitress. She smiled, saying, oh sure I can tell you how to get to it. You are friends with Jennifer and Carlo." "Yes I am.

I'm surprised you know them because I didn't think they came up very often." "Yeah, but Jennifer has been coming up here a long time. Her parents spend a lot of summers up here. I know exactly where their cabin is. I have been to it a couple of times. They had a big party up there last year and I helped cater it. Here I will get a pen and draw you a little map. It really is pretty easy to find. I will be right back." "Thanks Amy I appreciate it." Stevie thought to himself that this was going to be a lot easier they he thought. She is drawing me a map. Dam you have to love these upstate people. They are so darn helpful. Amy came back with a hand drawn map.

She went over the turns and told Stevie it should take about ten minutes to drive up the mountain. Stevie took the map and put into his pocket. He smiled at Amy, "Thanks so much. I will mention your kindness to Jennifer and Carlo." He was thinking that after he killed them he would tell them how helpful Amy was. He reached in his pocket and pulled out a ten-dollar bill and handed it to Amy. She was ecstatic, "Oh Thanks so much. That is very kind of you." "My pleasure Amy, have a great day." Stevie went out and back into his car. He took out the map and drove up the one lane road and up the mountain. He drove about ten minutes following the map. It was just like Amy said very easy to follow mostly a straight road with just a few turns. He came up around a tree line and a nice size lake was straight ahead. He followed the road and off in the distance he spotted the cabin. It was right on the lake. He didn't think it was safe to go any further without being noticed so he pulled the car over into and between the trees. He shut the car off and reached into the glove compartment. He pulled out a small revolver and a large hunting knife. He then pulled out a nylon rope and put the rope into his pocket. He put the gun into his belt. He kept the knife in his hand. He slowly got out of the car and cautiously walked towards the house. He went through the trees so he wouldn't be spotted. Stevie walked around the house but he stayed in the tree line so he would not be seen. He looked out onto the lake and he could see a small boat with one man in it fishing. It had to be Carlo he thought to himself. He was more intense now knowing he would be face to face with Jennifer after all these years. He carefully walked up to the back of the house and quietly stepped up onto the wrap around porch. He looked into a window and saw Jennifer just finishing slipping on her two-piece bathing suit. She picked up a brush and brushed her long hair. She then wrapped her hair into a pony tail and put on a button-down long shirt. She started walking out of the room. Stevie watched as she walked into the kitchen. He opened the window and took out the screen. He stepped up and through the window. He slowly walked through the bedroom and to the door leading to the kitchen. He stopped and watched Jennifer turn on the radio and pour a cup of coffee. She had her back to him and looked out the window out to the lake. He took a few steps towards her with his knife in hand. As he approached her the radio was pretty loud with the Beatles record of a Hard Day Night playing. He knew she could not hear him approach because of the radio. He then came within a few feet of her and a deep, sinister voice spoke, "I have to say you have aged very well and look the same as when I first met you." Jennifer laughed as she continued to look out at the lake, "Give it up Carlo, that voice, please stop watching those dumb horror flicks. I'm enjoying this beautiful day so cut the crap." "Such a sharp tongue you should be careful how you talk to me because I'm not Carlo." Jennifer turned around and was now annoyed with this stupid role playing. She was about to speak as she saw Stevie in front of her with a knife. She let out a scream as she dropped the cup of coffee. Stevie quickly grabbed her and put his hand over her mouth and the knife to her face. "Don't make a sound or I will cut your throat. Do you understand?" Jennifer shook her head up and down. "Good. Now I'm going to let you go so don't make a sound. I just want to talk to you." Stevie's voice was now calmer than threatening as he slowly let her go. "I know you must be surprised to see me after all this time. I have been meaning to get in touch but just haven't been able to do it until now. Now I want you to sit down in the chair and we will just talk a bit, okay?" Again, Jennifer shook her head as she was shaking. She sat down and just stared at Stevie. Stevie stood in front of her and smiled, "You must be enjoying your vacation away from the kid's right, just you and your wonderful husband. What's his name, oh yeah, Carlo that's it. You know, if my memory still is good he was the guy who shot me wasn't he?" Jennifer was too afraid to speak so again she just nodded. "Yes, that'd right, he shot me. He almost killed me and he walks with a couple of years. What a joke. The crazy thing is that it was because of you that I was shot. I thought we had something special that night but evidently, I was so wrong. You played me to get your boyfriend all jealous. Then he shows he is Mr. Macho by shooting me. You both must have enjoyed yourselves at my expense." Jennifer was not only frightened but confused. She took a deep breath and slowly started to respond, "Stevie I'm sorry for what happened but it was not like you are saying. We did connect that night and I was just trying to stop Carlo. I was not playing you I liked you and I was trying to get away from him back then. It wasn't until years later that I fell for Carlo. I felt guilty about that night and I tried to help him while he was in prison and then we fell in love. He is a totally different person from back then. He swears it was an accident when he wounded Danny and he never shot you." Stevie listened and then he came close to Jennifer's face and smiled, "No he didn't shoot me, he killed me. Before I came back I was dead. He killed me! Then when I came back I find out that you married him." As Stevie circled her Jennifer was terrified. He was insane. He was making no sense. He says, he was killed and came back. Jennifer looked around the room and tried to see if she had any chance to run. Her mind thought of Carlo he could be coming back any time now. If he doesn't realize that Stevie is here he could walk right into this maniac. I need to warn him somehow. I could scream but he might stab me. The only thing to do is play along with him until I can get a chance to run or hit him if he turns his back. She was shaking but she held herself together, "Please Stevie doesn't hurt me, I never wanted to hurt you. I cared for you and I am sorry the way things turned out. It was a long time ago and Carlo has changed. We have kids and we just want to live our lives. Please Stevie let me go. I promise I won't say anything about this. Please Stevie I'm a Mom, my kids need me." Stevie once again bent down in Jennifer's face and shouted, "Shut up! I don't want to hear your lies and your bullshit. So just shut up. I will tell you when you can talk. I have waited a long time for this moment and I am not going to let you ruin it with all your lies. Oh, how Carlo has changed who cares that he has changed. That doesn't change what he did to me. Nothing has changed except that now it's my turn to pay both of you back for what you did. I don't care about your kids, they mean nothing to me. Don't mention them again or I will cut you up. I have a plan for you sweet Jennifer I have a plan. So just shut up and listen to what I have to say. Do you understand?" Jennifer slowly nodded and whispered yes. "I thought you were different but I was wrong. I thought Danny and Jimmy were my friends but I was wrong about them. I knew Carlo was a piece of shit and I was right about him. Now it's time to even the score. I am not sure where Danny is but I will get him in time.

Jimmy, I know exactly where he is and with your help, I will get him, but Carlo is my first priority. That starts as soon as he walks through the door. First, I think me and you should have a little fun. What do you think?" Stevie took his knife and cut the top button off of Jennifer's top. Then he placed the blade against her cheek. He smiled, his eyes were blank yet penetrated Jennifer so her body began to shake uncontrollable. As Stevie got down on one knee in front of her with the knife in his hand Jennifer saw Carlo coming in the back door. He had an oar held up high. He waved his hand at Jennifer telling her not to look. He slowly walked up behind Stevie and swung the oar at him. The blow sent Stevie sliding across the room. Carlo grabbed Jennifer, "Run Babe I'll take care of him. Please just go and call 911." Jennifer leaped up and ran out the door. Carlo turned to Stevie as he was lying on the floor. The knife was knocked out of his hand and was a long distance away. Carlo reached down and picked up the knife. He then started to walk towards Stevie. He stuck the knife in his pocket and raised the oar saying, "Don't move, or I will bust your head open." It was obvious Carlo was deciding whether to hit Stevie or just keep him here until the cops come. He then decided it wouldn't matter if he got another whack at Stevie so he approached him slowly and brought the oar up ready to strike. Just as Carlo began to swing, Stevie took his gun out and fired four rounds into Carlo's chest. Carlo fell to the floor. Jennifer who just came back into the house because she wanted to get to the phone screamed in horror. She ran to Carlo and held his lifeless body and cried out,

"No please don't die. Carlo please doesn't leave me." Stevie grabbed a towel and wiped the blood off his head from the cut he received from the blow to the side of his face, "I am so sorry Jennifer I didn't want to kill the bastard like that. He gave me no choice. I wanted to enjoy his death this was very disappointing, really sorry about this. Well, now I think it's time for us to leave. This place is a mess, so get up we have to go." Jennifer looked at him wiping the tears from her eyes, "Go, are you crazy I'm not going anywhere with you. You are an animal you killed my husband you bastard." Stevie shook his head, "There is no reason for name calling and for your information, you will do everything I say." "You're crazy I am not doing anything you say. If you want to kill me, go ahead, I don't care." "Oh, you will care and you will do everything I'll tell you to do. You know those two children of yours well if you ever want to see them alive you will do what I say." Stevie reached into his pocket and took out the picture of them that he took from the neighbor's bulletin board. He showed it to Jennifer, "What a beautiful family you have oh, wait, you had. I have your kids and the only way they live is that you do what I say, understand?" Jennifer looked at the picture and she felt sick. She cried, "What do you want?" "Now that's more like it. First, no more questions from you, I have the kids and I'm the only one that can keep them alive. Second, you come with me and do what I say. You try to call for help or do anything that is against me, they will die. Do you understand?" "Yes." She replied. Stevie then grabbed her by the arm and lifted her up. "Come we have work to do." He led Jennifer to her van and they drove off.

Gulli pulled up to the cabin he looked at the clock it was 3:20. It took him a lot longer than he hoped. He pulled the car off by a large tree. He took his revolver out and started to walk towards the cabin. He saw there was just the one car in front. He slowly went to the back door and looked in the window. He saw no signs of anybody. He then walked into the cabin through the hall and into the kitchen. He looked down and he knew he was too late. Carlo was lying on the floor in a pool of blood. Gulli walked around the cabin and he knew Stevie was gone and it seemed so was Jennifer. He put his gun away and checked the body. He then went back to his car to call it in.

CHAPTER 33

"DESTINY"

I looked straight at the dark soul hearing its words louder and more clearly, "I warned you, but now you must die!" I started to panic and felt that I can't do this. Just as I was about to give up I heard a strong chant over the voice of the dark soul that was coming at me. "Angeli tutantur et dirige animam hanc tuto" Over and over I heard the chant. Then just as I was in a total panic, I see a white light brighter than any light I have ever seen appear in front of me. I looked at the light and I could see a figure inside becoming clearer. It was a man in white linen with a gold belt around his waist and a sash of gold around down from his shoulder. His eyes were a radiant bright blue, his arms and legs were muscular and bronzed. He looked straight at me and I heard him in my mind but no sound of a voice. I knew what he was saying without him talking. "Do not be afraid, I will guide you on your journey. You will be safe until we arrive then you will be on your own and determine your destiny." He then turned to Stevie the dark soul and put out his arms. He lifted his hands and he clenched them into fists. He stretched his arms and fists to the sky and with a swift blow he came down on the dark spirit. In a second the black cloud broke apart and disappeared. He then turned to me and offered his open hand. I knew he was saying take his hand and come with him. I was still scared but I reached out and grabbed his hand. It was like a rock, but yet his touched soothed me and calmed me. I felt safe and secure. In my mind I heard him say, "To close my eyes and see my destination. Concentrate and you will arrive." A few seconds later I was there. I looked down and I could see myself along with Danny and Stevie at the club. I looked at my guide and I heard him transmit to me again, "Now is your time to choose your destiny for once it is done it cannot be changed." A second later he was gone and I drifted down and entered my body.

CHAPTER 34

"CAREFUL WHAT YOU WISH FOR"

Jennifer sat next to Stevie with her eyes closed. He told her that he had her kids in a place that only he knew of. If anything happened to him her kids would die. She had no choice but to do what he said. They were driving to get Jimmy. Stevie wanted for her to go in and bring Jimmy to him. He didn't say why or what he was going to do but she knew it was not good. If she called the police her kids die, that was his promise. If she warns Jimmy and he doesn't come with her, the kids die. She realized that there was no guarantee that he would keep his word and let them go when she did what he asks. She was trying to think of some way to get out of this but she was drawing a blank. She was still in shock at seeing her husband die in front of her. Now her children in danger, this was a nightmare. Stevie drove in silence. He said all there is to say. He wanted Jimmy and then he would deal with Jennifer. As he drove he was thinking of different scenarios on how to punish Jennifer, each one sicker than the other. With each thought he smiled and would glance over at Jennifer. She just kept her eyes closed and prayed for help.

Jimmy listened in horror as Gulli was telling him what he had seen at the cabin. Gulli was driving back from upstate. "Jimmy, I have a feeling he also wants you. If that maniac shows up, call me immediately and call security. He might have Jennifer with him or he might have already killed her. He is capable of anything so don't be a hero and just notify security." Jimmy clenched his fist and banged on the table, "That bastard. I knew he was sick but this is beyond belief. I want to kill him myself." "Jimmy keeps calm. I don't think he is stupid so he might not risk coming after you. He might be on the run. He knows that we must be on to him now so he could go anywhere. I'm telling you to be careful just in case." "I hear you Gulli if I see the sicko I will notify security and call you." "Great Jimmy, I put a call in at the hospital to look out for him. I will call you as soon as I can. Take care." "Thanks, Gulli and please find him." Jimmy hung up the phone and looked out the window. He thought to himself, "I wish I wasn't in this dam wheelchair so I could deal with him myself. I hope he does come for me because I want him close so I can cut his evil throat myself." Jimmy wheeled over to his draw and took out a large steak knife that he had hidden and put it in his pocket. "Come to me Stevie and I will send you back to hell."

Stevie pulled the Van into the parking lot. He looked at Jennifer, "You understand if you let anyone know about me your kids will die. If you bring Jimmy to me, I promise you they will be safe and freed. It will be easy for you to alert Jimmy so if he does not come they die. I am in control, believe me, I have the power to set them free or kill them. The decision is yours. I will give you enough time to go in and convince Jimmy to come with you. If you are not back with him in fifteen minutes it will be too late to save your kids. Tell me you understand and you will do what I say." Jennifer softly spoke in between her tears, "Yes I understand. I will do what you want, then you will let me and my kids go?" "I told you what I would do now no more questions just do it!" Jennifer wiped her tears and stepped out of the van. She walked up to the hospital slowly. She knew Stevie was watching her so she picked up her pace and was now rushing towards the door. She was thinking of all different ways to stop this, but she couldn't come up with one that will make sure her children would be safe. She didn't trust Stevie to let them go, but what choice did she have. She could save herself and Danny but her children could die. She had no choice but to go along with what he wanted, if she could get a chance to hit him while he was confronting Jimmy that might work. With the help of Jimmy, she could get Stevie to tell her where he had her children. She walked through the door and went to the desk. She spoke with the receptionist and she headed to Jimmy's room. She was shaking badly but she knew she had to pull herself together. She went into the ladies' room and washed her face and tried to gain control of her emotions. She then opened the door and went down the hall to Jimmy. She softly knocked on the door, "Hello Jimmy" Jimmy turned towards the door, "Come on in." Jimmy watched Jennifer walk in, "Jennifer is that you?" "Jimmy, how are you?" "Great Jennifer, come in. What brings you here?" As he spoke he knew what brought her to him, it was Stevie. He somehow made her come to get me but it's okay. I will go along with his plan and when I get him I will put an end to the bastard. Jennifer weakly smiled as he could see the stress she was under. "Jimmy, I know this is crazy but I have a surprise for you and I was hoping you will come with me." Jimmy thought she was about to break so he made it as easy as possible on her. "Sure, Jennifer I love surprises. Just give me a minute and I will be ready. Jimmy wheeled himself into the bathroom and checked his knife. He looked in the mirror and nodded this is it. I need to stop him and now is my chance. Let's do this. He wheeled back out, "Okay Jennifer I'm all yours." She smiled and they both headed out the door. They went through the front door and down the walkway towards the lot. Jennifer led him down and around by the curb they stopped. Stevie came with the van and stopped right by them. Stevie jumped out and went over to Jimmy, "Jimmy so glad you could come with us." Jimmy started to reach in his pocket to get his knife but before he could get it Stevie came behind him. He had a rag with chloroform. He quickly grabbed Jimmy and held the rag over his face. He yelled to Jennifer to open the sliding van door. Jimmy struggled but then he was out. Stevie picked him up and threw him in the van. He told Jennifer to get in and they went speeding off. Jennifer stared at Stevie, "I did what you wanted so please tell me where my children are?" "Stevie stared straight ahead, "Don't worry, I will keep my word your kids will be safe." "Good now let me out." "Of course, I will but just let me go to a safe place and I will let you go." "What about Jimmy?" "Not your problem, so just shut up."

Gulli finally received the call he was waiting for. Jennifer's van was spotted heading east on Route 25A. "I'm heading there now. I was on the Long Island Expressway and I can be on 25A in five minutes. Send any cars to stop that van. He is extremely dangerous, so take proper precautions. He is armed and has already killed."

Stevie looked back and seen Jimmy moving as he was awakened. Stevie pulled the van off the road by an excluded area just before Route 25A ends. He drove through the trees and came to a stop. He jumped out of the van with his gun in his hand. He came around the side and opened the sliding door. He grabbed Jimmy and pulled him out. Jimmy was still groggy and could not put up a fight. Jennifer jumped out screaming, "What are you doing to him. Stop please stop." Stevie waved the gun at Jennifer, "Shut up and get back in the van. Don't make me shoot you. Do what I say." Jennifer stopped and stood still. Stevie continued dragging Jimmy and then stopped. He then kicked Jimmy in the ribs as he was lying there, "So you told the cops about me. You and your buddy Danny my good friends turned against me. Well, I will deal with Danny when he shows up. You should have just shut your mouth and I wouldn't have to do this." Stevie then bent down close to Jimmy he reached into his pocket and pulled out a rag. He wrapped the rag around the gun and as he started to point it at Jimmy. Jennifer came from behind him and kicked him in the back of the head. He jolted forward toward Jimmy and the gun fell to the ground. Jimmy then took his knife and stabbed Stevie in the chest. Stevie punched Jimmy and took the knife from him. He then reached up with the knife and started to lunge at Jimmy. As he reached up Jennifer fired the gun, hitting Stevie in the back. She fired three times as he fell to the ground. She dropped the gun and fell to her knees. Jimmy crawled over to her saying, "It's over, he's gone. Thank you, for saving my life." The sirens engulfed the area and Gulli came running over. "Are you okay?" "Yes, thanks to Jennifer." Gulli looked at Stevie and then at Jennifer. He lifted her up, "Let's get you taken care of." Jennifer cried out, "He has my kids and he said they die if anything happened to him." Gulli shook his head, "He lied. We have your kids, they are safe. We thought he might try to use them or hurt them so we picked them up and they are with your parents. We have them guarded and they are safe and unharmed." "Thank you. Thank God, he used me. He tricked me Jimmy I'm so sorry." Jimmy was sitting next to Jennifer and he hugged her, "You had no choice but it's over now you will be going home and he can never bother you again." Jennifer cried and hugged Jimmy.

CHAPTER 35

"DÉJÀ VU WITH A TWIST"

As I entered my body, I felt normal. I was back in the club just like I was twenty years ago. I looked around and I could see a few couples slow dancing. The room was smoky and dark. I saw Sal and Ray, standing a little away from me. Jimmy came over and was smiling. He showed me the telephone number he scored and he was happy. We now were waiting on Stevie. He was slow dancing to what was the last song of the night so we decided as soon as it was over we would grab him and hit the road. As the music stopped Stevie walked over to us, arm and arm with his new love. Her name was Jennifer she was pretty and very friendly. I pulled Stevie over and told him to get her number because we were ready to go. He was cool and knew it was time, so he took Jennifer by the hand to a corner they spoke a while and he was writing down her number, a score for Stevie. Just as he was writing down her number two guys came from what was I guess was the back door. One of them pulled Jennifer by the arm and away from Stevie. I knew right away this was not good. I knew Stevie was into her big time and he would not let this go. I told Jimmy to get the car and get ready to pick us up so we get the hell out of here real fast. Jimmy grabbed Sal and they went to get the car.

As all of this was happening, it was like I was watching a movie and I was part of it. It all went by so quickly it was difficult to think. I felt all this has happened before like that Déjà vu thing you hear about. I stood there watching Stevie is waiting for him to do something stupid but he didn't move he just watched as Jennifer and this guy were in a heavy conversation. I told Ray to come with me and we would get Stevie out of here. Ray and I went over to Stevie and I told him to be cool and let's get out now. Stevie smiled and said he was good he just wanted to wait just to make sure Jennifer was okay with this guy. Stevie seemed calm, so I started to relax a bit and said I would wait with him. Ray went to the door to see if they were ready with the car. Jennifer waved at Stevie and mouthed to call her she is okay. Stevie smiled, nodded his head and said okay. We both turned and started for the door, thank God no problem. I guess my instincts were wrong. As we started to walk towards the door, I knew there was more to this. I need to do something but I wasn't sure what it was. As we walked away and were a few feet from the door this jerk yells out, "You better get the out of here you asshole." Stevie stops short and turns back at the jerk; he starts to walk back at this guy. I see where this is going so I get in front of Stevie and tell him no don't be stupid just forget it and let's go. Stevie stops, looks me in the eye, smiles with that angelic look on his face and says I'm right let's go home. I take a deep breath and move away from Stevie towards the door. The rest happened so fast it was surreal. Stevie instead of following turns back at the guy and goes right at him. I was way too slow to react. I believed Stevie was coming with me and in a second, he goes the other way. I turn to try to go after him but he was already on the guy's face. As I watch I hesitate to react because something inside of me is telling me to back off. I can't help myself so I follow Stevie. Stevie punches him in the stomach and they both fall to the floor. Again, I feel confused part of me wants to do nothing but the other part forces me to react. I see him pull out a gun so I go to grab the gun. He fires three times and it hits Stevie in the chest. I punch Carlo and grab the gun. From behind one of Carlo's friend's opens fire and I feel a burning pain hit me in the chest. I fall to the floor. I'm thinking something is wrong, this is wrong... No this can't be something is very wrong. I'm not supposed to die. I try to speak, but nothing comes out. I see Sal hugging me and yelling for an ambulance. The pain in my chest stops and I feel nothing than the room starts to spin and everything goes black.

CHAPTER 36

"MIRACLE?"

Jimmy, Jennifer and their two sons Daniel twelve and Steven ten, stood over the side by side graves of Daniel (Danny Amindola) and Steven (Stevie) Bracken. Sal, Ray along with their wives and kids stood silently. Danny's brother Alex and his wife Joan stood with their two sons Alexander and Anthony. Father Thomas finished a prayer as they all said, "Amen." Jimmy bent down and picked up two stones placing one on each tombstone. He wiped the tears from his eyes and watched Jennifer, Alex, Ray and Sal does the same. Jimmy turned to Jennifer, "It's hard to believe that it's been twenty years." Daniel turned to Jimmy, "Dad, how did they die?" "It's a long story Daniel and someday I will tell you but not right now. It's funny the way life turns out. I know I owe a lot to Danny he saved my life." Father Thomas asked, "That night at the club he saved you?" "No, not that night it was a year later." "Jimmy, a year later Danny was already dead." "That's right. I know this sounds crazy, but he saved my life. It was in Viet Nam. I was there about ten months when I was on a search and destroy mission. We were looking for Viet Cong in a small village. I was part of a squad and we had just captured a VC prisoner. He was wounded and we were heading back to camp. We were under attack from VC and were moving through the jungle. I moved away from the rest of the guys because I was trying to contact the base. As I was on the radio it suddenly went dead. I saw a light appear in the dark jungle and in the light, it was Danny. I thought I was hallucinating as Danny told me to move away now. Come to me now. He kept saying it, so I did what he said and I started to run to the light towards Danny. As I ran I heard a loud whistle sound and then an explosion. It was a mortar round hit a few feet from where I was. I felt a pain and then I went down. I was told that if I was a few more feet in the other direction I would have been killed by the blast. Somehow Danny came to me and saved me. I was evacuated to a hospital in Cam Ranh Bay. I was treated for months before being sent home. I was going to the VA for rehab and that's where I met Jennifer. She was working as a nurse there and we became friends.

We had a lot in common, being there the night that Danny and Stevie were killed. She was broken up about it but it was good we were able to talk about it. She told me she was so sorry about what had happened. She was never really with Carlo they just went out a few times. She tried to tell him not to bother her anymore but he was persistent. He kept calling and always coming over. He was intimidating and had a reputation of being connected to the local mob. She didn't know he was going to be at the club that night. In a way Jennifer was relieved that Carlo would spend most of his life in jail. After a while Jennifer visited me even when she wasn't working. We became friends and then we started to date and the rest is history." Father Thomas smiled, "That is a miracle what happened." "I guess it was Father. I never talk about it because I know the shrinks would recommend therapy or worse for me, but that's what happened." Danny's brother Alex came over, "I never heard you tell that story. That is great to hear and I believe you. Danny died trying to save Stevie but Stevie died anyway. On his death he came and saved you. Danny was a special person and we all miss him so much. He never had a chance to live his life but he helped you live yours." "I suffered from shrapnel wounds and a couple of broken legs but with Jennifer's help I was able to get through it. If it wasn't for Danny I would have died or at best been crippled the rest of my life. We have a great life together we live in a great neighborhood and we have wonderful neighbors. We have an elderly couple next store to us that have been like grandparents to our kids. You know Father, I have some crazy dreams over the years about both Danny and Stevie. It's almost like I have dreamt about different lives. It's hard to explain, but it just seemed like my life could have turned out very differently. Danny and Stevie always seem to be in my dreams." "That's understandable because what you went through that night, losing your two friends and then Viet Nam and all you have been through. It's a testament to you that you have survived and have such a wonderful family, friends and life. I spent a lot of time in a remote part of England working in a monastery. I worked with a very special monk named Brother Aiden.

While working with him I witnessed many amazing events. He believed in good and bad messengers which were angels that altered the lives of many. In some cases, they saved peoples' lives by interceding and changing their course. He believed in alternate universes that can send one from one path in life to another. Just like what happened to you, with Danny appearing to you and saving your life. He in some ways was a good messenger that saved you an altered your life for the better. I knew a person like Danny, who came to me for help when he was at a crossroad in his life. With the help of Brother Aiden, I think we saved him and many other people from a very bad fate. One never knows how and when these messengers change our lives." "Father, did you ever meet Danny" "James that is a question I cannot answer."

THE END

ACKNOWLEDGEMENTS

I want to thank my oldest and dearest friend John Celano for all his help in writing this book. All the Viet Nam stories are based on John's personal experiences in the Viet Nam war. John and I grew up together and have remained closest friends for over fifty years. What John and his fellow soldiers went through in fighting for our country in a thankless war should never be forgotten. I did take a few creative licenses in some areas, especially in eliminating the colorful language that was commonplace with soldiers.

A big thank you to Maggie Stavola for all her helps in editing and proofreading.

To all my family and friends that inspire my stories.

www.ingramcontent.com/pod-product-compliance
Lightning Source LLC
LaVergne TN
LVHW021711060526
838200LV00050B/2609